OUT OF TUNE

ALL NEW TALES OF HORROR AND DARK FANTASY

Edited By

JONATHAN MABERRY

JournalStone
San Francisco

JOURNALSTONE
YOUR LINK TO ARTISTIC TALENT

JournalStone books may be ordered through booksellers or by contacting:

JournalStone Publishing

www.journalstone.com

ISBN: 978-1-940161-69-3   (sc)
ISBN: 978-1-940161-70-9   (ebook)
ISBN: 978-1-940161-71-6   (hc)

JournalStone rev. date: November 17, 2014

Library of Congress Control Number: 2014953318

Printed in the United States of America

Cover and Interior Artwork: Robert Papp
Cover Design: Cyrusfiction Productions
Edited by: Jonathan Maberry

As always, for Sara Jo

INTRODUCTION

Ask most folks today what a 'ballad' is, and they begin humming power chords from groups like Journey, Whitesnake, and Meat Loaf.

But let's take a step back from hair bands and glitter rock. Let's go old school. Once upon a time, a ballad meant something more. They spoke to a different part of our soul. They tied us to our culture or gave us glimpses into the past. Sometimes they opened doors to strange places. The ballads of long ago told stories. Sometimes fanciful, often strange, constantly intriguing.

Those old ballads told of doomed loves and damned places, of murder and romance, of love lost and lives imperiled. The balladeers enchanted our imaginations with faerie folk and noble knights, with lonely witches and deeply unfortunate romantic choices, with the seen and the unseen. Some of them even told the truth. Or, a version at least.

More often the ballads conjured in our minds a place where something deliciously dreadful happened long ago. Maybe it was the very spot on which you now sit, or a land glimpsed only through a parted veil at purple twilight.

Many of the ballads are so old that no one can really claim ownership, and all provenance is suspect or apocryphal. Often these are songs and stories told and retold, changed and reshaped, with new tunes and new lyrics imposed upon the seed of a story. Scholars have confounded themselves with trying to trace the roots of Appalachian songs all the way back to Scottish glens or Irish grottos or overgrown English gardens. Some ballads are so old they seem half buried in the myths of the ancients. Others are as fresh as the rise of Jazz and Blues.

One cannot say, with any real degree of certainty, that there is even a thread that ties all ballads together. There isn't. And yet, there is. It's less a connection of form or origin, and more a feeling. An awareness that these old songs and stories evoke in each of us.

Often, even at first hearing, we feel we *know* these songs. We've heard them somewhere before, we think; even when we likewise know we haven't. Their ghosts haunt the generations of songs that have come after them. Their dust is there. Their shadows.

OUT OF TUNE is not a collection of old ballads. No, sir. This volume contains only new stories. Prose, not rhymes. Stories, not songs. Fourteen tales spun by some of today's most talented writers. It's a witch's brew, no doubt. The stories are dissimilar in almost every way. Some are as bare as old bones, others are ripe to bursting. But they all share one thing. A thread. A ghost of a theme.

They are all inspired by old ballads. From England and Ireland, Scotland and Wales. And from America, too. Old songs, new stories. Not direct interpretations. No, those old ballads were whispers in the ears of these writers. Each writer took a thread from those timeless songs and in their own way spun new magic.

So, sit comfortably, pour yourself something nice, and dig in. And maybe—just maybe—you'll hear a spectral tune floating on the breeze as you read.

-Jonathan Maberry

TABLE OF CONTENTS

Folklore Commentary following each song—by Nancy Keim Comley

WENDY, DARLING

By
CHRISTOPHER GOLDEN

O n a Friday evening at the end of May in the year Nineteen Hundred and Fifteen, Wendy spent her final night in her father's house in a fitful sleep, worried about her wedding the following day and the secrets she had kept from her intended groom.

The room had once been a nursery, but those days were long forgotten. She had stopped dreaming the dreams of her girlhood years before, such that even the echoes of those dreams had slid into the shadows in the corners of the room. Now it was a proper bedroom with a lovely canopy over the bed and a silver mirror and an enormous wardrobe that still gave off a rich mahogany scent though it had stood against the wall for six years and more.

Some nights, though…some nights the tall French windows would remain open and the curtains would billow and float. On those evenings the moonlight would pour into the room with such earnest warmth it seemed intent upon reminding her of girlhood evenings when she would stay up whispering to her brothers in the dark until all of them drifted off to sleep and dreamt impossible things.

Wendy had lived in the nursery with Michael and John for too long. She ought to have had her own room much sooner, but at first their father had not wanted to give up his study to make another bedroom and later—when he'd changed his mind—the children were no longer interested in splitting up. By then Wendy had begun to see the Lost Boys, and to dream of them, and it seemed altogether safer to stick together.

That day—the day before her wedding—there had been a low, whispery sort of fog all through the afternoon and into the evening. Several times she stirred in her sleep, uneasy as she thought of Jasper, the barrister she was to wed the following afternoon. She quite relished the idea of becoming Mrs. Jasper Gilbert, yet during the night, she felt herself haunted by the prospect. Each time her eyes flickered open, she lay for several moments, staring out at the fog until she drifted off again.

Sometime later, she woke to see not fog but moonlight. The windows were open and the curtains performed a ghostly undulation, cast in yellow light.

A *dream*, she thought, for it must have been. She knew it because the fog had gone. Knew it because of the moonlight and the impossibly slow dance of those curtains, and of course because the Lost Boys were there.

She lay on her side, half her face buried in the feather pillow, and gazed at them. At first she saw only three, two by the settee and one almost hidden in the billow of the curtains. The fourth had a dark cast to his features that made him seem grimmer, less ethereal than the others, though he was the youngest. She had not seen them in years, not since her parents had gotten a doctor involved, insisting the Lost Boys were figments of her imagination. She had never forgiven John and Michael for reporting her frequent visits with the Lost Boys to their parents, a grudge she had come to regret in the aftermath of Michael's death in a millinery fire in 1910. How she had loved him.

By the time of the fire, it had been years since she had seen the Lost Boys. After the fire, she had often prayed that it would be Michael who visited her in the night.

"Wendy," one of the Boys whispered now in her moonlit dream.

"Hello, boys," she said, flush beneath her covers, heart racing. She wanted to cry or scream but did not know if it was fear she felt, or merely grief.

As if grief could ever be *merely*.

She recognized all four of them, of course, and knew their names. But she did not allow herself to speak those names, or even to think them. It would have felt as if she welcomed them back to her dreams, and they were not welcome at all.

"You forgot us, Wendy. You promised you never would."

She nestled her cheek deeper into her pillow, feathers poking her skin through the fabric.

"I never did," she whispered, her skin dampening. Too hot beneath the covers. "You were only in my mind, you see. I haven't forgotten, but my parents and Doctor Goss told me I must persuade my eyes not to see you if you should appear again."

"Have you missed us, then?"

Wendy swallowed. A shudder went through her. She had not.

"As I'm dreaming, I suppose it's all right that I'm seeing you now."

The Lost Boys glanced at one another with a shared, humorless sort of laugh. More a sniff than a laugh, really. A disapproving sniff.

The moonlight passed right through them.

The nearest of them—he of the grim eyes—slid closer to her.

"You were meant to be our mother," he said.

Wendy couldn't breathe. She pressed herself backward, away from them. It was their eyes that ignited a terror within her, those pleading eyes. She closed her eyes.

"Wake up, Wendy," she whispered to herself. "Please wake up."

"Don't you remember?" the grim-eyed one asked, and her lids fluttered open to find herself still dreaming.

"Please remember," said another, a lithe little boy with a pouting mouth and eyes on the verge of tears.

"No," she whispered.

The hook. Soft flesh against her own. The pain. Blood in the water.

Her body trembled as images rushed to her mind and were driven back, shuttered in dark closets, buried in shallow graves.

"Stay away," she whispered. "Please. My life is all ahead of me."

She did not know if she spoke to the Lost Boys or to those images.

"My fiancé is a good man. Perhaps when we are wed, we can take one or two of you in. He is kind, you see. Not like..."

A door slammed in her mind.

"Like who, Wendy?"

CHRISTOPHER GOLDEN

Hook, she thought. *My James.*

"No!" she screamed, hurling back her bedcovers and leaping from the bed, hot tears springing to her eyes. "Leave me, damn you! Leave me to my life!"

Fingers curved into claws, she leaped at the nearest of them. Passing through him, chill gooseflesh rippling across her skin, she fell to the rug and curled up into herself, a mess of sobs.

In the moonlight, she lay just out of reach of the fluttering curtains and cried herself into the sweet oblivious depths of slumber.

When she woke in the early dawn, aching and chilled to the bone, she crept back beneath her bedclothes for warmth and comfort and told herself that there would never be another night when she needed to fear bad dreams. For the rest of her life, she would wake in the morning with Jasper beside her and he would hold her and kiss her until the last of sleep's shadows retreated.

The sun rose to a clear blue morning.

No trace of fog.

The world only began to feel completely real to Wendy again when the carriage drew to a halt in front of the church. Flowers had been arranged over the door and on the steps and the beauty of the moment made her breath catch in her throat. A smile spread across her lips and bubbled into laughter and she turned toward her grumpy banker of a father and saw that he was smiling as well—beaming, in fact—and his eyes were damp with love for her, and with pride.

"Never thought you'd see the day, did you, Father?" Wendy teased.

George Darling cleared his throat to compose himself. "There were times," he allowed. "But here we are, my dear. Here. We. Are."

He took a deep breath and stepped out of the carriage, itself also festooned with arrangements donated by friends of Wendy's mother who were part of the committee behind the Chelsea Flower Show. A pair of ushers emerged from the church, but Wendy's father waved them back and offered his own hand to guide her down the carriage steps.

George stepped back. He'd never been sentimental, and now

he seemed to fight against whatever emotions welled within him. Amongst those she expected, Wendy saw a flicker of uneasiness.

"You look beautiful," he told her.

Wendy knew it was true. She seldom indulged in outright vanity, but on her wedding day, and in this dress…well, she would forgive herself. Cream-white satin, trimmed in simple lace, it had been one of the very first she had laid eyes upon and she had loved it straight away. Cut low at the neck, with sleeves to the elbows, it had a simple elegance reflected in the simplicity of the veil and the short train. Her father helped gather her train, spread it out behind her, and took her hand as they faced the church.

"Miss Darling," said one of the ushers, whose name she'd suddenly forgotten. She felt horrible, but suddenly it seemed that her thoughts were a jumble.

"I'm about to be married," she said, just to hear the words aloud.

"You are, my dear," George agreed. "Everyone is waiting."

The forgotten usher handed her a wreath of orange blossoms and then the other one opened the church door. Moments later, Wendy found herself escorted down the aisle by her grumpy-turned-doting father. A trumpet played and then the organ, and all faces turned toward her, so that she saw all of them and none of them at the same time. She smelled the flowers and her heart thundered, and she began to feel dizzy and swayed a bit.

"Wendy," her father whispered to her, his grip tightening on her arm. "Are you all right?"

Ahead, at the end of the aisle, the bridesmaids and ushers had spread out to either side. The vicar stood on the altar, dignified and serious. Her mother sat in the front row, her brother John stood amongst the ushers. And there was Jasper, so dapper in his morning coat, his black hair gleaming, his blue eyes smiling.

She no longer felt dizzy. Only safe and sure.

Until the little boy darted out from behind a column—the little boy with grim eyes.

"Stop this!" he shouted. "You must stop!"

Wendy staggered, a terrible pain in her belly as if she were being torn apart inside. She gasped and then covered her mouth, glancing about through the mesh of her veil, certain her friends and relations would think her mad—again.

But their eyes were not on her. Those in attendance were staring at the little boy in his ragged clothes, and when the second boy ran in from the door to the sacristy and the vicar shouted at him, furious at the intrusion, Wendy at last understood.

The vicar could see the boys.

They could *all* see.

"Out of here, you little scoundrels!" the vicar shouted. "I won't allow you to ruin the day—"

The grim-eyed boy stood before Jasper, who could only stare in half-amused astonishment. That sweetness was simply Jasper's nature, that indulgence where any other bridegroom would have been furious.

The third boy stepped from the shadows at the back of the altar as if he had been there all along. And of course he must have been.

"No, no, no," Wendy said, backing away, tearing her arm from her father's grip. She forced her eyes closed because they couldn't be here. Couldn't be real.

"Wendy?" her father said, and she opened her eyes to see him looking at her.

He knew. Though he had always told her they were figments and dreams, hadn't he seemed unsettled whenever she talked of them? *"Spirits," he'd said, "do not exist, except in the minds of the mad and the guilty."*

Which am I? she'd asked him then. *Which am I?*

Jasper clapped his hands twice, drawing all attention toward him. The unreality of the moment collapsed into tangibility and truth. Wendy breathed. Smelled the flowers. Heard the scuffling and throat-clearing of the stunned members of the wedding.

"All right, lads, you've had your fun," Jasper said. "Off with you!"

"Wendy Darling," one of the boys said, staring at Jasper, tears welling in his eyes. "Only she's not 'darling' at all. You don't know her, sir. She'll be a cruel mother. She'll abandon her children—"

"Rubbish!" shouted Wendy's father. "How dare you speak of my daughter this way!"

Wendy could only stare, not breathing as Jasper strode toward the grim-eyed boy and gripped him by his ragged shirtfront. She saw the way the filthy fabric bunched in his hands and it felt as if the curtain between dream and reality had finally been torn away.

"No," she said, starting toward Jasper…and toward the boys. "Please, don't…"

Her fiancé glanced up, thinking she had been speaking to him, but the boys looked at her as well. They knew better.

"She's had a baby once before," a pale, thin boy said, coming to stand by Jasper, his eyes pleading. "Go on. Ask her."

"Ask her what became of that child," said the grim-eyed boy.

Shaking, Wendy jerked right and left, trapped by all of the eyes that gazed upon her. Jasper frowned, staring at her, and she saw the doubt blooming in him, saw his lips beginning to form a question. Her father still glared angrily at the boys, but even he had a flicker of hesitation. In the front row, Mary Darling stepped from the pew and extended a hand toward her daughter.

"Wendy?"

Shaking her head, Wendy began to back away from those who loved her, retreating down the aisle. She tripped over her silken train and when she fell amongst the soft purity of its folds, she screamed.

"Ask her!" one of the boys shouted. Or perhaps it had been all of them.

Thrusting herself from the ground, whipping her train behind her, she ran. Her whole body felt flushed but she caught a glimpse of her left hand as she ran and it was pale as marble. Pale as death. At the back of the aisle, a few crimson rose petals had fallen, petals meant to be scattered in the path of husband and wife after the ceremony. To her they were blood from a wound.

She burst from the church, an abyss of unspoken questions gaping behind her, and she fled down the steps in fear that if she did not run, that yawing silence would drag her back. Pain stabbed her belly and her heart slammed inside her chest. Her eyes burned and yet strangely there were no tears. She felt incapable of tears.

At the foot of the steps, she tore off the train of her dress. When she glanced up, horses whinnied and chuffed. Her wedding carriage stood waiting. The driver looked at her with kind eyes and his kindness filled her with loathing.

"Wendy!"

Jasper's voice. Behind her. She dared not turn to look at him.

Racing across the street, she darted down a narrow road between a dressmaker's and a baker's shop. At a corner, she nearly collided with two more of the Lost Boys—*names, you know their names*—and she turned right to avoid them, racing downhill now. Another appeared from an alley to her left, but this boy was different from the others. He'd been badly burnt, skin and clothing charred, and unlike the others, he had no substance, flesh so translucent that she could see the stone face of the building behind him.

She wailed, stumbling in anguish, and fell to the street. Her dress tore and her knee bled, so that when she staggered to her feet and ran screaming—grief carving out her insides—a vivid red stain soaked into the satin and spread, the petals of a crimson rose.

"Mother," the burnt boy said behind her.

She did not look back, but glanced once at the windows of a pub as she bolted past. In the glass she saw their reflections, not only the burnt boy but the others as well, one with his head canted too far, neck broken, another beaten so badly his features were ruined.

Moments before she emerged from between two buildings, she realized where she had been going all along. Had she chosen her path or had they driven her here? Did it matter?

Wendy stared at the bank of the Thames, at the deep water rushing by, and all the strength went out of her. Numb and hollow, she shuffled to the riverbank.

Somewhere nearby, a baby cried.

Glancing to her left, she saw the bundle perhaps a dozen feet away, just at the edge of the water. The baby's wailing grew louder and more urgent and she started toward it.

She knew the pattern on its blanket. His blanket.

Kneeling on the riverbank, her bloodstained dress soaking up the damp, she reached out to pull the blanket away from the infant's face. His blue face, bloated and cold, eyes bloodshot and bulging and lifeless.

The sob tore from her chest as she reached for the child, lifted it into her arms and cradled it to her chest. Still she could not weep, but she pressed her eyes tightly closed and prayed for tears.

The bundle in her arms felt too light. Gasping for breath, she opened her eyes.

"No, please," she whispered as she unraveled the empty blanket. The empty, sodden blanket.

"Mother," a voice said, so close, and a hand touched her shoulder.

Wendy froze, breath hitching in her chest. This was not the burnt boy or the grim-eyed child from the church. This was another boy entirely.

Still on her knees, she turned back to see his face. Nine years old, now, his skin still blue, eyes still bloodshot and lifeless. Her boy.

"Peter," she whispered.

He thrust his fingers into her hair and she screamed his name—a name she had never spoken aloud before today. Wendy beat at his arms and clawed at his face as he dragged her to the water and plunged her into the river. She stared up at him through the water and his visage blurred and changed, became the face of his father, James, the butcher's boy. He'd earned his nickname with the bloodstained hook he used in handling the sides of meat in the shop down the street from the Darlings' home.

Her chest burned for air, the urgency of her need forcing her to strike harder at the face above her, which now became her own face, only nine years younger. The hands that held her beneath the water were her own, but she was no longer herself—instead she was a tiny infant, so newly born he still bore streaks of blood from his mother's womb. An infant conceived by a mother and father who were only children themselves, carried and borne in secret—a secret safeguarded by her brothers in the privacy of the room they shared, a secret which destroyed her relationship with them forever. A secret made possible by a father's neglect and a mother's denial.

Peter, she thought.

Starved for air, thoughts and vision dulling, diminishing, slipping away, Wendy opened her mouth and inhaled the river.

Blackness crept in at the corners of her eyes, shadows in her brain, and she realized she had stopping fighting him. Her arms slipped into the water and her hair pooled around her face. Bloodstained white satin floated in a cloud that enveloped and embraced her.

The hands on her now were larger. A man's hands. They

dragged her from the river and for a moment she saw only darkness, a black veil for a cruel mother.

"Wendy," said an urgent voice.

She saw him then. Not the little drowned boy, but Jasper, her intended. He knelt over her, desperate and pleading and calling her name.

Gathered around him on the riverbank were the Lost Boys, those cast-aside children, each murdered by his mother. Those dead boys she had met once before on the night she had drowned her Peter in the Thames. They had been visible to the people in the church, dark dreams come to life, but now they were unseen once more. Jasper wept over her, unaware of their presence...

Wendy could only watch him, standing a short distance away. Her dress felt dry now, but the bloodstain remained.

"No," she whispered, as the darkness retreated from her thoughts and she understood what she saw.

Jasper knelt there, mourning her, grieving for the life they might have had. Wendy saw her own lifeless body from outside, her spirit as invisible to him as the Lost Boys. Others began to run toward the riverbank—her parents and her brother John, the vicar's wife and Jasper's brother, an aunt and uncle. They seemed like ghosts to her, these living people, their grief distant and dull.

The Lost Boys circled around her, dead eyes now contented.

"Mother," Peter whispered, taking her right hand.

Another boy took her left hand. She glanced down and saw the grim eyes that had so unsettled her in her dreams.

"You promised to be a mother to us all, forever," the grim-eyed boy said.

Wendy blinked and turned toward the river. Somehow she could still see the swaddled infant floating on the water, sodden blankets dragging it down, just as it had on that night nine years ago.

"Forever," said Peter.

They guided her gently into the river, where the dark current swept them all away.

ON...THE CRUEL MOTHER

Child Ballad 20 (Roud #9), The Cruel Mother, is a 'murder' ballad. The heart of the ballad concerns a woman going into the forest and giving birth to two illegitimate children. She then murders them, either stabbing with a penknife or strangling them with a ribbon. She then buries them. In some versions she ties them together and buries them alive.

Later she sees two pretty children and rhapsodizes on how she would treat them most tenderly if they were hers, dressing them in fine clothing and feeding them only the best food. They answer that when they were hers and she treated them very differently and though they will be forgiven she will not and hell is her fate. In some ballads she must serve seven-year penance in hell.

In one significant variant a herdsman finds a child in the hollow of a tree. The child asks him to take it to the house where its mother is to be married that day. There the child announces that the bride is its mother. It then tells the assembled company that she has had three children. One she drowned, one she buried and one she hid in the hollow of a tree. In what Child calls a 'Wendish' version (i.e. Sorbian) the bride/mother has had nine children.(1)

Various musicians have recorded The Cruel Mother with singers such as Joan Baez.

1) Child, Francis James. The English and Scottish Popular Ballads Vol. 1. Mineola: Dover, 2003.

SWEET WILLIAM'S GHOST

BY
DAVID Liss

Maggie and I had been together for months, which is about as much as any relationship needs to drag on. Some guys, I know, are needy, and they're all about looking for that right woman. I don't have anything against that sensitivity of whatever, but let's just say I'm a little skeptical. I don't think there's any man alive who is happy with just one woman. Maybe he can settle, or trick himself into thinking he doesn't need anything else. More likely, I'm guessing, he's happy as shit for a while, and by the time he snaps out of it, he's got a mortgage and kids and responsibilities and all that bullshit. I saw that happen to my father, who looked at my mother like she was a piece of rotting meat. He didn't think I saw, but I did, and I vowed not to let that happen to me.

Even though I was on my guard, things went on with Maggie longer than I would have thought. It didn't hurt that she was a nice-looking woman. Pretty face with pale skin, black hair, and big-wattage blue eyes. I hardly ever notice a girl's eye color, not even if I've been with her for weeks, but with Maggie, it was almost the first thing I saw. Almost, because she's got a really nice body, and she works out in the gym where I'm a trainer. A lot of girls built like Maggie would strut around in micro shorts and sports bras, letting the world get an eye-full. She could pull it off, but she dressed like a fat chick when she exercised. That's fine. I understand she wasn't looking for attention, but I'm a trained professional. I know a woman in good shape when I see one.

I'd been watching her for a while, trying to figure out my

move. Guys tried to strike up conversations with her all the time, and she'd be polite, but she didn't want any part of it. She listened to music while she worked out, which made it easier to cut the chatter short. She'd pull out one ear bud when someone tried to get a conversation going, but stare at it the whole time, like she was itching to get back to the music. It made guys anxious, and they struck out.

I wasn't going to let that happen to me. When I moved in, it was going to count. I just had to wait for the right moment. One day I saw her at the squat rack, and I knew that was my in.

Not a lot of women bother with barbell squatting. It's technical and it's uncomfortable, and most people think it's for serious bodybuilders "only". Even so, there she was, at the rack, a pair of ten-pound plates on the bar, giving it a try. And doing it badly.

Your average lightweight gym member can't squat for shit, and as a trainer, I can tell you it's not worth teaching them. If a guy insists on hitting the squat rack when I'm training him, he usually cranks out half or quarter squats, and I don't tell him to do otherwise. Why bother? He doesn't want to hear he's doing it wrong. He doesn't want to hear that to do it right he's got to drop some weight and practice form. He wants to feel like he's moving a shitload of iron around, and he pays me to make him feel like he's the Hulk or something. That's the service I provide. I'm in the people business.

This woman wasn't paying me, though. I knew she was a class act. I saw the clothes she wore on her way in or out—skirt suits and shit and silk blouses and like that. She was some kind of professional. A lawyer or accountant or something. She was smart. I could tell from her eyes, from her hair, the way she carried herself. Whatever it was women like that talked about in their spare time—cinema and politics and the latest novel by some Indian lady—I wasn't equipped to handle. But squatting? That I could talk about.

"Excuse me," I said when she finished a set. "I hope you don't mind my saying this, but you're form is wrong. You'll hurt your knees."

She looked at me, like she wanted to hear what I had to say. Her eyes darted over my body in my shorts and polo shirt. She took out both ear buds, rested them in her palm. I'd passed the test, and with good reason. I am tall and I am fit. Women like to look at me, and I don't see the point of pretending otherwise. Her gaze shot up to my face, which isn't so bad either, and she tried to keep it there. She laughed self-consciously and shook her head.

"I'm not surprised," she said. "I read an article about squatting in a magazine, and I figured I'd give it a try, but it's harder than it looked."

"Harder than it looks, but easier than you think," I said. "You have to go all the way down. Thighs parallel to the ground. Can I show you?"

She let me show her. Just like that. Hands on her shoulders, then my palm pressed flat against the small of her back. She might as well have gotten naked right there, because even if she didn't know it, or pretended not to know it, I had just closed the deal.

§

A few minutes of my time there, a few conversations around the gym the next few times she comes in, and suddenly she hires me on for sessions twice a week.

I'm not an idiot. A woman in that kind of shape doesn't need a trainer. Unless you're a movie star or an athlete, no one in good shapes needs a trainer. This woman sure as hell had no business paying someone to toss her a medicine ball while she stood on a balance board. She didn't need for me to count off while she did some bullshit on the TRX. She hired me because she wanted to sleep with me.

Maybe she never intended to go through with it. Most people don't jump in the sack with every person they've got the hots for. I get that. Still, she was flirting—flirting with me and flirting with the idea. Maybe that's all she wanted to do. Maybe at first she thought the thrill of having a guy who looked like me put his hands on her twice a week was enough to scratch her itch.

And make no mistake, Maggie loved it when I put my hands on her. I felt her shiver and tense, I heard her let out her breath when I would adjust her form or correct her posture. Even so, she put up plenty of barriers. She mentioned her fiancé at least twice a session. William this, and William that—how kind, how smart, how sweet. It was as if to say she was spoken for, and she would not have any flirting. For all that, she asked me about my weekends. She fished for information about my social life. She touched my forearm with her fingertips during casual conversation. I know the drill.

It turned out I was right the first time. Maggie was a lawyer, though not like the kind you see on TV, talking to juries and solving crimes and shit. She was a corporate lawyer and sat in her office reading contracts all day, which sounded dull to me, and she admitted it was not the most exciting thing in the world. I was also right when I guessed she was smart. She liked movies, the more foreign and colorless the better. She liked to read books. Her fiancé, William, was some kind of high-powered engineer, specializing in environmental cleanup. He was a big deal. She was proud of him. He mattered. She loved spending time with him. She was looking forward to a life with him and starting a family with him. His awesome importance made her absolutely untouchable. No matter how much she might be attracted to another guy, no sane woman would mess up the sort of future she had with a guy like her sweet William.

Maggie and I were sleeping together within three weeks of her first session. Smart guys with smoking-hot girlfriends take note. I don't care how compatible the two of you are. I don't care how much your souls intertwine or whatever. If she's better looking than you are, she's going to step out with someone like me. Know that going in.

§

That's how it went for two months. William worked long hours, and he traveled all the time, so Maggie and I didn't have to work too hard to find opportunities to slip off to my apartment, which wasn't far from the gym or from the house Maggie shared with her fiancé. I had to do a little cleaning up for Maggie, throwing away pizza boxes and shoving laundry in the hamper, but whatever. She was worth it. After a while, she canceled the training sessions. They were too much of a tease for both of us. All that distraction with heavy weights—that's a recipe for an accident. In the interest of safety, we limited our interactions to me pounding the shit out of her whenever we could both slip away.

It wasn't like we were in love or anything. We were attracted. We liked to have sex with each other. That was it. She was out of my league, and I was out of hers, which made it hot. She felt like crap about what she was doing to William, while I didn't care, and that was also hot. Once a week she would tell me that we should stop, that she really loved him. I'd tell her that I would hate to let her go, but I wanted her to be happy. When I said that, I'd see something darken in her lovely face—the knowledge that I could simply walk away and not look back. I think that's what kept her around. Maggie wanted me to be desperate for her, and until I was, she wasn't going anywhere.

Then, one day, lying in my bedroom on a Saturday afternoon, Maggie looked up at me. "William's going to be out of town for three weeks," she said. "He's got an extended assignment in Glasgow. Some old factory has apparently been leaking who knows what into the soil for decades."

"Thank God for William," I said.

Maggie raised an eyebrow at me like I was being a dick. I didn't like that look, but as she wasn't wearing anything, I let it slide.

"You'll be able to come over to my house," she said. "I can cook you dinner."

"I can take or leave dinner," I told her, and that was true. I didn't want to play house with Maggie. I wanted to hook up with her a couple of times a week. Maybe more, but I wasn't interested in bringing her flowers and the two of us selecting the right wine to go with her French whatever. Maggie knew where I stood. I was taking advantage of her and helping her to shit all over her happy future, so I figured the least I could do was to be up front about it.

"Come on," she said, forcing a smile. "It'll be fun. It'll give us a chance to see."

"To see what?" I asked. But I already knew the answer.

She slapped my butt playfully. "To see how we do together."

"I think I already know," I told her, but that wasn't true. I didn't know, and I didn't want to see. I wanted her to keep sleeping with me. I didn't care if she broke up with William. That was her business. I had no interest in taking William's place.

§

Maggie lived in a snooty part of town where none of the neighbors knew each other, so my coming and going wasn't a problem for her. No one there gave a crap about her business. That's what she said. I saw a few housewives eye me as they pushed their baby strollers down the street, but if Maggie didn't mind, then neither did I.

Before William had been in Scotland a week, I was coming over every day, sleeping there every night. Maggie would text me when she was on her way home, and I would meet her at the house. As it turned out, she never made me dinner—it was always take out or prepared stuff from the grocery store. Then we would have to figure out what to with long hours together. It was a weird transition, at first. We had only ever flirted or had sex. Suddenly, we were a real couple, washing plates and choosing side dishes. I hadn't thought we were up to it, but it turned out I liked it. We would watch some old movie, and Maggie would talk about what this scene or that meant when the film first came out, or what the director was trying to say, and it was actually kind of interesting, stuff I hadn't thought about before. Then I would make some comment or ask some question, and Maggie would look at me like I was really smart, or at least smarter than she had given me credit for. It was like she was taking me seriously, and the truth was, I enjoyed it. I kept acting like I didn't, but I did.

One day over some salmon filets she bought she said to me, "What would you do if William confronted you?"

I shrugged. "What would you want me to do?"

"Would you hit him?"

I chewed my fish thoughtfully. "Yeah, probably. I mean, if I had to. If he got all in my face."

She looked down at her plate. I could tell she liked that. Smart women like that sort of thing because the guys they're usually with don't know how to protect themselves.

I was in her bed when the call came in. It was maybe just after midnight. I watched as she answered, as she went quiet and pale, as she put a hand to her mouth. I watched as she considered dropping the phone, or opting out by collapsing or something, but that wasn't Maggie. Maggie dealt with things. She took a long breath, and then grabbed a pencil and began to write down information. Then she hung up the phone.

"There's been an accident," she said, her voice mechanical, slow, precise. "William is dead."

But I already knew that. I knew it as soon as she put her phone to her ear, maybe as soon as it rang. I knew it, and I wasn't sure how I felt about it. Okay, maybe I was sure. I was glad.

§

I stayed out of her life for a few weeks. William's family decided he should be buried in Scotland, which it turns out was where he was from. I hadn't know that, but I liked it. He was buried far away. There would be no regular trips to set flowers at his grave. Perfect.

Maggie spent more than a week there, and then, when she returned, her time was taken up with friends and relatives and well-wishers. I understood that she didn't want to deal with me. Her fiancé was dead now. He had become Saint William, and all the things that had bothered her about him before—his being safe and unassertive and in mediocre shape—now seemed irrelevant. She had loved him and planned to live the rest of her life with him, and I was a reminder of how she had spurned and humiliated him, even if he hadn't known it. William was forever, but not me. A year from now, she wouldn't remember my name.

Except that a month after the funeral, she called me up. "I need to talk to you," she said. "Can you come over?"

When she answered the door, she was wearing sweat pants and an oversized t-shirt. That's woman code for "I'm not going to fuck you," by the way. I looked at her and her sad smile, and I knew that this was where I did not want to be. I thought of a million excuses I could use to get out of there now—an appointment forgotten, a friend with an emergency—but I let them slide.

Maggie poured us some white wine with a foreign name and sat across from me in her cavernous living room.

"I didn't want us to end on bad terms," she said.

"Who says we have to end at all?" I asked.

She turned away, and I could see she was crying. They were silent tears, and I could pretend not to have noticed.

"I can't be with you anymore," she told me, still not looking in my direction. "After what we did to William."

"We didn't do anything to him," I told her. "He never knew. He never had any feelings about us because we kept us a secret."

She turned her head toward me, hard and sharp. "I was going to marry him," she said. "Don't think I wasn't. If he showed up here, right now, I would marry him."

"Well, that's nice," I said as kindly as I could manage, "but he's not going to show up." I was starting to feel like I didn't even want to bother to sleep with her that night. It would be all sad and awkward afterwards, and it seemed like it was way more trouble than it was worth. The smart play was to agree with her, tell her I understood, give her a brotherly hug and get the fuck out of there. It was like there was this little guy in my brain, shouting into cupped hands what I should do, but I ignored him.

"William is gone," I said. "I know you feel guilty, but you never did anything to hurt him, and now he's not around anymore. But I am."

I came over and sat by her. She stiffened and pulled away from me, but I knew this was a game at this point. I began to kiss her neck. At first she shoved me away, told me to stop, but pretty soon we were upstairs and those baggy clothes were lying on the floor. Big surprise, right?

§

That's how I basically moved into her house. It was just a temporary thing. It had to be for a guy like me because I loved my freedom too much, but even so, I liked having Maggie around. At least, I liked the old Maggie. The post-William Maggie turned out to be kind of a mope. She didn't talk much. She didn't want to have sex unless I forced the issue. She sat silently at meals.

Why didn't I walk the hell out of there, you're wondering, and it's a good question. I'm not sure I have the answer. I think I wanted the old Maggie back. I think I believed if I waited long enough, the old Maggie would return. This half-dead thing would be a memory, and she would be fun again.

Two weeks into this, my patience was starting to wear thin. Maggie acted almost like she didn't want me around. I'd say, "Do you want me to move out?" and she'd say, "Yes," and I could almost believe she meant it. She'd tell me she didn't want to have sex, and then we'd have sex anyway. I started to think that I didn't understand women all that well.

Maybe that's why things started with Amanda. You can't argue that was wrong on my part. I mean, it was how I met Maggie, so was she in a position to complain? Anyhow, it's the way of things. People meet, they get together, they move apart. That's just how it goes, right? Amanda wanted more and more of my time, and she was new, a country not yet conquered. Maggie was just Maggie. Nothing she did or said really surprised me anymore. I still liked the things she did and said, but so what? I like tacos, but I'm not going to spend the rest of my life with a tortilla stuffed with chicken.

So, I was waiting for the right moment to let her know that I was done, that I was moving out, that it wasn't personal. I figured I'd keep the whole Amanda thing to myself, since there was no upside in that. But that was about the time the business with the ghost started.

§

I was about to start the talk. You know the one. I've been thinking, Maggie. Where is this really going, Maggie? That kind of bullshit. Not fifteen minutes earlier, Amanda sent me a text asking if I could meet her for a drink. A drink would lead back to her place—make no mistake about that—and I liked the idea. Amanda was tall, trim, big in the shoulders and chest, and I was getting worked up just thinking about her.

Maggie and I were sitting on the couch, with the TV on, but not really watching anything. Maggie was staring into the distance. This is it, I thought. This has got to be the end of our little experiment. I'm sliding into bullshit relationship mediocrity, and if I don't get the hell out now, I'm screwed forever.

I took a breath and opened my mouth, but Maggie spoke first.

"I've been seeing someone," she said.

This announcement surprised me. I won't lie to you. Maggie

sat next to me, her legs tucked under her body, her arms wrapped around her chest. She kept her eyes down, and her loose hair covered her face like a veil.

"What the fuck?" I asked.

I know what you're thinking, and you're right to think that. Why was I making a fuss about this when I was the one who was about to kick her to the curb? She was making my life a whole lot easier right now, and I ought to accept a gift when it's offered. Somewhere in the recesses of my mind, that little guy with the cupped hands was trying to tell me all this, but I wasn't listening to him again. I was angry. How could Maggie be stepping out on me?

"I guess I can't be surprised," I said. "You fucked around on William, and now you're fucking around on me."

She raised her eyes, and I saw something there that scared me. Not physically scared, like she was going to stab me or anything. I saw a kind of darkness and chaos, the look of a person who warped all the rules when she was around.

"You don't know what you're talking about," she said. "I've seen William."

"William," I repeated, feeling more and more like a deflating pool toy. "Dead William?"

Maggie kept that dark, chaotic glare on me. "Yes," she said. "I've seen him. His ghost."

When I'd gone through the roster of how Maggie might respond to my leaving, I'd considered the possibility that Maggie might go crazy, but not that she might *be* crazy. Here's as much supernatural shit as I believed: she could sense something was up with me. She could feel me pulling away. Maybe she'd caught a whiff of Amanda's perfume, or maybe she had just seen a look in my eye, but whatever it was, she knew. She might not even have known that she knew, but some nugget of female predatory instinct was driving her to get her claws in me deep and not let go. This crap about a ghost was just her way of trying to nail me down.

"I don't believe in ghosts," I told her.

"Yeah," she said, picking up a glass of wine and draining half of it. "There's nothing like seeing one to make you rethink that position."

Here's what she told me. It was four or five days ago, after nine, and I was still at the gym, since I had a late client—go ahead, see if you can guess her name—and Maggie was at home. Her father and brother were in town for a visit, which I'd been avoiding, having clients at convenient times. They had been over for dinner, so when she heard a noise downstairs, she thought it was one of them coming back for some forgotten bullshit. It had sounded like there was something moving around the house, but when she looked around, there was no one there.

Then, she said, came the knock at the door. When she opened it, there was William.

She put a hand to her mouth to scream, but she says she didn't. Maybe it's true. I don't know. Women are always going to tweak those kinds of details, right, to make themselves seem less stupid. But the thing that matters here is that it was William, standing there like he had never died doing his important crap that no one cared about. He wasn't beat up or bleeding or standing with some industrial pipe sticking through his head. It was William, like he was still alive.

This is how the brain works. Not just Maggie's brain, you understand, but pretty much everyone's. Was William dead? Yes. Had he been dead for weeks? Affirmative. Did Maggie have any doubts about that? Negatory. Yet, she stood there and thought that maybe there had been a big mistake. Maybe William had never been dead at all. Maybe he had spent all this time eating haggis and oak cakes and now he had decided it was the right moment to head back to the US of A and rescue his fiancée from her meathead boyfriend.

I didn't get all the dialogue, but she said he talked like William. He sounded like him, both in his voice and his wording. Maggie invited him in, and he said no. He could not enter the house. He was there, he said, because he sensed she needed help. You believe that crap? She needed help. Like, from what? Did she need help looking at her stupid contracts at work? I don't think so. She needed help with me. This dead asshole can't even stay buried, right? He has to come crawling out of the grave to mess with my shit. Like he would have had the balls to mess with me while he was still alive. Don't tell me this doesn't raise your blood pressure too.

Maggie swears she didn't suggest it, but out of the blue William starts talking about why they can't get married. He starts talking about how he lives in a coffin now, and there's no room. He's getting all worked up as he lists all the reasons why two people can't move into a coffin, but the last isn't really necessary, is it? I mean, if you say you live in a coffin, I'm not about to suggest shacking up. You pretty much barred the gate at coffin, right?

Who knows what Maggie would have said. Maybe she'd have tried to talk him into some other arrangement, but they were both startled by the headlights of my truck pulling into the driveway. I wasn't looking up. I was minding my own business, thinking that maybe I should have showered before coming over. I kind of brushed past Maggie and hit the bathroom. By the time I came out, she was in bed with the lights off, pretending to sleep, and I pretended to believe it.

Now she was crying, but I'm actually good with tears. I hugged her, even though it was like hugging a goddamn statue. I made her some tea. Crying women love the shit out of tea. Who knows why? Coffee and tears do not mix, but tea and weeping go hand in hand.

"He says he'll be back," Maggie said, sipping her tea.

"He's not coming back," I told her, "because he was never here. You just dreamed it."

"I didn't dream it. It was real."

My phone started buzzing from an incoming text. Amanda wondering where I was. I was busy. That's where the fuck I was. Didn't the fact that I was not where I said I'd meet her pretty much demonstrate that? I never understand why people don't get the obvious.

I tried to take Maggie's hand, but she pulled it away. That made my nice guy routine a little harder to maintain, but I was trying. I was really doing my best.

"I know you're upset," I told her.

"No," she said, her voice even, sharp as a scalpel. "No, don't talk to me that way. He was here." Then she smiled at me, and for the first time, I was scared. "You'll see when he comes back."

§

I didn't believe her. Not really. Even so, I thought something was going on. Maybe Maggie was crazy. Maybe someone was trying to scam her. Maybe—and this one felt the most likely to me—she sensed I was pulling away and was trying to come up with a plan to keep me around. As plans go, this one was pretty fucked up, but women do some crazy shit when they're desperate.

In the meantime, I'd sent Amanda a few texts, politely telling her to fuck off, that I had things to do. At first she got angry, but when I didn't answer her messages, she just left me alone. I figured that was how it would go.

The next night, Maggie and I sat in near silence. She opened a bottle of wine, and we both drank a little too quickly. Then she opened another bottle of wine.

"Maybe we should dim the lights," I suggested.

"It's not a séance," she said testily. "He'll either come or he won't."

I drank some more wine.

At a little after 9:30 there was a knock at the door. It wasn't a *Christmas Carol* banging or a timid and ghostly tapping. It was just a knock, just like anyone rapping his knuckles against the door. I thought to say that maybe ghosts don't use doorbells, but I kept my mouth shut. I'm good that way. Instead, I watched as Maggie, now looking like a ghost herself, rose from the couch and shuffled over to the door. Her hand rested on the knob for a moment, and then turned it.

I had never met William, but I'd seen pictures of him, and there he was—thin and pale with his unkempt hair, too smart to groom himself. Death hadn't hurt his looks much, but they hadn't improved them either. The fact was he looked like a person. There was nothing floating or transparent about him. He was there, like he'd never died.

"I wanted to see you again," he said. His voice sounded normal, not ghostly or groaning or filled with weird echoes.

For all that, I knew this was a ghost. I was looking at a ghost. This was the spirit of a dead man, a soul, that which remained of the human form after crossing the barrier of death. I took out my cell phone and began recording the conversation. If nothing else, I figured I could take a video that would go viral. I'd be the guy who recorded a conversation with a ghost. That could get me on

TV.

"I wanted to see you too," Maggie said. "I miss you so much."

Like I wasn't fucking sitting there.

I looked at the video feed on my phone. There was Maggie talking to William, and it occurred to me that this video was going to look like a whole lot of who cares. Two people talking. That's it. This was not going to go viral on YouTube because there was nothing special about it.

I stood up to walk over to them, but I found I couldn't move my feet. It was like they were glued there and I was watching some freaky movie. I was standing behind Maggie plain as day, but Dead William didn't seem to notice me. Neither did Maggie. It was like they were the only two people in the world.

"I want to go with you," Maggie said.

"You can't," William said. "My home is a coffin now."

"I'll come to you," she said. "If I come to you, will you marry me?"

"If I marry you, you'll die," William said.

"Then we'll be together," she said.

He shook his head. "It's not what you think," he told her. "You don't want to be dead."

"I don't care what it is," she said.

Suddenly I found I could move. I lunged forward, moving toward the two of them. For a minute William turned his gaze in my direction, but he didn't see me. He looked through me as though I were the one who was dead. Worse, he looked at me as though I didn't matter, as though I were insignificant to him.

Fuck that dead asshole, I thought. I slammed the door. Maggie looked at me, shock on her face. She threw open the door, but William was gone.

"What the hell was that?" she demanded.

"There was no point," I told her. "I thought we were going to get some ghost video, but he just looked like a regular person. And then I needed to stop him."

"Stop him from what?" Maggie said.

"He was, I don't know, hypnotizing you or something. You were talking like going to live in his coffin was an okay idea in your book."

"He wasn't hypnotizing me," Maggie said. She turned away

from me, so I was talking to her back. "I want to go with him. I want it."

"Because he was doing something to do you," I said. "Messing with your head."

"No, it's because he's the man I was going to marry. You think I want to spend the rest of my life with you? You seduced me into cheating on William, you practically forced me to let you live with me. If I knew of some way to make you leave, I would do it, but you're the one haunting me. Not William. Going to live in a hole in the ground in Scotland would be a relief."

I stood there, staring at her, unable to believe what I was hearing. I had stuck around for her. I made her tea, and now she was turning against me?

"What are you telling me?" I asked. "That you would rather be dead with him than alive with me?"

"Go be with your other girl," Maggie said and turned her back on me. "I wish you had moved in with her already, but you won't. You'll come back here, like you always do. When William comes back tomorrow, I'm going with him. At least I'll be away from you."

§

I had the last of my shit in my gym bag and had already loaded up my truck. "You've gotten rid of me," I told her as I stood by the door.

She sat on the couch, staring ahead, not looking at me.

"If you didn't want me around, why didn't you say anything?" I asked.

"I did tell you," she quietly. "You didn't listen."

I shook my head. "Just promise me you won't have him coming around anymore."

"You want me to call an exterminator?" she asked.

I didn't have much to say to that.

I grabbed my bag and left. I was done with her. The shit she had said to me was unforgivable, and I wasn't going to put up with it. No fucking way. Except after about a week, I gave in. I called, but she'd disconnected her phone.

I decided to drive by her house, and there was a real estate agent—a real fat one—setting up one of those lawn signs. You'd have thought she was deadlifting the way she was huffing and sweating.

I don't like people to see that I give a shit about anything, so I played it all casual. "What happened to the lady who lived here?"

The fat real estate agent looked up and wiped at her forehead. "It's very sad," she told me. "The woman passed away. Her family wanted the house sold as soon as possible."

"That's fucking bullshit," I told her. I might have said some other things, pushed her around a little, but she was asking for it, laying that on me like that, so suddenly. It wasn't kind at all.

I went home and looked it up on my computer. There it was, the obituary in the paper. Maggie had died the night after I left. There had been an undetected heart problem, and she dropped dead, standing by her door. The paper played it up real tragic, like her fiancé had died a few weeks before. They treated it like it was some amazing story of love, like one of those plays you have to read in school or something. They especially got off on how Maggie had just changed her will, saying that when she died she wanted to be buried in Scotland, next to William.

I was not about to let that asshole win. No fucking way. Without getting up from the computer, without worrying about how much it cost, I bought a plane ticket to Glasgow for the next day. I'd buy a shovel or something there. They must have shovels in Scotland. Once I found that graveyard, I would show them both that getting away from me is not as easy as they think.

On...Sweet William's Ghost

Sweet Willam's Ghost is Child Ballad 77 (Roud #50). The Aarne-Thompson Tale Type Index lists it rather wonderfully as #365 — Supernatural Opponents, Specter Bridegrooms.

A ghost, usually named William, comes to the window of his lover, usually called Margaret. There he asks for his 'faith and troth' back (i.e. her promise to marry him). Not knowing that he is dead, she asks him to come and kiss her, wherein he sometimes answers that if he does her days will not be long. In a few variations, she asks that they go to the kirk (church) and marry. He then tells her that he is dead. She returns the troth and follows him to his grave, asking if there is room in there for her as well. She then either dies on his grave, does not have long to live, or goes away weeping. (1)

In some versions she refuses to return his troth unless he tells her what happens after death to unbaptized children, women who die in child birth, and those who commit suicide.

This belief of the dead betrothed coming to visit their intended was evident even in the nineteenth century. Sir Walter Scott wrote of a woman who, arriving too late to see her dying fiancé, asked to see his body. She touched his hand and thus, superstition tells us, escaped a visit from his ghost. (2)

Sweet William's Ghost was recorded on Kate Rusby's 2003 album, *Underneath The Stars,* and is the name of a musical project out of Portland, Oregon.

1) Child, Francis James. The English and Scottish Popular Ballads Vol. 2. Mineola: Dover, 2003.

2) Child, Francis James. The English and Scottish Popular Ballads Vol. 2. Mineola: Dover, 2003.

BLACK IS THE COLOR OF MY TRUE LOVE'S HAIR

By
DEL HOWISON

"unstable souls ... they are the children of curse"
— 2 Peter 2:14, 1599 Geneva Bible

In the far corner of a forgotten stone garden stands a most unusual grave statue. A chiseled sandstone child, solemn and expressionless, she watches the seasons pass without comment. Dismissed in the dark extremity of this hallowed place by the statues of crying angels draped over the gravesite or stone urns and granite wreaths that are placed closer to the sunshine and front gate, the lone child stands erect, arms at her side, staring straight ahead. Nothing so simple has ever been so unnerving. Where other monuments were entwined by nature in this forgotten garden, the girl stands clean, the ground about her dead and brown as if Mother Earth has offered up the final rejection, allowing no peace. The original carving, although graced with great artistic emotion, is somewhat crudely set as if it was toiled upon by unskilled hands. From the direction she faces, the winds and rains have wiped away many details of her surface and the only inscription offered to the curious meanderer is hard to read and incomplete.

Mara L rr
 orn 1889 - D ed 19 0
To soon   was taken   om hi wo
Bl k is th c l r of y   tru   ov s h   r

Her face remains mostly intact though softened with time and weather. Her mouth wiped clean. If one were to walk around the likeness, they would notice very distinct long locks of hair that are carved with exquisite care, flowing down the backside of the image. The hair was so attended to by the sculptor that it feels like the predominance of his time was spent away from her face. The flow and placement of each shock fills one with awe for the workmanship that does not appear elsewhere on the effigy. The love that is exhibited here is wrapped in great sadness, as all extraordinary loves are in order to exist at all.

The shadow of maternity had hung over the shack for more than seven months before the fateful night arrived. Elwin could hardly wait for the birth of his first born. He had spent the last few years of his life anticipating and hoping this moment would come. The only woman who had been willing to shackle herself to a poor dirt farmer was lying in the next room, screaming with pain. It had been Hell on Earth living with her, and after their initial sexual encounter on their wedding night, the opportunities to procreate had been few and far between. There had been no lovemaking or joy. Any sexual satisfaction he encountered had been in the bed of a neighbor. He had rejoiced that one of the quick, awkward thrusts his wife had allowed him had actually worked.

As she felt the pain from the poison course through her body, she realized the time was nigh and revenge was tasting sweet. Her agony rose and fell like waves cresting and each time catching her breath was harder and harder. But she savored it, knowing that the last minutes of her life had been in her hands, her call. It could be minutes or might be hours but it would be over.

"Elwin, go," she said. "Fetch the undertaker and be as quick as you can."

"Undertaker?"

She almost sat up in bed with the pain and her declaration.

"Yes, the undertaker."

"What? What are you talking about?"

"I'm talkin' about I'm gonna die and I'm taking your sweet, precious baby with me. You wanted me to have your baby like some kind of breeding stock. Well, I did that. You took an oath to be true to me and you couldn't keep your damn pecker in your pants! I'm takin' her by taking me."

Elwin began to cry.

"What did you do!"

"You cheating slob. There's only one thing you love more than yourself. You love your baby, just not enough left over to love me for carrying it. I believe your baby is already dead and I'm just pushing it out. I will be following shortly and with that I take your heart for all eternity. I take what you wouldn't give me!"

She winced with pain and then looked him straight in the eyes through her sweat and the heat.

"It makes me happy. It makes me real happy. I'm taking your heart, Elwin."

She shouted and grabbed her stomach.

"Oh God!"

Elwin stuttered a moment, looking at his wife, and then headed for the door.

"I'm going to get Miss Orpha," he said

"Miss Orpha is a Yarb Doctor. She cain't help you none. It's too late. I don't need no witchin' around my family. If it was illegal to be peddling her mumbo-jumbo, I would have had her throwed her in jail. You are too late. Too damn late! Why don't you just run to your whore instead?"

She doubled up with pain and then grabbed her stomach as if it might explode. Her breathing was short, forced. Her face strained, turning darker in color, and sweat as if from a soaked rag ran from her face. Her voice came out soft between the exhalations of her breath.

"You gave me the original pain. Now I'm giving it back. I'm ending my suffering and that of the child. I swear again on the ghost of my father, as I did our wedding night, that you will find no pleasure in me or your offspring."

She practically raised up out of the bed in anger and spit at him as she spoke.

"I curse you! You will have nothing! You are a poor excuse for a man."

Then the pain grabbed her and knocked her back into the damp mattress.

"Death, be quick about it!"

He ran to the barn where the wagon sat and left to fetch the midwife. His wife grabbed the sideboards of the bed and held on as tight as she could manage. She prayed the child would try to emerge before they returned. Then, if it were living, she would kill it with her own hands. She could feel it was not dead yet. But he would have nothing.

While Elwin stood to the side, helping with clean water and towels, Orpha worked on the child. She leaned up between his wife's legs, and her hands and trained fingers manipulated the baby inside. She cocked her head as if listening to something but the only noise was the wife's laboring.

"It's coming," she said.

"The child?" he asked.

"Four, three, two..."

She paused and then the thunder rattled the cabin. She smiled at him.

"Wipe me," Orpha said. "The storm. Have you never waited on the storm by counting from the flash?"

He moved forward with a damp cloth and blotted the sweat from her forehead and out of her eyes.

"I hadn't noticed," he said, confused.

"You are negro scum," his wife shouted and spit at Orpha.

She shook her head more from what she was feeling rather than the running perspiration. She was unhappy with her discoveries.

"Kill me!"

His wife was screaming throughout the ordeal but Orpha paid her no heed. They had tied her ankles to the frame at the foot of the bed, legs spread wide. She would offer them no help and Orpha didn't want to be kicked.

"The child is kneeling breech," she said to Elwin.

"Is that good?"

"It is a sign, like the storm. There's evil in this birth. She'd be better dead."

Orpha watched his face. Clearly he did not understand what she was speaking of. "If the child lives, it will be evil."

He walked in circles trying to get his thoughts in order. "She must live! You must save her. She is all I've got."

"I have never willingly brought evil into this world."

"I'm the father. I can train her and teach her in the way of goodness."

"You are a poor excuse for a man," his wife told him for the second time that night.

"The bond is here," Orpha said, and with two fingers she pulled out a taut section of the umbilical coming from the opening of his wife, showing it to Elwin. He turned his head away. "Look, the child is not tight inside. There is room for the cord to slip along the sides of the walls and come out first. I am trying to push it back up, past the child. The feet and the ass are coming out together. If they pinch the cord, the child will suffocate before birthing. I will have no say in that. That would be God trying stop the child. If I try to pull the babe down and out before the cord can slip out sideways, the force will either pull loose the baby's limbs from the sockets or split apart your wife. I can't save them both."

"Save neither, witch!" his wife cursed at Orpha and tried to wiggle about.

"I am here to do what I have been trained to do."

"You are betraying my wishes, you old crone!"

She pulled out her hands and carelessly wiped her forehead, leaving a splattering of blood and fluid behind. "I am betraying my own soul. Your crazy wishes do not concern me at this point," she said to his wife.

Orpha wiped her hands with the gingham rag she kept in her apron.

"It won't happen. It can't happen," Elwin rocked his body and called to the heavens. "You must save her."

Orpha looked at him with disdain. "The child should be buried while there is still life in her, standing up, so that God can take the child's soul before he loses it to Satan. You are making a big mistake here."

The thunder took another shot at gaining their attention.

"You are so simple. Even for being a man, you are so simple." Orpha shook her head. "You understand nothing of the ways of the Devil."

"I understand that all I've ever wanted is a child. I will not have another chance. I'm poor, growing older every day and no woman looks at me. I have to save that child."

Orpha shook her head, then reached into the pocket of the wifery apron she wore and pulled out a handful of objects. She pushed aside the personal items from the top of the scarred wooden dresser and laid her items out to see. To Elwin it looked like some Ozark dirt and a few bones and jewelry laid scattered on the wooden top. His wife screamed and he finally found his voice.

"What are you doing?"

"What I've been prepared to do," Orpha said as she placed certain items in their own small pile. "The Devil has given us a choice and you are stupid enough to take him up on it."

She looked back at his wife struggling against the ties.

"The child has the chance."

She took a pinch of the dirt. With two fingers she spread the soil in a line crossways on his wife's stomach just above the hairline.

"What is that?"

"Blessed dirt to help counter the jimsonweed your wife ingested. If we are unlucky enough, one soul will remain with body tonight. The bone yard shall make the choice."

"But my wife...You must save her too."

"I must do nothing of the kind," she said and with her finger and thumb spread the belly dirt out into a wider line. "Salvation is elusive."

He was scared. Elwin stepped up and pushed at her. "I don't want any of your hoodoo magic in my house."

He was puffed, asserting himself. She spun on him, freezing him with a look. After the pause he shrank back against the wall into the shadows.

"You stay there," she hissed at him. "You stay there, little man, and let me do my work! You fetched me. Now I am here. I do your bidding, not mine! So leave me alone before I change my mind."

When all was still again, except for the vulgar screaming from the bed, Orpha turned back to her objects.

"Yes, I am a midwife," she said. "But I am also a Granny woman. I'll use every tool at my disposal. But on a night like tonight, it may not be enough."

The thunder answered in response. She spoke low and slow.

"You stay out of my way, little man, whilst I try to save at least one Missouri life this evening."

She took a necklace from the pile and placed it over her head, about her neck. Her movements were deliberate, unhurried and ceremonial as if there were none in agony within the confines of the room. Her fingers moved over the drop that hung from the beads, fingering the amulet's familiar surface, focusing her ritual. Her lips moved but there was no sound to be heard except for the high-pitched swearing of his wife and the drumming of the rain.

"Can you help her?"

Elwin's attention continued to be split between Orpha and his wife. He was growing more frantic by the moment, feeling helpless in this nightmare.

"I can," Orpha said. "But we don't know yet whether or not it is a she. Do we?" Her toothy smile shrank him back yet again.

"All we know is that the bairn is bedeviled and your wife has caused herself and the child great suffering. It must be removed and the pain will cease. Then we will find how the poison has affected it."

She kissed the periapt and turned the necklace around so that the pendant hung down her back. She faced the bed, her countenance taking on such a dark tone and emotion that Elwin would not have thought it was the same woman who had walked through the door with him. The umbra that bisected her face seemed to be part of her skin tone and gave a great lurid depth to the lines that etched her appearance. From the other pocket of her apron, she pulled a sizable knife with a serrated blade. She paused and then looked at Elwin.

"You must be strong," she said, looking him up and down. "Although, I am aware that is counter to your soul."

He looked at the glinting metal and then to his wife.

"For the cord?" he asked Orpha.

"No," she replied. "For the womb."

In the years that followed the birthing, Elwin was visited often by Orpha to "watch the child's progress. " While he was grateful for the assistance, he felt wary of their secret talks and long, woodsy walks. But he couldn't deny that there were things, "girl things" as Orpha called them, that he just didn't understand. Still, darkness draped the house and neighbors seemed to shun his land. He had lost his position at a local feed-seller and needed to make do with odd jobs and farm pickup work. To help out their income, he carved in wood and chiseled in stone making things for people. The house was poor in the poorest of areas.

Despite Orpha's continued warning to destroy the girl, she grew, thrived, and seemed happy. She would bring her father rabbits and squirrels along with any other small animals she had caught to help with their meals. She wouldn't trap them but instead killed them with sticks and rocks in the most violent manner. It put him off but he never turned down the food, for their needs were greater than his morals. Whenever he would speak to Orpha about this, she would ask him if he was ungrateful for the food. He wasn't, of course. Beggars could not be choosers, she said. He didn't want to lose his daughter's love and Orpha would shake her head, pointing at him, warning the day of reckoning was due.

"The Devil is a strong demon," she would say. "And you are a weak man."

If Elwin attempted to offer excuses, he was put off by Orpha and charmed by his daughter. Mara was a charmer. Her jet black hair carried the ghost of her mother and the shine in her eyes was mischievous and lost at the same time. She had but to touch her father's arm to calm him or stroke his cheek to take him to a happier, unquestioning place. Elwin was too tired to fight her as long as she was happy. It was all curious and the whiffs of a spirit that lingered in the cabin since the death of his wife rested like a blanket of silence and foreboding. He could not get out from under the weight and it kept him silent.

But he worried about Mara every day. There was more in his household than his mind could hold. In his heart he knew the time was near. Were he a religious man he might have prayed for guidance. Instead, once or twice a month, he would hitch the wagon and go to the Joplin library. There he found books on folklore and superstition and witchcraft and children born under a bad sign. He would stutter his way through them, moving his lips as he silently read to himself. He found that there were two options, the fight to win her soul, which he knew he couldn't win, and an out he couldn't force himself to take. Either he would drive out all that the blood of her mother and the poison that the jimsonweed had instilled in her or he would have to bury her, alive, pleading for forgiveness, her head pointed towards heaven. When the showdown for the soul of his daughter came, he would not lose for lack of preparation.

As Mara pinned the clothes to the line, Elwin watched the wind move her shiny dark hair across her back in small waves. The glistening was diamond in its sheen and the volume was unworldly in its fullness. When she turned and looked at him, Elwin smiled back in a learned reaction. Keep her happy. Let her know you were her rock, her only parent. He needed her to answer to him only.

As she had gotten older, she understood her power more and more. She really could do anything she wanted, even if she was a little unsure of what steps to take to make that happen. She removed the final clothes pin from her mouth and slid it over the dangling piece of material, holding it securely on the line. Then she stepped back to admire her work.

"Another job is finished, Mara," Elwin said. "Well done."

"Yes," she said. "That's the last time I'm going to do that."

Elwin watched her face cloud as she walked over and sat in the wooden chair next to him. The clothes danced on the line.

"That's the last time I do anything I'm really not parcel to."

"Ah, but were life that easy, child," he said.

She turned to him, intense and meaningful. "But it is, Papa." She played with her hands a moment, thinking what to speak. "I can make people do things if I want."

A childish statement all the more chilling for its innocence.

"What do you mean, Mara?" he asked.

But he knew what she meant.

"It's a feeling inside. It builds and builds until I want to pop. So I have to let it go to make myself better."

She turned her head slightly away and smiled at him with her eyes. She would be able to charm them all. He could feel the smile travel up his spine and sit between his shoulder blades, pecking the base of his neck.

"The other morning when you left to go to Alexander's Store, I sat out on the step and watched the woods. A squirrel, a fat red-brown, stood on that lower limb of the oak there."

Mara pointed at a branch some forty feet from where they sat. Her head cocked slightly as she spoke as though she were seeing the entire incident over again

"He chattered at me. I believe he was mad that I was sitting and watching him or maybe he was upset that I had killed and eaten his brother. I yelled out at him, 'Be quiet!' But he continued on with his talk."

She stood up from the chair as she told her tale and took a step toward the tree in reenactment.

"I said, 'Be quiet,'" she said and continued her slow step to the tree. "Finally I became so furious that I held out my hands, open wide like claws but flat, and screamed at the top of my lungs to frighten him off. He froze still for a moment and then dropped to the ground, still. I did it without stick or stone, Papa."

Mara turned back to her father, once again looking like the little girl she was.

"I just wanted to quiet him. But I killed him."

Elwin stood up and hugged her. "No, no, Mara. You didn't kill him. It was just a strange thing and he happened to die at the same moment you shouted. That's all."

Elwin put his arm around her shoulder and they turned to walk back into the house.

"Do you really think so, Father?"

"I do."

"That is odd. I thought it was me."

"No, no. Just a strange thing. Life is like that sometimes," Elwin said and stepped up on to the stoop.

Mara stopped and looked up at him above her. "Yes, I suppose that's true," she said, nodding her head. "So now that makes four strange things altogether this week."

She walked up the stairs past him and into the cabin. The chill returned to Elwin like an old companion.

When the first child turned up dead, the news spread quickly through the hollow. He'd been found fresh as life, like he was sleeping there in the grass. The was no sign of violence, no injuries, not even any out-of-the-ordinary bug bites. It was just an odd thing that the doctor couldn't explain.

"Sometimes these strange things just happen," was all he could say. "God calls us when we least expect it."

Elwin heard the talk at Alexander's Store and knew the boy's family. A layer of dread covered his heart as he walked the ridge to the cabin. When he arrived, he cupboarded the meager supplies and stepped out to look for Mara. She sat on a stump out back looking into the trees.

"What are you doing?' he asked as he sat down beside her.

"Watching."

"For what?'"

"For dinner."

"You don't have to today, Mara. I made enough chore money to buy us a few groceries."

Elwin pulled a long strand of grass from beside the steps and stuck it in his mouth. He looked at her face as he spoke.

"I heard about Paul today at the store."

She squeezed one eye tight for a split second as if he was giving her a headache but continued searching the trees.

"You know about your school friend Paul?"

She turned and looked at him. "He was not my friend."

"He was ten and he is dead," Elwin said. "He is much too young to be dead."

She watched his eyes and then looked back into the trees. "He was older than our dinner," she said.

"That's true. But he was a person not a rabbit."

"The rabbits never laughed at me," she said and stood.

She walked into the cabin, leaving Elwin alone on the steps. He sat trying to figure what he knew and what he did not want to know. It is hard for the most rational of people to digest things that hang just outside of daily experience and Elwin decided he had more library reading to do. That was it. That was all. He just needed more book learning.

Some weeks later, when Elwin had been planting most of the morning, he heard about the dead horse. He was sitting on a stone next to the road, drinking some water he'd brought to the field with him when the county agent went by and stopped to talk. No reason he said, just seemed like the horse's heart up and stopped. Strangest thing. Doc can't figure it. There had been mention of a young child being glimpsed in the pen shortly before it happened but nobody knew for sure. Elwin knew but he didn't say so, not even to himself.

"Took you too many years to admit it," Orpha said. "But now judgment is here, ain't it? You conceived her during your spell of sinning and your wife tried to destroy her because she knew of your sin. It all says 'Devil' in great big letters."

"Can you help me? Another child cannot die because I was too weak to stop what needed to be stopped."

Orpha went back to her stove and whatever she was cooking. She poked it with a fork to let the grease drip down its sides. It hissed when it hit the bottom. She looked up at Elwin from the open stove.

"You never want to let things heat up enough to pop. You can ruin a lot by letting it get that far." She stood up and set the big fork on the cutting board. "I did warn you," she said. "It's true that all prophets are liars but I knew what I was talking about. I've been through this before."

Elwin leaned his head against the door jamb of her cabin and began to cry.

"Orpha, you've got to help me. I can't do this alone."

She jumped down on the ground next to him and grabbed his face with both hands. Inches from him he could smell the rot on her breath.

"I tried to help you! You rebuked me. Now things is dying and you come crawling to me. Well, damn you! Help yourself!"

He jerked and pulled away when some of her spittle sprayed his face from her anger. He wiped his lips with the back of his sleeve.

"You've got to help me. I've got nowhere else to turn."

Her eyes, like burning coals, seared through him and then she quickly turned away and climbed back into her cabin. She walked to the corner of the room and grabbed a spade.

"You know what you have to do."

She tossed the shovel at him and he grabbed it. He looked at it in terror, knowing it was the only solution to his problem.

"God has already damned your soul, Elwin. Salvation is a fickle thing."

She slammed the cabin door shut. He stood looking at his daughter's murder weapon.

Secretly digging the hole in the back corner of the cemetery was easy. There was no keeper, nobody to notice his activity. He had contemplated burying her somewhere out in the woods but knew he needed consecrated land so God would take her soul. Getting the reverend to bless new ground would have come with its own problems and suspicions so he had chosen ground that was already blessed.

The night of the deed was cloudless and still. It was darker than the inside of the well and Mara lay peaceful on her blankets. Elwin approached her with the clothesline he had torn from the trees out back. His work rag from the barn stuck out of one pocket. He tried to move without creaking the boards by stepping as close to the walls as he could, where the boards had less give. He crept to her side of the room and looked down at the only thing he had ever loved. She was beautiful. Her black hair even seemed to shine in the darkness, catching light from some unknown place. He stood for a long time looking at her, breaking up inside of himself.

With a final, deep breath, he committed himself by jumping on her and pinning her to the ground before she could awaken in the confusion. Being sure to stay clear of her hands, he tied them behind her and then began binding her legs together. She screamed and thrashed but he was too much for her. There was no one to hear her cries in the woods. He then ran the rope from the top of her leg bindings to her hands and over her shoulders, bringing it back down on the other side. She was now prevented from bending and had to remain stiff. He would lower her into the hole feet first, like a fence post, and she would remain erect, head toward heaven, as he shoveled the dirt in on top of her. He would save her and she would wait for him in heaven.

Elwin retrieved the work rag from his pocket and stuffed it in her mouth. He secured it by wrapping a length of rope about her face. Then he picked her up, slung her over his shoulder, and took her out to the wagon in the barn. He laid her gently in the back and climbed up top. Giving the reigns a shake, the horse began its journey to the stone garden and the final resting place of Mara.

At the gravesite he lifted her out of the wagon and carried her over to the hole. She had managed to slip a couple of her fingers free and touched his arm. He turned and looked into her face and almost abandoned the entire plan. Her eyes pleaded with him and the tears ran down Mara's cheek. The child was begging for life. The rope he had wrapped about her head to keep the rag in place had chafed her fine white skin and the redness was almost raw to bleeding. He stopped in the grass and set her down as his body heaved in agony over what he was doing. When his sobbing had subsided, he looked down at her and realized how much he loved her. He must save her. Her soul was all that mattered.

Picking her back up, he carried her to the hole and laid her next to it. Elwin grabbed her under her arms, and then he twisted her about until her feet were dangling over the edge of the cavity and he tipped her slowly in. He slid her down until she came to a stop with her head about a foot below the surface of the ground. Standing up, he looked around for Orpha's shovel. Using the side of it, he scooped the dirt into the hole and over the head of his child. It fell into the pit, filling up around. She wiggled and tossed as she began to breathe in the dirt through her nose. Then, suddenly, she was completely consumed by the soil.

He patted the mound flat and smooth, then set the spade aside. He knelt beside the dirt tomb and prayed to God. He was now a religious man.

"Thank you for giving me the strength."

There he left it in the Almighty's hands.

Three months later, Elwin was carving on the slab of sandstone that he had set on top of her resting place, hiding the churned ground from prying eyes. Some townspeople felt it was a memorial placed in the back of the old cemetery to a missing child who would never be found. He was a sad spirit and the local folks mostly left him to his own devices. It was that afternoon when he heard the news. They had found another dead child.

On...Black is the Color of My True Love's Hair

Black is the Color of My True Love's Hair is not in the Child Ballads—instead it is listed in the Roud index as #3103. The Roud Folk Song Index is a database of nearly two hundred thousand references to nearly twenty-five thousand songs compiled by Steve Roud. It includes all the Child material and is now maintained online by the English Folk Dance and Song Society. (1)

There are many different versions of this song, starting with the title—from Black is the Color, Black is the Color of My True Love's Hair, But Black is the Color of My True Love's Hair, Black Black is the Color of My True Love's Hair, and even Black Black Black is the Color of My True Love's Hair. (2). There are versions from both the male and female perspective.

The basic plot of the song is the singers' desire and longing for their love. The '"True Love" has, as the title alludes to, black hair. Their eyes, face, hands, and even the ground under their feet is adored. The singer longs for the time when they can be as one.

Recent singers include everyone from Christy Moore on her 2008 album to Nina Simone. There is even a downloadable ring tone.

1) Roud Folksong Index. 2013. 25 September, 2013. <http://www.efdss.org/library-and-archive>. English Folk Dance and Song Society.

2) Roud Folksong Index. 2013. 25 September, 2013. <http://www.efdss.org/library-and-archive>. English Folk Dance and Song Society.

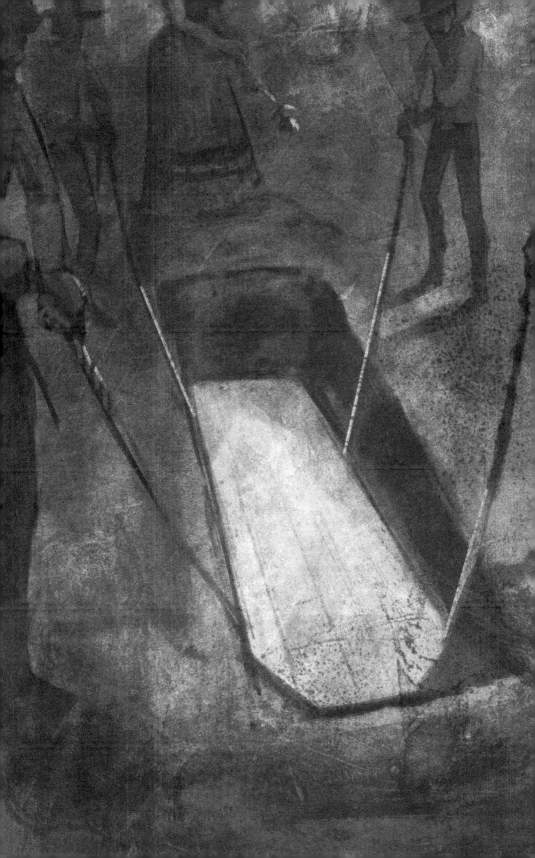

John Wayne's Dream

By
Gary A. Braunbeck

"Music is the art which is most nigh to tears and memory."
— Oscar Wilde

"It (music) expresses that which cannot be said and on which it is impossible to remain silent."
— Victor Hugo

Man, it's bad tonight—sick, miserable, choke-on-this ugly—the worst it's ever been, worse even than when you were drying out in the hospital, and you need tonight's meeting before you decide to break the goddamn seal on the bottle stashed in the trunk of your car with those Other Things, Things you can't help but think of in upper case, that's how bad it is; it's so bad you can't bring yourself to name them, even silently to yourself, that would mean you're actually, seriously, no-shit-Sherlock considering the repellant thoughts and ugly pictures that are kicking so hard across your mind, these things you know damned well ought to turn your stomach but don't, not even a little (they've caused you to actually smile when you're alone and once even chuckle into your cold coffee), and if you decide to do it, the Things will make it so easy, easy, easy-peezy, so you have to think of those Things in upper case because to name them, to admit you have them because of the thoughts and pictures in your mind, that's what scares you right down to the marrow of the bones in this sad-ass body you've been walking around in for—what?—fifty-three years and however many months and days, this sad-ass body that at least had enough willpower to drag itself down here to the church basement and the all-too familiar door halfway down the hall, the one you're standing in front of right now; so you take a deep breath, close your eyes, force the thoughts and pictures to the back of your mind, hoping they'll stay there, God grant me the serenity to make it all fuck off, and as you grasp the doorknob and begin turning it, you see the piece of paper that's been hastily taped to the frosted glass—

AA Meeting Canceled
Tonight Only:

Ghosts Sing Sad Cowboy Song for the Whole Broken World—and you feel your jaw actually drop like the anvil-mouth of some cartoon character as you read the words a second time, hand still gripping the doorknob, but before you can react, you hear it start from inside the room: that song ... and on a guitar, of course—a steel-faced dobro-style resonator, from the sound of it, just slightly out of tune, causing the melody to sound all the more distant and empty and hopeless; gritting your teeth, you pull your hand away from the doorknob and step back as if moving two feet away will stop the sound from reaching you, but reach you it does, just as loud, just as cheerless, no goddamned different from any of the hundreds of times you've heard it played or played it yourself by request, by request, by request only because that's the only way anyone in their right mind would play the song, sure as hell not by choice, nosiree, like King Lear always said never, never, Never, Never, NEVER.

"Are you going in?" says a voice to your left.

She's younger than most of the people you've seen at the meetings; her face is round, its skin slightly pink beneath the surface, no tell-tale loopy blue lines of broken veins in her nose, no too-bright sheen in her eyes, no crow's feet, nothing to indicate that she shares your disease—hell, she looks like someone who should be playing the Julie Andrews part in *The Sound of Music*, not a recovering drunk.

"The, uh ... the meeting's been canceled," you say, not so much pointing at as absent-mindedly flipping a finger toward the makeshift sign.

"I know," she replies. "I'm here for the ghosts' concert. Isn't that why you're here, _____?"

She calls you by name. You have never seen this woman before. She's so fresh, so genuinely pretty, so clean—no, it's more than being clean, she seems … absolutely unspoiled. You might have a small graveyard of brain cells relegated to the back plate of your grey matter, but you're not so far gone that you'd forget a face like hers.

She smiles and brushes past you, reaching down and turning the doorknob. She's pressed against your side, her hand almost touching yours, but doesn't seem the least bit shy or embarrassed by it.

"I always loved this song," Unspoiled says. "It's been one of my favorites for … oh, I don't remember how long."

You just stare at her, not knowing a courteous way to respond. C, F, G, A-minor and D-minor; the whole goddamn song's based on various combinations and repetitions of those five chords—hell, the intro alone looks and feels like the most goddamn boring tune ever written—

```
/ C - - / G - - / Am - - / G - - /
/ C - - / F - - / C - - / G - - /
/ C - - / G - - / Am - - / G - - /
/ C - - / F - - / G - - / C - - / - - - /
```

—Snoozeville, right? Yet somehow those five basic, dreary, mind-numbing chords—chords you could teach a genetically-retarded monkey to play—manage to give body, soul, shame, and voice to the pain of the saddest songs ever … and wouldn't you know, it was Dad's favorite?

Of course you know that, you know damn near everything about good old Dad; you know too goddamned much about good old Dad—Christ knows he talked enough during those last few days, lying there in his bed with a bedpan under his ass and a catheter running up into his urethra, trickling bloody urine into a plastic bag. Sometimes he'd give you a half-hearted smile, but he wasn't the same man, the one who used to berate, humiliate, and mock you, the man who could always find fault in everything you did, who knew just the right thing to say to make your accomplishments seem inconsequential in everyone's eyes including your own, who could diminish you with less effort than it took to pick his nose; no, this wasn't the same man at all. This was just a sick old bastard making a last-ditch effort to get his bad-tempered ass into heaven.

"Have you heard this song before?" asks Unspoiled, staring at you with a curious intensity that, goddammit, reminds you of good old Dad toward the end.

You'd take him to the county cemetery where his parents and sister were buried, and as he sat there in his wheelchair staring at their headstones, you'd study his face and see him wondering if there was something that he'd missed, something he could've done to spend a little more time with them, to save them from feeling alone and frightened during their last few days of life, maybe even wishing that one or all of them could still be here to comfort him and, for a little while, get his mind off the disease that now counted down the clock that told of the time he had left. You don't know, maybe he came here to study their graves the same way he'd study his own face in a mirror, naked and defenseless. Why won't you look at me and Mom that way, you'd wonder. We have some time left—not much, but some—and maybe we could repair some things—okay, okay, okay, be realistic—if not repair, then at least spackle over some of the cracks so that when we drop the bag of meat that used to be you into the dirt, we might feel some kind of loss instead of relief. Is that too much to ask at this point?

"Did you know," says Unspoiled, "that this song has actually been around for centuries, in dozens—maybe even hundreds—of variations?"

You nod your head. "Actually, yeah ... I did know that." Because good old Dad, he'd told you about that dozens—maybe even hundreds—of times ... when he wasn't a zombie.

He'd sit for long hours in front of his bedroom window, staring out at the same neighborhood he'd known for most of his life, searching for something hidden, something unnoticed until now, something that would reveal whatever secrets there were to be revealed. Close by, Mom and you waited for him to complete this final voyage into himself, hoping the old emotional wounds might at last heal so that he would maybe, maybe, maybe, please

God just once turn and smile over his shoulder, telling the two of you, without the burden of words, that he'd returned from this last nightmare, this final batch of self-recriminations that had made him a sadistic stranger to you for too long; and now, now that he was returned to you for however brief a time, you would go outside into the warm spring light, your mother and you each holding one of his hands, and you would thank the day for its blessings as it fell into twilight, and you would remain there, in shadows, as before, hands joined. "I don't even feel sick," was among some of the last things he said, along with, "What I wouldn't give for a hamburger and cold beer right about now." And of all Final Requests, he asked you to get out your old guitar and play that fucking song for him because, he said, it helped him to relax, to breathe easier, to fall asleep the way a man ought to fall asleep—no drugs, no siree, just a good, hard-working man falling asleep because the good, hard work took it out of him today. He would say that the Duke, the Duke never took to pills or liquor to fall asleep in his movies. The Duke was a Man, a Man's Man, and boy, wouldn't it be nice to just once have the kind of dream that the Duke must've had when his head hit the pillow at night, the kind of dream only a strong, solid, all-American Man's Man dreamed? "Maybe I'll have it tonight," he said to you that last night as you strummed those five horrible chords on that shabby guitar you'd bought second-hand from a pawn shop when you were twelve. "Maybe tonight I'll dream John Wayne's dream."

Part of you wanted to smash that guitar to pieces right there and then, go all Pete Townshend on the thing and scream "Don't you remember his last movie, Dad? The Duke, your Man's Man, was a goddamn walking corpse, being eaten away bit by bit from the bottom of his bowels by the same thing that's gobbling up your guts—fuck! He spent most of that movie fractured on Laudanum. That's how he went to sleep, but you don't remember that, do you? No—all you remember is that Jimmy Stewart told the Duke it was not the way he'd choose to go out, and that the Duke, your Man's Man, the great All-American Cowboy, he took Stewart's advice and went out in a blaze of glory, guns blasting away and bad guys dropping all around, blood and bodies littering the saloon floor, and you sure as hell aren't going out that way, are you, Dad?"

GARY BRAUNBECK

No, he sure as hell didn't. But that doesn't have to mean you'll go out the same way, his son who was such a private embarrassment to him; his son who never walked into the sunset with his best girl at his side; his son who never counted off twenty paces with a cheating gambler in the street before whirling around and putting the scoundrel down with a quick, single, justified shot; his son who never rode high in the saddle or talked real slow and deliberate or strolled with the swagger of a Real Man who made decisions and stuck with them out there where the tumbleweeds blew across silent, dusty streets where the womenfolk and children could walk in safety once again, knowing it was Real Man who'd done what needed doing.

"Hey, Dad, look at those bad guys fall. Look what I decided to do. Am I a Man in your eyes now? Am I worthy to sleep the sleep of the Just, of the Heroic? Am I worthy to dream John Wayne's dream?"

Unspoiled leans her head to the side a little and says your name again. "Are you all right?"

"I was hoping for, you know, the other meeting that was supposed to—"

She grabs your hand as she pushes the door open. "Oh, this will be much better than one of those dreary meetings. Those meetings are for everyone." She pulls you into the room. "This, tonight, is just for unfortunate rakes—just one, actually. This is just for you."

You stare at her, hoping her crazy won't explode and get all over you. "Imagine what that means to me." What the hell is that supposed to mean? You have no idea, but it's too late to take it back.

She laughs and pulls you into the room. It's mostly dark except for one bright circle of light shining down onto the middle of the floor; in the center of the circle is a folding chair. She leads you there, pushes you down, and kisses the top of your head.

"Now don't you move. We went through an awful lot of trouble to put this show together."

Before you say anything, she's gone—snap!—into the shadows. You stand up and walk back to the door, but it isn't there any longer. Okay, okay, okay—maybe you just lost your bearings. That has to be it. You're just a little confused because of

Things in your trunk and the unbroken seal on the bottle and the thoughts and pictures in your head, that has to be it, you're just ... Shit—you're probably just losing it, finally, just like everyone said you would someday. You stick out your arms and start feeling around the walls, doing your best Helen Keller to find the door because it has to be here someplace, but after a minute or two, you find nothing and you're even more confused than you were before you stood up, so you go back to the chair and you just sit because you don't know what else to do.

The sound of an old-fashioned projector clatters to life somewhere behind you, and your gaze follows the beam of light to the far wall where someone—Unspoiled, maybe?—has pulled down a screen, and you watch as a grainy black-and-white home movie comes into focus and shows you a scene that you know damn well took place dozens of times in your youth but could not possibly have been filmed because your family never had the money to afford a home-movie camera:

You see a variation of yourself—so much younger but only a little stronger than the man he eventually became; he's standing in the corner of a room, head down, studying his feet as if expecting some great revelation to come thundering up from the earth's core and show him a Great Truth that will set his spirit free.

Sitting a few feet away in his favorite chair, good old Dad is pointing at the young man who would have to settle for becoming you; he's got a beer in his hand and a cigarette dangling from the corner of his mouth.

A conversation repeated so many times and with so few variations it has surpassed the realm of mantra and become the refrain of the inharmonious tune that has been and is your life:

"A man makes a decision and he sticks with it, boy."

"Yessir."

"A man does what he says he'll do. No more, no less."

"Yessir."

"How old are you now?"

Christ, you really didn't remember, did you? You think now "Twenty-three, sir."

"Twenty-three, and what have you got to show for it?"

A decent enough music career—playing clubs, upscale restaurants, sometimes getting enough put aside for some studio time, a couple of self-produced albums selling okay for digital download on some minor music sites. Friends. A place of my own. "I think I've got a lot to show for it."

"You ain't famous, now, are you? I mean, what's the point of doing what you do if all you're gonna settle for is being small-time? A big fish in a little pond?"

"I like my life."

"You're weak, boy. A real man, when he makes a decision to do something, he does it. Your problem is you never decided to be anything more than second-rate because you ain't got the guts to be a real man and decide to be something more."

Why didn't you just say you were ashamed of me? I could've worked with that. "I thought you'd be pleased that I make a decent living at something I love to do."

"Don't talk to me about doing something you love. Doing something you love don't get you shit in the long run. It just makes you weak, makes you a fella who's happy to settle for something. Hell, the Duke never settled in any of his movies. I thought you'd learn something from you and me watching all his movies when you was a kid. The Duke's movies, they taught good lessons. Taught you how to be a man."

Still looking down at the floor, waiting for revelations to thunder. "Because when he made a decision he always stuck with it."

"Goddamn right he stuck with it. Duke always went out a winner, a hero, a man you could respect. Because he knew, the Duke did. A real man, he makes a decision and sticks with it."

"Yessir."

"Does what he says he'll do, no more, no less."

"Yessir."

The film finishes, the light goes out, and the projector shuts off. Deep down in your bowels, you feel the need churning. Leave. Open the bottle. Do it. Take the Things and just do it. Don't go out like good old dad. Don't go out like the Duke. Christ, it hurts! If someone had jammed a knife-blade entwined with barbed-wire into your stomach and twisted it, it wouldn't hurt as much as this need.

"Goddammit," you whisper to yourself. "I want a drink. I want a drink. Just one. One drink. That's all."

The unseen guitar begins playing again, the same five chords, and each chord snarls into your head and your balls like a diamond-tipped drill. You want to get up and get the hell out of the room—and if you can't find the door, you'll beat a goddamn hole into the wall with your bare fists ("Just like the Duke would do," comes the echo of a voice that sounds like your own), you'll kick and claw and chew your way out if you have to, you'll—

—Unspolied appears as the screen is raised up. She's sitting on a stage several feet off the floor. Her body is all wrapped up in a white sheet of some kind, its material thicker than something made from cotton; it looks almost like a tarp. Only her face and one hand are visible.

The music from the guitar fills the room, a sentient force, and as you look into Unspoiled's eyes, you can feel her grief, even from this distance. She smiles at you, a smile that bespeaks an errant wish—that a young woman might never grow old, never lose the radiance that kissed her face when a suitor came to call, never see her beauty dissolve little by little in the unflattering sunlight of each morning, and never know a day when the scent of fresh roses from an admirer did not fill her rooms; as she begins to sing, you stare into her eyes, eyes with sad dark places around them that tell you she has often hid behind a scrim of gaiety to conceal a lonely heart, and both she and her song become every night you've sat isolated and alone, wishing for the warm hand of a lover to hold in your own as autumn dimmed into winter and youth turned to look at you over its shoulder and smile farewell.

> "When I was a young girl, I used to seek pleasure
> When I was a young girl, I used to drink ale.
> Right out of an alehouse down into the jailhouse,
> Right out of the barroom down to my grave."

As she sings, other forms move forward from the shadows: a knight in the remains of ruined armor, his sword in one hand, his bent and twisted visor in the other; behind him comes a cowboy, classic and tall, spurs jangling with each step, holding his stained and tattered hat in wind-burnt hands; an older woman dressed in mourning black; a group of soldiers in uniforms crisp and funereal, carrying the shroud-covered form of a fallen comrade.

GARY BRAUNBECK

The words each of them sing are different, but the melody—the morbid, heartsick, soul-beaten melody—remains the same; it doesn't matter if Unspoiled is singing of one morning in May or the soldiers are singing of Saint James' Hospital or if the knight sings of the maiden fair who passed on her physical ruin to him under the guise of love; it doesn't matter a damn if it's a cowboy dying in the street or a young woman perishing alone in the countryside; it doesn't matter if it's a soldier who got a dose from a passing lady of the night or a mother discovering her prodigal daughter by the side of the road; it doesn't matter how the words are changed or if the rhythm is ever-so-slightly altered or even if the words are in English, it doesn't matter if it's a bad girl's lament or a sorrowful young girl cut down in her prime or if she's riding on horseback or the man is a soldier loyal and true or the cowboy knows that he's done wrong and so must pay penance; it doesn't matter if the pipes and fifes play or if anyone bangs the drum slowly; all of them eventually arrive at the same place. Send for the preacher to come and pray for me/Send for the doctor to heal up my wounds/For my poor head is achin'/my sad heart is breakin/My body's salivated and I know I must die/Hell is my fate/I'm a-feared I must die/There goes an unfortunate lad to his home/I'm shot in the breast and I'm dyin' today/All gone to the round-up/The Cowboy was dead/For I know I must die/die/die/ die/die ....

The lights snap to black and the figures on the stage are gone, as is the music. The ghosts have sang their ballad, they have revealed the truth that a young man once, while staring at the floor, wished would thunder up from the core of the world and set his spirit free.

You feel a hand on your shoulder and look up into Unspoiled's dimming eyes.

"Do you understand now?" she asks.

"It doesn't matter," you say. "It doesn't matter if your intentions were good. It doesn't matter if your heart was true. It doesn't matter if you understood right from wrong."

"Yes ..." Her voice is filled with bliss.

"It doesn't matter if you loved well or not, if you kept that love or lost it, it doesn't matter. You—all of you—all of us—the whole goddamned broken world—it doesn't matter, because we can't help but be what we are, and what we are, in one way or another, will end us before we're ready, before we can be forgiven, before we can feel worthy of the life that is inside and around us."

"Yes …" Her voice is now Bliss itself.

"None of us will ever measure up," you say, rising to your feet, feeling tall and proud and strong. You smile at her, running your rough hands through the curls of her hair.

"Am I your best gal?" she asks.

"Always by my side."

"It's hard to be a man."

"To be a man means you make a decision and stick with it." When had you left the building and gotten back into your car? When had you driven here, to this restaurant/bar full of people who have no idea that it all means nothing?

You raise the bottle to your lips and drink deeply of the whiskey, just like the Duke would, whether or not the streets of Laredo waited outside the saloon doors or not. The bad guys were everywhere and always would be.

Hey, Mom! Hey, Dad! Look at me standing proud.

You climb down off your horse and pull the Things from the saddlebag. You rack a round into the shotgun, and chamber rounds into the four pistols. No hesitation, no doubts.

For I am a lonely cowboy, and I know I've done wrong …

Jimmy Stewart told the Duke he wouldn't want to go out that way, and the Duke didn't, but good old Dad couldn't lay claim to a blaze of glory at the end, could he? No, he couldn't.

But you can.

You can be a Man, a Man's Man who doesn't make his mark with guitar strings and meaningless words in best-forgotten songs.

Time to be a Man.

You push open the doors to the saloon.

Hey, Dad—look at the bad guys fall!

As you walk and talk real slow, just home from the prairie green, tall and proud as the villains and scoundrels perish, tall and proud like a man ought, tall and proud, with guns blazing, the soft light of home beckoning welcome, welcome home, home at last, home in John Wayne's dream.

On...Streets of Laredo

The Roud Folk Song Index proves that #23650, usually known in America as 'The Streets of Laredo,' is a ballad that people have been loving and adapting for centuries. For example The English Folk Dance and Song Society lists no less than 195 versions. (1)

The well-known ethnomusicologist and folklorist John A. Lomax wrote that it may have gone back as far as 1790.(2)

In its first incarnation as 'The Unfortunate Rake/Lad' the song is about a soldier dying of a 'disorder' that should have been treated with 'pills and salts of white mercury'—aka syphilis. He asks that he be brought to his grave accompanied by young girls singing, drums and fifes playing, and muskets fired over his coffin. (3)

Especially after its arrival in America, the ballad evolved. In some the gender changed from male to female and instead of the sympathetic "Unfortunate Rake," the name became "The Bad Girl's Lament."(4)

Possibly the most famous version of this song in America is The Streets of Laredo, which is often referred to as a 'Dying Cowboy Lament.' Lomax writes that as it moved to the Southwest, it took on local references that obscure its British origin. Now it mentions cowboys, gamblers, a dram house, and a card house, among others, and features the protagonist instead of dying of syphilis, unsurprisingly, dying of a gunshot. The protagonist asks that cowboys and whores (in the bowdlerized version, pretty 'maidens') carry his coffin to the grave. Yet, however obscure this ballad's origins became, there's still a glimmer of the British military in the line "Oh, beat the drums slowly, and play the fife lowly." (5)

This ballad is popular with many musicians. Johnny Cash, Don Edwards, Joan Baez, Eddy Arnold, Arlo Guthrie, Prefab Sprout, Susanne Vega, and Bing Crosby have all recorded versions.

1) Roud Folksong Index. 2013. 2 October, 2013. <http://www.efdss.org/ library-and-archive> English Folk Dance and Song Society.

2) Archive of Folk Culture. 2013. 3 October, 2013. <http://www.loc.gov/ folklife/LP/CowboySongs_opt.pdf> Library of Congress.

3) Mainly Norfolk: English Folk and Other Good Music. 2013. 3 October, 2013.
<http://mainlynorfolk.info/lloyd/songs/theunfortunaterake.html> English Folk Dance and Song Society.

4) Smithsonian Folkways. 2013. 4 October, 2013. <http://www.folkways. si.edu/the-unfortunate-rake/american-folk-struggle-protest/music/ album/smithsonian> Smithsonian Center for Folklife and Cultural Heritage.

5) Archive of Folk Culture. 2013. 3 October, 2013. <http://www.loc.gov/ folklife/LP/CowboySongs_opt.pdf> Library of Congress.

BEDLAM

BY
GREGORY FROST

The storm-tossed seas that night sank ships up and down the coast. Hulls smashed on reefs and rocks, crews dove or were flung headlong over rails, drowning unnamed and ungraced. Tangled in seaweed, bodies rocked in hard-pushed foam along beaches, Death being no kind nurse with gentle cradle for the loose-limbed and pale corpses. Tomorrow would bring new wailing as the dead and lost were claimed.

Lightning flashed and flashed again, tossed barred shadows down into the depths. Water sprayed like from a cannon's mouth.

In among the water devils and the churning dark, one prow shot up as if it had sprung from the deep, not ridden down trench and up wave. The tattered ship cut the night impossibly. It made straight for safe harbor and a quay that could have been no more than myth to those on board. The lighthouse on the point had been doused and darkened by the almost-sideways rain. What human hand could have guided any ship to so invisible a berth?

"Hard-a-lee!" shouted Tom, their captain. "Cling tight, you aloft!"

His crew was young as tyros on a maiden voyage, stripped naked or reduced to rags by the tempest, and bony as starving beggars, all. Their eyes pulsed a luminous blue as if sea creatures had slithered up into the sockets. They secured the lines and clung to the rails and up against the shrouds, the sails all reefed. He trusted in them, and they in him to bring them in across this wild, infernal sea.

And so came sailing into port a shape like a mound

bearing three huge crossed spars as if Golgotha, ripped free of Jerusalem, had come scudding from ubiquitous darkness to a new destination.

Then the air seemed to shudder. A huge gust, and the storm had outpaced them, pushing on, ahead and over land. The final waves pitched and washed over them, slammed Tom against the wheel again. He heard mad laughter in it as if the sea were taunting him. He spit out spray and gripped the handles, but didn't so much steer as let the ship have its way.

Swells and lesser waves rolled beneath them, but moment by moment these, too, lost strength, until by the time they dropped anchor and it thumped the sand fathoms below, the surface had calmed as if no storm had ever passed.

Suddenly swallows winged across the sky, and in the black distance ahead appeared the small fairy lights delineating a town. Dripping wet, Tom followed the birds' flight past a crack in the clouds, his sharp-edged face presented to the burst of moonlight as the clouds pulled apart.

His sailors looked where he did with animal eyes, stung salt-red and wild, creatures not long out of the torrent, hardly longer out of hell. Doused in the faint light, they cheered him and laughed wildly. They had survived it all.

"Rum all around," Tom called. "But lower me a boat first." While most of them scurried for kegs, he scuttled across the foredeck and ducked under the bowsprit, where he leaned out beside the ship's figurehead, its lacquered arms bent and ending in a curl of claws that were ready to grab the wind, its grinning face stretched wide with sharp teeth and its eyes the yellow of a gorgon that might turn any opposing ship to stone. Its ample breasts peaked in nipples of iron, which had rusted over time so that they seemed to have bled in streams down the belly to where carved flesh became scales and joined the hull.

"I go in now," he whispered to her, his only confessor, "to fetch my love, my Maddie, who waits and has waited." He thought the gorgon smiled at his words. "She *has* waited," he insisted.

On deck below, the spindly boys dipped their cups into a cracked keg and then poured them back, empty of anything but spray and air. Yet they swayed as if affected by true spirits, pushing, wrestling one another for a place in line, a second or a third drink. Looking down upon them like a cleric from his pew, he said, "My bonny boys."

He climbed down and walked through them ignored, like a ghost himself, then climbed over the side and down the Jacob's ladder to where the lowered rowboat awaited, cast off the ropes, unshipped the oars, and began to row. He skimmed alongside the ship, and beneath the carved scroll bearing her name: *Bedlam*.

With each stroke of the oars, his moon-drenched body, barely whole at the start, seemed to take on mass and muscle. His ragged clothes knitted as though invisible silkworms were spinning their threads about him.

§

Along the rocks of the seawall he strode. The town above was mapped in his head. Where the plat had come from, he didn't know, didn't ask, didn't care.

As with each stroke of the oars, once he'd tied up at the quay, each step he took along the rocks put a finish upon him, blushed his face with color, oiled and curled his wild hair beneath a tricorner hat, drew sharp the line of his short, dark beard.

He started up one set of steps, but a tree had been uprooted in the storm and fallen across them. Above it he saw a man watching him, an odd bald fellow with eyeglasses, who waved to him as if they knew each other, gestured him to come up as though the huge tree didn't bisect their path. Tom raised his chin, seeming to assent, but he retreated down the steps, circled farther around and climbed up to the town along a dirt path so hard-packed that the rain had slid down it as if it were glass. As he climbed the slope, the wind picked up, gusting at him, sea spray or rain slapping him in the face. He ducked his head and let his hat take the brunt.

He entered the town now from its stern. The buildings cut off the wind again. Ribbons of his breath steamed into thick night mist.

At first he was alone, but even as he reached the wider paths, there were few people about and most of them drunk—who else would have braved this night but those whose need drowned common sense? They stumbled past, and he, like a darksome wind with purpose and destination, heard their jumbled, unvoiced dispatches, collected snippets of gossip out of the black air, gathered to him the capricious voice of the town. It told him everything.

The man with glasses was now down upon the rocks, calling out, seemingly seeking him where he no longer tread. "Village fool," he muttered. He chuckled to himself and pressed eagerly on up the hill.

A path of cobblestones appeared ahead. It glistened in the storm's aftermath like jewels and he fairly danced along now, higher up the hillside, past an inn and some shops, then in among individual hovels and homes. Time was of the essence.

He knew the place, his destination, though he had never seen it before this moment. A fine, small house. She'd married well, he thought, though he knew already the full story. Golden light fluttered in the front window—a fire burning in the warming hearth.

Awhile he stood outside in the darkness and just watched through the distorting glass as she bathed her two children in a tin pan with a sponge. Young boys, both, and he thumbed the empty scabbard at his hip where his long knife had previously dwelled. Its blade, lost to him, had tasted the meat of children before. "Pork pies" was what he'd called them. He flung the memory off. Two boys. They might, only a few years hence, join his crew. Some other night than this. A sly grin crossed his face but he wiped it away as the boys put on their nightshirts and she urged them ahead of her up into the loft. Then, from the top of the ladder, she climbed down, her skirt pulled high up, her legs and feet bare, palest thighs arresting his heartbeat for a moment, pulling him taut with honest yearning. He moaned softly with want, and her name slipped from his mouth swaddled in breath. In the ripple of the glass, she looked as young and beautiful as ever she had.

She stepped down and paused as if thinking what she had to do next, and as she did, she looked straight at him out in the cold night. He knew what she saw, lit gold by the fire of her own hearth and edged sharp in moonlight. He was a phantasm drawn from her memory.

Her fingertips pressed to her lips, peeling them apart. Such pearls, her teeth. He remembered.

Her eyes gleamed wet with joy and she ran to the door, flung it back and then herself into his arms.

"My Tom, oh, my Tommy! It can't be!" she cried.

"Maddie," he laughed. He caught her around the waist and swung her about. Hips thicker than he'd known, but not from bearing sons. Her smell—of soap, babies, and honest sweat—filled him up with lust he'd thought he would never feel again.

He set her down. She stood on tiptoe on the wet stones.

"I thought you dead. They told us—"

"They lied. To you, to everyone. They spoke from rumors, stories passed from ship to ship. We never sank—we don't know how. We were boarded, right enough, taken, yes. I was beaten plenty. They plundered us and would have done so again, but not with this crew, my Bedlam boys. I'm captain now and we sail on my command to anywhere you like."

"Anywhere *I* like. . ." She said it as if she'd misheard him. Then, "Why did you not send word? I waited forever."

He opened his arms. "This is it. I *am* my word. You were in my thoughts across the whole of the Atlantic. It's forever your face in darkness, in moonlight, when I close my eyes. I had to come—to collect you, to carry you off and give you the whole of the world."

"But, Tom, not knowing it, I married. I'm a *wife*." She gestured back at the house. "Two sons, and a husband who's away on—on business. Time has passed for you and me, though I swear, you look not one day older than I remember."

"No, we can't be severed. You are Proserpine and I've come to lead you out of the darkness of Hades that you don't know you're in. I never gave up in all this time. It's you and no one else, Maddie Maudlin. I know you've never stopped loving me. How else did I see you everywhere? I could feel you, even were my grave a hundred fathoms down. I saw it in your eyes through the window just then when you turned and I see it now, right here. Everything that ever existed 'tween us. You *want* to come with me." He held his hand out as if to take hers.

"But my boys—"

"They ain't yours, are they? They're his, from before. Nor's he your rightful helpmate." Then he laughed, his white teeth gleaming, as if none of it mattered. "I've a ship, a crew. We're invincible, can't be sunk by God nor nature. I'll give you the world, a thousand ports of call, if you'll only cast off this other life and join me."

She pressed a hand to her cheek. "How can I do that?" She glanced back through the open door. "My—the children. My husband."

His eyes gleamed sharp. "And where's he now, tonight?" She started to answer but he interrupted. "You stumbled in the telling. I'll tell *you* what he's away on. Riding his tender mistress in a room above a tavern the next town over, where they meet as often as he can steal away, and you pretend not to suspect so as to be able to go on." He clucked his tongue. "Let's go back inside. You stand for me in that tin pan, and I'll wash you clean, and we'll remark upon the bruises and the marks of his belt."

Horrified, she stepped back from him. "You only just arrived, how can you say—how can you know any such a thing?"

"One hears things in the wind and in the dark. Such as your new name, which I'll never call you by, nor where you reside." He opened his arms as if it was obvious. "How do you think I came here so directly?" When she didn't move, he added, "I saw the stripe on your thigh from his buckle as you got down, is how. Won't be the only mark. It never is." He clutched her hair, drew her face close. "You know *I* won't leave marks like that on your beautiful flesh." Her eyes were wet, but it was she who pressed her face, her lips, to his. Her hunger came to the fore now, drew him like an undertow inexorably away, and he let go and drowned with her.

He wiped a hand on his mouth, half-astonished by the intensity of her feelings. He turned quick, and pointed. "See, out there my waiting ship!"

It stood, still as something painted upon the night sky, sparkling with inviting lantern lights. They seemed to dot even the masts.

He licked his lips. Her taste lingered. "Let him have his boys and his belt. I have a whole ship full of boys who'll admire you — no—worship you. Worship you as I do." He offered his hand to her. It was flawless and strong. He curled his fingers, relishing the feeling. "Come with me, Maddie Maudlin. I've so much to share. Treasures and pleasures. But you must come now. Tonight, before midnight."

"Why's that?"

"Why, the tide of course. We must sail upon the tide before midnight, else find ourselves stranded here when the next storm hits."

She looked into his eyes then, and her expression shifted like a sail catching a favorable wind. He watched his promises flow into the curve of her lips. "Swear," she said, "you'll take me all the way to Italy, where the white lilies grow."

"Of course, of course. Anywhere."

She went back inside, lifted a poker and stirred the fire till it jumped up hot and bright again. She climbed the ladder a final time, stood at the top, her back to him. He watched, his will guiding her to sever each adopted tie. The resolve was his, though she would think it her own.

Down again, she snatched up her shawl and closed the door on the life lived in that house, and all its deceptions.

"None could ever hold a candle to you, my Tommy." She ran one slender hand over his taut, cold cheek. His eyes nearly closed at the sensation so long forgotten.

He took her by the hand and drew her through the curving, sloping streets of the town. He was the current now, pulling her out to sea, and she didn't resist.

"It's late," he said. "It's very late. Hurry."

Wind already was swirling in from the sea again. The spray stung him.

At the steps down to the seawall, the "village idiot" reappeared, closer now, running across the uneven dirt to catch up. The moon shone on his balding head. His eyes were like an owl's, magnified behind the lenses of his eyeglasses. "Thomas," the man called. "Stop now. Come back, for your soul's sake. Stay and ride it out with us."

"Get away, you." Tom quickly dragged Maudlin down the stone steps to the seawall.

"How does he know you?" she asked.

"He doesn't," he replied, and pressed on. "He never did."

"Thomas!" 'Twas as if the wind called from above.

They hurried along the wall, out the quay. In the distance,

the glittering ship rose and fell now, the sea coming to life again as if agitated at his return.

He set her in the rowboat, clambered down and sat with his back to her as he hauled hard and fast on the oars. Facing the shrinking town, he stared at the man, who just stood there, leaning on the wall in a helpless way.

The water slapped Tom in the face. It seemed to leap over the gunwale to strike him. The whole sea wanted him back, didn't it? He craned his neck. Maddie sat with her shawl over her head, her face in its shadow, bowed as though in prayer. The ship rose and fell behind them, closer with each stroke. The gorgon watched their approach.

He saw his own hands losing their flawless shape. But he'd got her and no mistake. Not the ocean, nor her careless husband nor, any force of God she prayed to could stop him.

They glided alongside as he shipped the oars and made a grab for the rope ladder dangling where he'd left it.

With his head down so that she wouldn't see the change in him before she was on board, he urged, "Go up, my love, go up." She climbed ahead of him, barefoot still. The cold of the sea did not chill her. He only looked up when she was halfway and wouldn't see how his teeth showed through one cheek, and the sockets of his eyes glowed.

Boys' faces leered over the chain-wale. Their arms reached out for her.

Tom climbed along after. With each step he took, the Bedlam transformed around him, planks rotted, snapped, came unpegged. Moss grew up like a beard on either side.

Above, the sails unfurled without any hand tugging on any halyards. The sheets fluttered, tattered but swollen, pregnant with blue fire. The Bedlam boys' eyes burned with that same blue, and his own. "Yes," he mumbled. "Down and down, to hell we go, my Mad Maudlin. I'll show you where your white lilies grow before our final port of call, yes, I will." He slid over the side and onto the broken deck. "Oh, I've—"

"Got you now," she finished for him.

The naked boys smirked from around her skirts and under them, too. Her eyes gone the yellow of the gorgon's. Its polished face burnished her features.

"Mad!" he cried. "I swear! I'll show you—"

"No," she said. "Never can you show me a thing. That power was lost the day you drowned, my darling." She cocked her head. "Went mad did your Maudlin when you died. Off the sea wall she threw herself. Couldn't wait for your bones to wash up, so sent hers out to find you instead. An' here we lie, entangled below."

She turned to her crew, *her* boys. He was just one among them now. They all had ports of call and turns to take.

"Weigh anchor," she ordered. The sky cracked with jagged lightning. The wind bulged in the blue burning sails. It carried to his ears one final time that faded voice on the shore, a single shouted "Thomas!"

Then the sea rose up like a cobra, higher than the yardarm, and as he opened his mouth to scream, it slammed hard upon him, and them. She stood at the wheel, and the ship plunged downward to darkness.

His ears breached with the wail of a million souls drowned along with him.

§

Wailing echoed down the corridors. Lightning flashed and the thunder, right atop them, shook the very foundations of the hospital, and behind the terrified shrieks, one woman's voice screaming, "Tommy!"

The wild boy with the pail was ready to fling more icy water down on the patient tied to the iron frame below, but the physician raised his hand and called, "Enough!" He lumbered forward, removing his glasses and wiping at the misted lenses, at his own eyes. He leaned over and squinted dolefully at the soggy face.

Blue eyes stared wide, but somewhere far past and above him, all the way to the stars.

"Lost," said the physician. He put his glasses back on. "This time he's lost." To the two attendants he said, "Dry him off and take him back to his ward. And get your damned monkey down from that ladder before he strikes one of us with his pail. We won't have further need of him." He shook his nearly bald head, and walked over to the table in the corner where his notebook lay.

He should have sat down and written up his notes immediately, but he couldn't face them. It was too great a burden tonight. He'd hoped. . . but he'd failed again. Even "hydro-therapy," as they were calling it, hadn't revived Thomas. If anything it had flung him out of this world altogether—not that his journey had been far to begin with.

The attendants—senior patients themselves—were cautious in wiping down Thomas. They didn't untie him until they were done. One still wore a bandage from the last time, when he'd been bitten by the savage madman. Rumor was the fiend had stabbed and flayed dozens of children before he'd been caught and locked up here. Another rumor had it that he was the doctor's only son, and that was why he was given every imaginable treatment from bloodletting to this water-dashing.

The attendants hauled him upright and dragged him out between them. They didn't bother to dress him. He wouldn't notice. Last time it had been a week before he'd come to what passed for his senses, claiming to be the survivor of some shipwreck. It looked this time like he wouldn't be coming back at all, and you didn't waste a gown on the mindless ones.

Lightning flashed again through the barred windows, making them jump as they left the chamber. Yowling filled the air.

Down the narrow corridor of Bethlem Hospital they staggered, though the patient hardly weighed more than a sack of bones. The near-naked boy who'd flung pails of water capered ahead of them as though leading a parade.

Wretched creatures ogled from cells on both sides, some grasping after them, but most laughing, howling at the sight of the naked man. Some threw their own stained nightshirts through the bars.

Across the walls obscene figures had been drawn—not all of them by the incarcerated—including a voluptuous female with fanged teeth and a snake's body. The word BEDLAM had been gouged out in huge letters beside her with a spoon.

At the sight of the procession, the woman stopped her cries and then began to sing:

"Tom o' Bedlam's home again
No escape in the deep.

Maudlin's mad with lust and sin,
All Bedlam boys do weep!"

The physician, following them, told her, "Hush up, Madeline."

She stepped back, curtsied, then raised her gown and pressed her sex against the bars at him. The Bedlam boys across the way yipped and strained to get a look.

The attendants pushed open the doors at the far end and a chill wind blasted down the corridor, snuffing out wall candles one by one. The hall went dark and the yowling recommenced. Then the doors shut, the bolts snapped, and one by one, they fell silent to listen to her soft chants, flowing like an undercurrent beneath their noise.

She was whispering singsong; it rose and fell. "I got you now, Tommy, got you, I got you." The susurrus bore them along, snaking through the cold darkness, drawing them from their cells. It might have been any of them she claimed—at least in their imaginations.

"Got you forever now, my love," she sang, "an' here we'll lie, together."

On...The Demon Lover

Known as 'The Demon Lover,' 'The Carpenter's Wife,' or 'The House Carpenter,' Child Ballad 243, also classified as Roud #14, was described by Child as "A Warning For Married Women, being an example of Mrs. Jane Reynolds (a West-country woman), born near Plymouth, who, having plighted her troth to a Seaman, was afterwards married to a Carpenter, and at last carried away by a Spirit, the manner how shall be presently recited. To a West-country tune called 'The Fair Maid of Bristol,' 'Bateman,' or 'John True.'"(1)

According to respected British folk singer and song collector A.L. Lloyd, the ballad was first printed as a broadside in the 17th century and before then was part of oral tradition.(2) There are many versions of this ballad—Child's description is a good general outline. The details change from version to version: the number of years between learning of her lover, often named Jamie Harris', death and her marriage, whether the one who comes to her is a spirit or the devil, the number of her children, how she dies and whether her husband simply mourns her or commits suicide.(3)

Shirley Jackson uses the name Jamie Harris throughout her short story collection THE LOTTERY AND OTHER STORIES. One of the stories, THE DAEMON LOVER, Jackson recorded in 1960 for Folkways Records and is housed by the Smithsonian Center for Folklife and Cultural Heritage.(4)

The many who have sung the ballad most recently include A.L. Lloyd, Bob Dylan, Joan Baez, Natalie Merchant, and Pete Seeger.

1) Child, Francis James. The English and Scottish Popular Ballads Vol. 4. Mineola: Dover, 2003.

2) Mainly Norfolk: English Folk and Other Good Music. 2013. 9 October, 2013. <http://mainlynorfolk.info/lloyd/songs/thedemonlover. html> English Folk Dance and Song Society.

3) Child, Francis James. The English and Scottish Popular Ballads Vol. 4. Mineola: Dover, 2003.

4) Smithsonian Folkways. 2013. 10 October, 2013. <http://www. folkways.si.edu/shirley-jackson/the-daemon-lover-and-the-lottery/ prose/album/smithsonian>. Smithsonian Center for Folklife and Cultural Heritage.

AWAKE

BY
JACK KETCHUM

In the dream he was lying on what could only have been a
pebbled goat-path high above a whitewater sea pounding the
rocks below, lying in the embrace of a beautiful young woman
naked as he was, the path so narrow and so dangerous that the
slightest move beneath her could send them both tumbling over
the edge. He asked her to *please let go* and she said *no, not this time,
I don't think so* and they began to fall.

He startled gasping up off the couch thinking *what the hell
was* that *all about?* and in the flickering light reached first for the
dregs of his scotch and then for a cigarette. On the flat screen in
front of him a hard-faced cop stood by while his partner squatted
in front of a distraught woman in a chair, her arm on the woman's
shoulder.

He threw back the scotch and lit the smoke.

Right away he started coughing.

The cough took its usual course. Dry at first and insistent and
repetitive as a single staccato note played over and over on the
piano. Until finally it modulated into a wet cough and the ball of
phlegm that released him from its grip.

Everybody knows they're going to die, he thought. *It's another
thing to have a schedule.*

It was interesting.

His father had died of emphysema so he knew the drill. The
progress of the thing.

He knew how it ended.

It was a nasty way to go, struggling for each breath. Until

eventually your heart just threw in the towel. He gave himself a few more years. Maybe ten if he was lucky. But a simple head-cold could kill him too.

When the wet cough stopped happening he was in very deep shit.

His piss-hard-on was insistent too.

He took another drag on the Winston and stubbed it out. He shouldn't be smoking at all. But then there were a lot of things he shouldn't be doing.

The woman on the flat screen was quietly sobbing now. He muted her and hauled himself off the couch.

Maddie had left the light on for him in the hallway. That was good because the scotch was still working its dull magic.

It wouldn't be the first time he'd walked into a wall.

A dozen barefoot steps to the bathroom. A dozen more to their closed bedroom door and his daughter's open one, opposite. The usual. Lights off in both rooms.

In the bathroom he could hear himself wheezing.

The wheeze was roughly B flat. His piss in the bowl a clear A sharp.

He coughed again and the wheezing stopped.

He shook himself and zipped his jeans.

In the living room the cops were roaring silently toward a New York City brownstone. He tried for a moment to place the neighborhood. Couldn't. They shot the thing here — he'd see the crews on the street every now and then — and sometimes he could make out a landmark, a Grey's Papaya or a Love Cosmetics or, often, the Chrysler Building. But to him most all brownstones looked the same.

He lived on the eighteen floor of a decades-old high-rise. You couldn't miss it. He kept waiting for them to shoot there but it had never happened.

He reached for the bottle of MacPhail's and poured himself a short one. He'd need a clear head in the morning but he needed sleep too. You weighed one against the other and decided. Tonight it was sleep.

But an hour and two pours later he found himself grinding yet another Winston into the ashtray while the same cops in another episode grilled a wealthy matron about the supposed suicide of her husband and he was no closer to sleep than he was to Yellowstone National Park.

The sessions were eating at him.

He knew they weren't right

He, Lambert, Georgie and Kovelant were halfway through their fourth CD and the heads were fine, they caught the melodies nice and tight, the segues out of two-four and the ensemble turns were all fine, but his piano breaks just weren't making it. They were wooden, lacked the mix of fire and subtlety he was known for. They were competent. But they fucking bored him.

Nobody in the band was saying so but he'd been playing with them long enough to know what they were feeling. *What's wrong with Fahner? And what the hell are we doing playing jazz takes on Appalachian folk ballads in the fucking first place?*

It was his idea. Seemed like a good one at the time.

Still did. It was different. Dark, moody.

Maybe, he thought, *it's the COPD. Maybe it's that good old death-sentence telling me I'm as good as croaked and might as well just lie down, already.*

His first three CDs were solid hits. By jazz standards nowadays, big ones. At the moment he was the critics' darling. There was something to be said for quitting while you were ahead, he knew that. But he had bills to pay. And he wasn't quite ready for the piano-bar circuit, not yet.

He wasn't ready for *that kind* of applause.

Probably he should talk to somebody. Anybody. He hadn't. Not a soul.

Nobody in the band knew. During the sessions his Advair and Ventolin inhalers had the cough under control. Hell, they were *all* smokers. They *all* coughed, he no more than the rest of them. His producer didn't know. His agent didn't know. He'd hidden away the inhalers from Maddie well enough so far, usually in the piano stool, where neither she nor his daughter Leslie were likely to go.

The thought of his thirteen-year-old daughter digging around in his sheet music made him smile.

That would happen on the day that bears started reciting iambic pentameter and the menu at Le Bernardin offered up a side dish of Cheese Doodles.

Leslie used to love to listen to him play. She'd sit on the bench beside him. He taught her *Chopsticks. Twinkle Twinkle Little Star.* For Christmas, *Deck the Halls.* But that was years ago. She was hitting her teens now. And he was not Beyonce or Justin Bieber and certainly no Lady Gaga.

His little girl was growing up.

Last month she'd wanted a tattoo. Maddie was furious at the very thought. Actually screamed at her. He asked her what kind of tattoo. She said a rose. A red one. With thorns. She pointed to the back of her left shoulder. *Right here,* she said.

Well, he said to Maddie, *at least she's not asking us permission to pierce her tongue.*

He thought he was being funny. Maddie missed the joke.

But basically he agreed. He was not about to let her deface her body.

No way.

When he considered it now though, he thought that her choice of said adornment had been appropriate, at least. *A rose. A blossomed rose.*

Because she was blossoming too, wasn't she? From skinny little kid to young woman. Her hips had begun defining themselves in graceful waves depending from her waist. Her breasts slowly building beneath her skin.

Another coughing fit set his nose to running and sent him headed back into the bathroom. Respiratory disease invaded not only the chest but the throat and nasal passages as well. He wondered if Maddie had noticed that they were going through a whole lot more toilet paper lately.

Maybe I should talk to somebody, he thought. *A shrink. I'm pretty certain all this is depressing me.*

He sat down on the toilet and blew his nose, wadded up the paper and tossed it into the tank. Blew it again. He was quiet about it. He didn't want to wake Maddie. He sure wasn't ready to talk to *her* yet. He didn't know if he'd ever be.

There were *problems* with the marriage.

That's what Lambert and Georgie called them. *Problems.* Because they'd been having them too. Of the four of them only Kovelant seemed to have escaped the grim net of marital woes. But then Kovelant didn't fool around on the road or after sessions either.

Fahner wondered how he managed it. Jazz, when it was good, left you horny as a goddamn rabbit. It went with the territory. Jazz just…*jazzed you up.* The operative word being *up.*

But twice now Maddie had found out about it. Twice wasn't too many times, all things considered. But he guessed it was sufficient. A good day for them now was a day in which they were cordial to one another. Not openly hostile or aggressive.

But not exactly friendly either.

He didn't want a divorce. A divorce would devastate Leslie.

And he loved his daughter with all his heart. All his body and soul. He loved her as much as he loved his music and maybe even more.

He couldn't hurt her. Not in a million years.

In the hallway he gazed at her open door.

Maybe he should see somebody.

She lay awake thinking about what she was about to do.

There was a grim satisfaction to it, almost a sense of pride, now that it was in motion. Doing it this way. So many times she'd thought about it. Only she always seemed to falter, her nerves seemed to fail her at the last minute. But over the past few weeks she'd heard him noodling that goddamn song often enough, pointing the way.

And the idea had simply harpooned her. The *song* had harpooned her. *Her anger* had harpooned her and now she was finally pulling taut on the line.

It was one thing to screw around behind her back. There was a reason that she'd always considered the word *groupie* a diminutive. She could live with that. Had for many years now.

But this was another thing.

This was a dull muted rage in her that had been with her for so long she could barely remember when it began. She never spoke of it. She simply *accommodated* it as the Christian thing to do. She had her faith. Even if he never had his own.

Phil Fahner was a pagan through and through.

She'd loved that about him once.

She thought back to their first days together. The thoughts should have been sweet ones but they weren't. She'd been working as assistant to a painter, famous and prolific in the '60s but quietly losing it now that he was well past seventy — and sometimes losing it not so quietly at all.

It was an appointment-book and go-fetch job. Far beneath her talents and abilities. Get him into the town car on time. Take his strange, worried, sometimes furious calls at two or six in the morning. Pick up his paints and supplies at Lee's Paints on 57th Street. Deliver his paintings or sketches or lithographs.

Even shop for his wife for god sakes! Jesus! *What she'd been through!*

He was a rough, erratic taskmaker.

There were many, many times that she needed a drink after work and since she didn't drink alone — her father had, and look what happened to *him* — there was a quiet little bar on 68th Street not far from her apartment which was like those bars in Greenwich Village where you walked a few steps down off the street into dim lighting and some good quiet jazz and could sit among well-mannered upper-middle-class New Yorkers, and a woman could have a glass or two of Chardonnay and talk with the other customers without feeling like some tramp looking for a pickup.

He and his bassist Lambert and drummer Georgie *did* get to chatting her up, though. And they were smart and fun to talk to, so when the three of them got off their barstools to have a cigarette outside and asked if she smoked too — she did in those days — they invited her to join them. It was a warm spring night, just getting on to dark. At some point Lambert and Georgie faded back down into the bar while she and Phil Fahner — *the* Phil Fahner — lit another smoke and talked further about her job and her own painting and she felt this attraction. This magnetism. So that when he asked her out for dinner *the following night* she accepted.

Drinks and dinner, that was all it was for a couple of weeks and then it was drinks and dinner and bed and he was a very good lover, very attentive to her.

And she thought, *he was attentive all right. He played her like a full-sized upright. All the keys.*

So that when he asked in bed one hot sweaty August night why she didn't just dump the fucking job and marry him and do her own painting she said yes, and two months later they were at the City Clerk's Office.

And about a year after that she was pregnant.

Thirteen years ago, that was. Thirteen years was a long time. The good and then the bad. Then the very bad.

Thirteen years, to this.

There were far too many more years ahead of them for this family.

It had to end.

She could almost cry but she had stopped crying. She had always hidden the crying well, she thought. She had her makeup. Or else she had a cold, just the sniffles. But it finally stopped entirely only weeks ago when she heard him practicing for the session, playing that song over and over, and she recognized the lyrics within the melody from a record she'd owned in college, the harpoon deep into the body of the whale.

Tonight she would set the whale free.

Her daughter Leslie had awakened to her touch slowly, as though drugged. She'd always been a deep sleeper, a bed-wetter in fact from the ages of seven through nine.

And that had been her first clue. The bed-wetting beginning so late.

She should have seen it years ago.

If she had, they wouldn't have been here now. Here in this bed.

Her daughter rubbed her eyes as she woke and said *whaaa?* and she pressed two fingers to her lips. Lips warm with sleep.

I want you to go into our room, she whispered, and get into bed.

Huh? she said.

Don't ask me any questions, she said, just do as I say. I love you. We're trading places. You understand?

She watched as her daughter's eyes went gradually wide. Then after what seemed a very long time she nodded. Just the smallest nod of comprehension, of something that had passed between them. But it was enough. She slipped off the bed and started across the room.

Be sure to close the door in there, she said. And turn off the light.

She waited until she heard the door click shut and then

reached for the stainless steel kitchen knife she'd honed early this morning which lay beneath her scarf on the night table beside her, lay down and pulled the covers over her and turned her back to the hall and the open door.

The song ran 'round and 'round in her head. An old Appalachian folk ballad. It was a comfort to her. She heard Joan Baez, her sweet thin soprano. She heard her girlhood.

> *"Don't sing love songs, you'll wake my mother.*
> *She's sleeping here right by my side.*
> *And in her right hand a silver dagger.*
> *She says that I can't be your bride."*

She didn't know exactly what she would do with the knife but breathed easily for the first time this long day and night and waited for him to come.

On...Silver Dagger or Katie Dear

As with so many beloved ballads, The Silver Dagger, Roud #711, has been shaped and changed by people as they sing and interact with it. Even though it's termed a Murder Ballad, the only death that takes place is a suicide. Like Romeo and Juliet, it deals with young love thwarted.

To look at three versions can give us a taste of how people change it to suit themselves. A version recorded by the Smithsonian has as its plot a 'comely youth' who courts 'a lady fair and bright.' Desperate at how her parents do their best to separate the lovers, the girl wanders out of the city, pulls out a silver dagger and stabs herself through 'her own true heart.' Dying, she calls on her act to be a warning never to part 'young true love.'

As she lies dying, her true love finds her. She bids him farewell, saying that they will meet on Mount Zion. Her lover then uses the dagger to kill himself. (1)

The theme of two daggers held by the girls' disapproving parents, silver for mom and gold for dad, is also common. In a ballad collected by Byron Arnold, Mrs. Hester—from whom he collected the ballad, couldn't bring herself to kill the young lovers. In her version of 'Katie Dear,' Mrs. Hester has the lover request that Katie ask her mother whether Katie can be his bride. Katie refuses, saying her mother has a silver dagger with which to stab "my true love's breast." The same request transferred to Dad is answered the same except his dagger is gold. Rather than end with a stabbing, Mrs. Hester rather confusingly has Katie say, "Oh, won't you be glad, my own true lover, When you and I become as one?" (2)

The Louvin Brothers version of Katie Dear includes both daggers and death. As with Mrs. Hester's version, the lover's request for Katie's hand in marriage is met with assurances that her parents keep daggers nearby for just such occasions. Heart-broken, he stabs himself with the golden dagger. After saying good-bye to her parents, Katie uses the same dagger to end her own life. (3)

Other than the Louvin Brothers, this ballad has been recorded by Joan Baez, Ian and Sylvia Tyson, Gillian Welch, and the Chieftains on the album Down The Old Plank Road, The Nashville Sessions.

1) Smithsonian Folkways. 2013. 10 October, 2013. <http://media. smithsonianfolkways.org/liner_notes/folkways/FW03831.pdf> Smithsonian Center for Folklife and Cultural Heritage.

2) Arnold, Byron. An Alabama Songbook: Ballads, Folk Songs, and Spirituals. Tuscaloosa: The University of Alabama Press, 2004.

3) Bluegrass Lyrics. 2013. 9 October, 2013. <http://www. bluegrasslyrics.com/node/1665>.

JOHN HENRY, THE STEEL DRIVIN' MAN

BY
JEFF STRAND

It happened in West Virginia, or maybe Alabama, around 1869, or maybe a decade later. This ain't a story about facts.

They say that no man alive could drive in steel like John Henry, and I believe 'em. With a hammer in his hand, he'd pound those spikes into the rock like you or I might stick a toothpick into freshly baked angel food cake.

Oh, he'd had muscles to spare when he was a slave, but he'd gotten even stronger after he was freed. He wasn't building the railroad all by himself—that would be crazy—but he was doing more work than any other steel-drivin' man, that's for damn sure. And believe me, the steel-drivin' men were not lazy people.

Too bad they all were gonna lose their jobs.

That's because some enterprising fool had invented a steam-powered hammer. How could a human being compete with such a machine? These poor workers and their families were gonna starve to death, all on account of "progress."

Well, John Henry, he put forth a challenge: he would race that mechanical hammer, and prove that a man could beat a godless contraption. And if he won, the workers would keep their jobs.

The race began, and oh, how the other workers cheered him on! Not to mention his wife, Polly Ann, who not only cheered louder than the steel-drivin' men but looked better doing it. John Henry's hammer, it came crashing down over and over, sparks a-flying, drivin' those steel spikes with the power of a god. Now, John Henry was a God-fearing man and would not have made that particular comparison himself, but to the outsiders watching the whole spectacle, it seemed appropriate.

Thing is, that steam-powered hammer was doing a mighty good job. I suspect that when John Henry put forth that challenge, he'd secretly hoped that the machine would break down after six or seven spikes and he'd win by default, but nope, it was pounding in those spikes at a rapid pace. Despite his muscles and his passion, John Henry was falling behind!

"Keep driving in that steel!" the workers shouted. "We believe in you! Don't let us lose our jobs!"

By now, John Henry had worked up a sweat of such quantity that more perspiration emerged from his pores than a normal man had of all body liquids combined. Oh, he was feeling the ache all the way down to his bones. His vision was starting to get kind of blurry at the edges, and that damn steam-powered hammer was generating so much dust his lungs burned with every breath.

But if you think John Henry gave up...well, you don't know John Henry.

He doubled his efforts. That's right, when any other man would have quit, John Henry hammered in those spikes even faster than before! I wish I'd been there to gape in amazement. He hammered and hammered, and though you might think that a couple of those spikes were crooked or not quite in all the way, you would be wrong. Every one of those spikes would have passed the railroad owner's inspection. John Henry was not a man to do slipshod work.

And then he caught up to that steam-powered hammer.

And then he passed it.

That's right, he passed it. Technological advancement was completely pointless when John Henry's hammer was at work. He was suffering, suffering bad, as if his arms might rip right off his torso at any moment, but John Henry was going to beat that infernal machine!

Yet with only three more spikes left to hammer, John Henry thought that he was going to die.

"Don't die!" shouted the other workers. "You've only got three spikes left!"

John Henry was so exhausted and he'd sucked in so much dust that for a moment, he wasn't sure that the voices of his co-workers were going to inspire him enough to finish the task. But then he heard the voice of his beloved Polly Ann making the same general point that the workers had made, and he knew that he could pound in those last three spikes.

Slam! Two spikes left.

Slam! One spike left.

John Henry, he raised his mighty hammer, and he let out the loudest grunt any human being had ever grunted up to that point in history, and he swung that hammer down and drove in that last piece of steel.

He'd won the challenge! He'd beat the machine! The workers were going to keep their jobs!

And then John Henry, with every ounce of energy in his body used up, dropped his hammer, fell on the ground, and died.

§

"John Henry, wake up!"

John Henry opened his eyes. "Huh?"

It was Polly Ann, crouching over him. Her beautiful brown eyes were filled with concern. "We think you may have been dead, but we resuscitated you!"

"I saw a bright light," said John Henry. "I was floating toward it, and some angels were beckoning, and then suddenly I was right back here. I think you did bring me back to life. Thank you, Polly Ann."

Charles, who was a steel-drivin' man just like John Henry but not as efficient, patted him on the shoulder. "We're glad you ain't dead, John Henry. Because we need you."

"Why?"

Charles pointed. "They've done invented an even bigger and faster steam-powered drill! They say it can do the work of twenty men! We're all gonna lose our jobs if you can't beat it!"

"I'm very tired," said John Henry.

Charles and Polly Ann took him by the hands and pulled him to his feet. "You're our only hope!" said Charles. "You've proven that a man can beat a machine once! Now we just need you to prove it one more time!"

"We can do this tomorrow, right?"

"No! The challenge is now! You've got to win, John Henry, or we're all going to lose our jobs worse than before!"

"That doesn't even make sense."

It took three men plus Polly Ann to lift the hammer, but they put it back in his hand. John Henry looked out at the faces of the workers and knew that he couldn't let them down.

Like I said, I wasn't there. But if I had been there, do you know what I would have seen in John Henry's eyes? Resolve. Resolve not to let down the other workers. Sure, he'd exhausted himself to the point where a medical professional would have declared him legally dead, but that was at a time when they didn't necessarily have the proper equipment to make such a declaration with complete accuracy. People used to get buried alive all the time.

An ugly thing, being buried alive. You may think there are worse ways to go, like when they chain each of your appendages to four different horses and then send those horses on their way in four different directions, but that's got nothing on the horror of waking up alone in a coffin, six feet under the cold ground.

But you know what? If that happened to John Henry, he would've busted his way right out of that grave, dusted himself off, and gotten right back to work. That's the kind of man he was.

Anyway, John Henry didn't get buried alive. He got to his feet, and he stared at that steam-powered hammer, which was all shiny and new, and he could feel the strength flowing back into his arms. He pointed at the hammer and said, "I'm sending you back to the scrap heap."

Well, everybody applauded and cheered, except for the driver of the steam-powered hammer, of course. He frowned a little.

And John Henry, he drove in those spikes like a man possessed. He'd been half-dead, and yet he worked like he'd spent the past week relaxing on the beach in a hammock, sipping drinks out of a hollowed-out pineapple. How many people do you know who could do that? I think you'll understand that I mean no disrespect when I say that, in similar circumstances, you probably would have just let those men lose their jobs. I know I would have. "No," I would have said. "Just let me die all the way in peace."

They weren't lying when they said that this steam-powered

hammer was faster than the old one. Hell, that thing was twice as fast. It was so fast that a few of the workers admitted that though they didn't want to lose their jobs, they could see that the machine was indeed more efficient than human labor, with the added benefit that nobody had to suck dust into their lungs, and, yeah, they were still hoping that John Henry won the race, but they could understand the perspective of those in charge.

John Henry worked twice as fast as before without sacrificing quality. Slam! Slam! Slam! Slam! Slam! Inanimate objects or not, you almost had to feel sorry for those steel spikes.

The driver of the steam-powered hammer started to get kind of nervous. He was going to look like a real jackass if he lost to a half-dead man, and the financial implications of losing this challenge were dire. Railroad owners would cancel contracts all across the nation, and he'd have to lay off thousands of workers in his factories.

"John Henry's pulling ahead!" shouted Charles. Actually, John Henry had pulled ahead a couple of minutes ago, but Charles had been too flabbergasted by that fact to speak until now.

A big ol' cloud of dust had formed, so thick that the spectators couldn't see what was going on. But when the dust cleared, do you know who'd won the race?

That's right, John Henry.

Did you know that some railroad workers would swing their hammer so hard and so often that their intestines would come out? Yep, their intestines! Can you imagine that? But not John Henry. His torso was strong enough to keep those intestines inside where they belonged.

But he fell to the ground, closed his eyes, and everything went dark.

§

"John Henry...?"

"Go to hell."

"John Henry, wake up. It's me, Charles."

"I'm pretty sure I just asked you to go to hell."

"John Henry? It's me, Polly Ann."

"You can remarry after I'm gone. It's okay. I give you my

blessing. Be happy."

"John Henry, open your eyes!"

John Henry didn't want to, but after some more coaxing, he finally opened his eyes. Charles and Polly Ann were crouched over him, looking concerned.

"Is everybody still employed?" he asked.

Charles and Polly Ann both nodded.

"Good. That's good."

"How are you feeling?" asked Polly Ann.

"Like somebody set my whole body on fire, and then took their sweet time in extinguishing me. I don't fear death. Death right now would be like a cold glass of lemonade on a hot summer day."

"Don't die," said Charles. "We need you."

"I can't help anyone."

"They say there's a man who can control the elements. A practitioner of the dark arts. By manipulating the earth, wind, water, and fire, he can drive in spikes faster than any steam-powered hammer! Maybe he doesn't use the water or fire. I'm not sure how it works, but unless you can beat him, we're all gonna lose our jobs!"

"My hammer's right there. Have fun."

"No, John Henry, you're the only one who can win the race!"

"If that's true, then maybe we need to accept the idea that progress isn't such a bad thing, even when there's collateral damage. You shouldn't continue to use outdated methods when a better option exists just to maintain the status quo."

"Come on, John Henry, you can't really believe that!"

"Do you want technological advancement to remain stagnant? This could be your chance to acquire some new skills."

"Please, John Henry! Don't let us down!"

John Henry looked into their eyes, and at that moment he knew that he had to accept this challenge. He had to show the world that supernatural abilities couldn't replace a man with a hammer.

The practitioner of the dark arts looked pretty much the way you'd expect a warlock to look. He wore a black cape, had a pointy mustache and pointy beard, and laughed a lot even when nobody told a joke.

John Henry lifted his hammer high above his head, and the challenge began.

John Henry was my father.

I kept trying to find a good place to insert that piece of information, but there really hasn't been one, so I apologize for just blurting it out like that. I assure you that you're getting an unbiased telling of the events, even though I'm his son.

Well, the warlock waved his arms, and cyclones appeared! Their winds were so strong that the other workers had to step back and shield their eyes, lest rock particles slam into their irises at a hundred and forty-five miles per hour. John Henry's eyeballs were more resilient and he kept his eyes wide open so he could see what he was doing.

With those cyclones, the warlock could lift spikes into the air and slam them down four or five at a time! He kept cackling with laughter the entire time. John Henry wanted to laugh right back at him, but he could hardly breathe.

Several of the workers shouted words of encouragement, trying to inform John Henry that they felt he was the superior competitor in this race, but their voices were lost in the swirling winds.

My guess is that a couple of the workers felt that it was worth sacrificing their wages to watch a warlock summon cyclones with his hands, but nobody ever admitted to it.

Some men, when faced with what seems to be an unwinnable challenge, drop into the fetal position and tremble. Well, John Henry trembled a bit, but he didn't drop into the fetal position even once. "I'm going to beat that warlock," he said, figuring that it didn't count as talking to himself if he couldn't hear his own voice, "and I'm going to save everybody's jobs. Then I'm going to take a nap."

He wondered if the cyclones would stop if he bashed in the warlock's face with the hammer. Then he decided that such a thing would not be true to the spirit of the challenge.

So John Henry, he began driving in that steel even faster than before! If you'd been there and been wearing protective eyewear, you would have gasped at that steel-drivin' man, I promise you that. I would never use language unbefitting a gentleman, but anybody standing there that day could be forgiven for taking the

Lord's name in vain.

And when the cyclones dissipated, do you know who'd won the race?

Nope, it was John Henry!

The workers cheered and applauded even louder than before. "That John Henry, he's done it again!" they shouted.

The warlock, he was a sore loser, and he flung a lightning bolt at John Henry's head, intending to vaporize him. But John Henry, he held up his hammer at the last instant, and the lightning bolt bounced right off it, and that warlock became the one who got vaporized.

The workers stopped their cheering and applauding. Even if the victim is an evil warlock, you need to show respect after the loss of a human life.

Unfortunately for John Henry, you can't work that hard and just walk away whistling a merry tune. He got dizzy, collapsed, and then everything went dark.

§

When he opened his eyes, it was still dark.

And cold.

He lifted his hand. His fingers touched wood.

Dear God, they'd buried him alive.

Now, John Henry was braver than you or I, but don't let that fool you into thinking that he didn't let out a howl of primal anguish. Anybody else would have done the same, and there was no shame in it.

And then he cried.

I'll be honest—I wish he hadn't done that. It was a predicament to be sure, but that doesn't mean you need to go and blubber about it. Maybe I would have wept and maybe I wouldn't have; I just feel that, all things considered, a man should be a man when it comes to these matters.

I've never shed a tear in my life.

Perhaps there's something wrong with me. My wife thinks so. "It just ain't normal!" she wailed at our son's funeral. He drowned in the pond out back. I was supposed to be watching him. But that's not the story I'm here to tell.

Most men, upon waking up and discovering that they'd been buried alive, would claw at the underside of the coffin for a while, and then go back to sleep until their oxygen ran out. But not John Henry. They'd buried him with his beloved hammer. He picked up that hammer, and even though there wasn't much room to maneuver, he went and busted his way right out of that grave.

"John Henry!" Charles shouted. "Thank goodness you're out!"

Polly Ann gave him a great big hug and a kiss. "I love you so much, John Henry!"

"Why were you two standing around by my grave?"

"We were about ninety percent sure that you were dead," Charles explained. "It wasn't enough not to bury you, but it was enough that we felt we should keep watch for a while, just in case."

"I appreciate that."

"And now we need your help," said Charles. "They say there are dragons! With one tap of their enormous talons, they can drive in steel faster than any man alive! We're all gonna lose our jobs!"

"Why would you lose your jobs?" John Henry asked. "Surely they need workers to ride the dragons and make sure they don't fly off and kidnap maidens."

Charles shook his head. "They've got this new invention, this newfangled thing called hypnotherapy, and those dragons wouldn't touch a maiden even if she were rubbing up against their scaly tail!"

"There have to be other jobs out there."

"There aren't! We need you!"

"What about the poor dragons? Why should they be unemployed?"

"Please! Just one more race! That's all we ask!"

"My hands are covered with blisters," said John Henry, "and those blisters have even bigger blisters on the tips, and those blisters have even bigger blisters on the tips!"

"Exaggeration is not an admirable trait in a man," said Charles.

"You're right. I'll do it. I'll drive in that steel faster than that dragon!"

"Dragons. Plural. Four of 'em."

"Well...then...all of us workers will be racing as a team, right?"

Charles shook his head. "Nobody said it was a fair challenge."

Now, John Henry could have crawled right back down into that grave and nobody would have thought less of him. But that's not the kind of man he was. He stood up real tall, and he puffed out his chest, and he held his hammer up high and he vowed that he would beat those dragons, or die trying!

You may think you know how this story goes. "No man could beat a quartet of steel-drivin' dragons!" you're saying, "so clearly John Henry lost the challenge, and all of the workers lost their jobs, and everybody was sad."

Well, that's not how it happened.

He swung that hammer so fast that even the wings of a hummingbird had more visual clarity. And when the dust settled, it was a tie.

But you know what? One of those silly dragons had driven in a spike all crooked, so John Henry was declared the winner!

Hooray for John Henry!

Seriously, that was one hell of an impressive accomplishment. I don't care how jaded you are to superhuman feats of strength and endurance...that was impressive. It's difficult for my mind to even process what he did. He beat four dragons! Four! If he'd beat only one dragon, the world would be shouting "Oh my God! John Henry beat a dragon!" But he beat four of them! That just doesn't happen!

The dragons were taken away and put to death. All of the workers gave John Henry a great big pat on the back and told him what a fine job he'd done. He'd never shaken so many hands in his life.

He didn't even try to die this time. And before too long, sure enough, Charles hurried over to him, his eyes wide with panic.

"John Henry, we need you! They say they've got a man who can drive in steel faster than a steam-powered hammer, a more advanced steam-powered hammer, a warlock, and four dragons! We're all gonna lose our jobs!"

"Oh?"

Charles gave a frantic nod. "You have to beat him in a race! You're the only one who can..." He trailed off. "John Henry, you're gonna steal our jobs!"

"Or you could let me die."

"Yeah, I think maybe we'll do that."

And so, John Henry shook Charles' hand, and then he gave Polly Ann a hug, and he went off to die in peace. They say that late at night, if you're real quiet and you listen real close, you can hear the sounds of his hammer. Though I guess that means he's stuck doing this shit in the afterlife for all eternity, so it's not such a happy ending.

On...John Henry

Roud #790 the ballad, John Henry, is the most well-known and most-often recorded American folk song. (1) The English Folk Dance and Song Society list over 900 versions. (2) In the ballad, John Henry is a huge man who worked for the railroad (usually the song takes place in West Virginia, others place it in Alabama). (3) In order to build the railroad, tunnels had to be built through mountains and John Henry's job was to pound holes into rock where explosives would be placed. The bosses decided to bring in a steam-powered drill in hopes of speeding up progress. John Henry challenged the steam drill and its operator to a race to see who could drill faster. John Henry won thanks to his superhuman effort but it cost him his life.(4)

John Henry can be read in many ways: one is as a Luddite tall-tale with one man beating a steam machine that threatened to take away his job. As John Cephas, a blues musician from Virginia, states, "It was a story that was close to being true. It's like the underdog overcoming this powerful force. I mean even into today when you hear it (it) makes you take pride. I know especially for black people, and for other people from other ethnic groups, that a lot of people are for the underdog." (5)

Folklorist John Lomax writes how John Henry was often used as an inspiration by African Americans. While talking with a family on Fenwick Island, the father came in from work wet and exhausted. The family needed food that could only be acquired by rowing two miles to Bennett's Point. The father referred to the story of John Henry and trudged back out into the rain to row to the store. Later, another man rowing Lomax, in foul weather and against the tide, stated that if John Henry could beat the steam drill, he could row them back home. (6)

As one would expect, many people have sung this popular song. The Roud Index lists Woody Guthrie, Leadbelly, and Doc Watson (7), while Hugh Laurie and Johnny Cash can both be found on YouTube.

1) NPR.Org. 2002. 9 December, 2013. <http://www.npr.org/programs/morning/features/patc/johnhenry/index.html>. Present At The Creation.

2) Roud Folksong Index. 2013. 27 November, 2013. <http://www.efdss.org/library-and-archive>. English Folk Dance and Song Society.

3) ibiblio. 2013. 4 December, 2013. <http://www.ibiblio.org/john_henry/>. A collaboration of the School of Information and Library Science, the School of Journalism and Mass Communication and Information Technology Services at the University of North Carolina at Chapel Hill.

4) NPR.Org. 2002. 9 December, 2013. <http://www.npr.org/programs/morning/features/patc/johnhenry/index.html>. Present At The Creation.

5) NPR.Org. 2002. 9 December, 2013. <http://www.npr.org/programs/morning/features/patc/johnhenry/index.html>. Present At The Creation.

6) Lomax, John A. and Alan Lomax. American Ballads and Folk Songs. New York: Dover Publications, Inc., 1934.

7) Roud Folksong Index. 2013. 27 November, 2013. <http://www.efdss.org/library-and-archive>. English Folk Dance and Song Society.

FISH OUT OF WATER

BY
KEITH R.A. DECANDIDO

I knew something was wrong when I saw the twenty-eight-foot Coast Guard boat coming toward us.

I cut back on the throttle to slow us down. It wasn't a collision course, but if the Coasties were coming this way, going the way they came from might not be such a hot idea. It was a Response Boat–Small, one of the new Defiant Class, and if an RBS was here, it probably meant something and/or someone went missing at sea. After double-checking the code painted on the other boat's hull, I grabbed the radio.

"USCG 25119, USCG 25119, this is *Groucho* on 16, over."

"*Groucho*, this is 119, over." I recognized the tinny voice that squawked over the radio as Boatswain's Mate 1st Class Cole Howard, who worked out of the USCG station located on Marathon Key.

"119, *Groucho*, wasn't expecting you guys out here. Something we can help with?"

"*Groucho*, 119, thanks very much. Don't suppose you've seen *Soleado*? It's a rec boat that usually launches from the Azucar Di—"

I interrupted before he could start describing a boat I already knew quite well. "Cole, it's Cassie—have those jackasses gone missing *again*?" Over Thanksgiving weekend, boats from the Azucar Dive Shop up on Big Pine Key had gone missing twice. In fact, Cole was the one who found them the second time.

"*Groucho*, 119, that's affirmative." Formal as ever, was Cole. "Last radio contact was at 1100 hours." Then he got less formal and more skeptical and sardonic when he added, "Said they saw a mermaid."

Last time they said it was the Loch Ness Monster, so at least they were getting more local. On the other hand, I numbered among my close friends and acquaintances the ghost of a wrecker captain, an immortal barfly, and four Norse gods, so I really wasn't in any position to poo-poo someone who said they sighted a mermaid. Or Nessie.

"119, *Groucho*, I've got six tourists who really want to dive Pickles Reef. Okay if I proceed there?"

"*Groucho*, 119, that is in our search pattern, but not for a bit. Proceed as planned, but be advised that we've received reports of an odd storm front over that way. Nothing on the radar, but a few boats radioed in tornado warnings."

That didn't make sense on any level. For starters, I'd checked the weather before we came out. And for another... "119, *Groucho*, those boats do know we're in the Florida Keys, right? We don't generally get tornadoes."

"*Groucho*, 119, wanted to mention it just in case. Good sailing."

"You too. Out." I thumbed the radio off and hit the throttle, zipping around the RBS.

The half-dozen tourists who had come to the Seaclipse Dive Shop on Stock Island and hired me to take them scuba diving were a bunch of martial artists from a dojo in Denver visiting Key West for the week. The woman who seemed to be the ringleader, a short, lithe Filipino named Isabel (all the others called her "Senpai Bel"), poked her head into *Groucho*'s tiny bridge. "Everything okay?"

"Yeah, just touching base with the Coast Guard about a dive boat that's gone missing." I filled her in on what happened. "So good thing you went with us instead of Azucar."

Bel smiled and shook her head. "Our *kaicho* told us we should try Azucar, but it was too far up the Keys. We wanted somewhere closer to Old Town. Don't usually go against his wishes, but *damn*."

"Anyhow, we'll be at Pickles Reef in no time."

"Can I ask you something, Ms. Zukav? *Kaicho* told us the reef was named for the pickle barrels at the ocean floor. What he didn't tell us was why the barrels were left there."

My bosses at Seaclipse didn't warn me when I took the part-time job as dive-master last year that the job description included playing tour guide for the entirety of south Florida, but I quickly became quite the expert on the history and trivia of the Keys. "So many ships got wrecked on the reefs around here for centuries, there's no way to get everything back up above water. And these barrels are full of concrete, so hauling 'em up would be a major pain. No one's really sure where they came from—might be a wreck, might be a construction project gone bad. They used to think it was concrete to construct the forts they started to build during the Civil War, but they did an analysis a few years back that shows that it was a type of concrete made between 1890 and 1925. Might've been for the railroad they built through the Keys."

"What railroad?"

I smiled. "You guys drove down from Miami, right?"

Bel nodded. Flying into Key West International Airport was often more expensive than flying into Miami International Airport and renting a car. That had the added bonus of getting to drive on Route 1 through almost all of the Keys, which is some of the most scenic driving you'll ever see.

"The Overseas Highway is mostly on what used to be the railroad that went from Miami to Key West. It opened in 1912 and closed down after it got hammered by a hurricane in 1935. They built the road over the same right-of-way." I shrugged. "Anyhow, I'd rather they focused on cleaning up the actual litter that people throw down there. There's so much sh—so much crap down there..."

Smiling, she said, "It's okay, Ms. Zukav, you can say 'shit.'"

I laughed. "Sorry, first dive I ran, I made the mistake of saying 'fuck' in front of some Southern Baptists. Had to give 'em their money back. As a general—" I cut myself off when I caught sight of a boat in the water ahead of us. It wasn't on our exact course, but we'd pass pretty close. It was running a dive flag—the red flag with the white diagonal stripe that's become the universal sign for a boat filled with divers—but the motor was silent and it was bouncing around in the ocean as if it wasn't anchored.

Squinting at the boat, Bel asked, "Should we let that Coast Guard guy know?"

"Let's make sure they're okay, first," I said as I changed Groucho's course toward the dive boat, which looked more and more like Soleado the closer I got. "First time they went missing last weekend, it was another one of their boats that found 'em, but BM1 Howard found 'em the second time. He let 'em off once with just a warning, which means he's gonna rip several new—" I smiled at Bel, reveling in my newfound permission to speak freely. "—assholes this time. Probably close the shop for a major inspection, and whatever else he can do to make their lives a living hell."

Giving me a questioning look, Bel asked, "So you're gonna let them off?"

"There are about eighteen reasons why they might've gone quiet, starting with the radio breaking down."

"Cell phones?"

"Reception can be spotty out here. They also could be damaged in some other way that's not their fault. I'd rather not sic the Coasties on 'em until we know for sure they deserve it. Like the song says, we look after our own." I pulled up alongside the boat that had the word SOLEADO stenciled on its bow. "Mind giving me a hand?"

With the help of my very able-bodied tourists, I was able to tether Soleado to Groucho and then drop anchor so we'd all stay in one place for Cole to find us if we needed it. Groucho wasn't rated for towing, so if they were damaged, we'd still need help from the Coasties, but I wanted to know what was happening first.

Besides, it could've actually been a mermaid. Since moving to Key West, I'd dealt with a dragon, several different water fae, a half-dozen ghosts, what's left of the Norse pantheon, the spirit of the Calusa tribe, and a UFO on Dry Tortugas. I figured it'd be best to make sure it was something that the mundanes could handle before I called them in.

Okay, the Norse pantheon remnants I mentioned? I'm one of them. While I was "born of Midgard," as my friend Ginny, a.k.a. Sigyn, put it, I'm actually a Norse fate goddess—one of the Dísir. As a Dís, I tend to attract weird-ass shit, and sometimes I even can *deal* with the weird-ass shit. Cole was *way* too straight an arrow to handle an actual mermaid without his head exploding, so I needed to do triage on Soleado first.

Mind you, I had no idea if there actually *were* mermaids. I only found out I was a Dís seven months ago, and it didn't come with an instruction manual.

Once we secured the other boat, I jumped across to their deck. *Soleado* was a twenty-nine-footer just like ours, though it was made by a different company, so there were variations in design. However, the basics were the same: bridge fore, deck aft, galley and head below. I didn't see anyone in either of the former two places, so I climbed down belowdecks to find five people all standing crammed into the galley. They were all wearing some dive paraphernalia, but nobody was fully geared up—and nobody was fully un-geared up, either. One guy had a single fin on one foot, one wore a regulator but no mask, one had half his neoprene suit off—it was like they had all been interrupted in mid-prep and came down here.

I stared at the one person I knew, Al Martinez, one of the dive-masters at Azucar. He was the one wearing only a single fin. "Al, you okay? What happened?"

"I got a wife, back in Tampa, an' two kids. Ain't gonna be seein' her no more."

I frowned. "Al?"

The Asian couple crammed in on either side of Al then each said something in what I think was Korean; at the very least it sounded like how my Korean neighbors back in La Jolla always sounded when they chatted in their native tongue. After they said their peace, the other two—a couple of brunettes who looked related, probably sisters—spoke up.

"My fiancé's back in Ann Arbor. We'll never get to be married."

"My husband's waiting for me in Chicago. He'll be a widower."

I blinked. Even by my standards, this was weird.

Bel called from the deck—she had followed me across, apparently. "Everything okay, Ms. Zukav?"

"Lemme get back to you on that." I reached out to the dive-master. "Hey, Al, it's me, Cassie—from Seaclipse? Let's get you guys outta there, okay?"

But Al didn't move, he just said, "I got a wife, back in Tampa, an' two kids. Ain't gonna be seein' her no more."

KEITH R. A. DECANDIDO

That started the whole litany again, first the Asian couple, then the sisters.

Hesitantly, I grabbed Al's arm by the neoprene and tugged a bit, but he refused to budge.

I felt like there was something else I should do. This had all the earmarks of a spell cast over them. But my knowledge of spellcraft was limited to the fact that I was able to cast one if someone spent the better part of a day showing me how, and I only did *that* once. I needed to know a helluva lot more before I could try to cast a counterspell—and by "a helluva lot more," I meant "something."

I hopped back up onto the deck, asked Bel to keep an eye on the creepy quintet in the galley, and radioed Cole.

Once the RBS showed up, I untied *Groucho* and took the paying customers on to Pickles Reef, leaving Cole to handle Al and his clients. Bel and her friends paid for a reef dive, and they got a reef dive. Since there was an even number of divers, I stayed on the boat while they dove, since you always go down in pairs. (No certified diver would *ever* go down alone, and no reputable dive shop would ever let anyone go down alone.) Had I been in the mood, I could've been a third for one of the pairs, but these guys had some kind of teamwork bond stuff going on, so I let them do their thing.

I was fondling my smartphone when a call came in from BM1 Cole Howard's cell. I smiled and hit ANSWER. "Hey, Cole, what's up?"

"Just thought you'd want to know, we got Martinez and his customers out of the galley. They're on the RBS now. They just keep doing the same thing over and over, talking about who they left behind at home."

"You got a Korean speaker on board?"

"Yeah, me." I could hear Cole's smirk from here. "They were saying how they were going to leave their three kids orphans. And the boat was clean—no drugs, nothing untoward at all. All we found was a cooler full of non-alcoholic drinks, the first-aid stuff, dive equipment, and three iPads covered in waterproof casings."

I chuckled. One of Seaclipse's biggest sellers were the waterproof casings that allowed you to bring your smartphone or tablet underwater with you so you could take pictures with it. Those actually sold better than the disposable underwater cameras. As a veteran phone fondler, I totally got why people didn't want to be separated from their devices and wanted to have their underwater pics right there at their fingertips, but I never risked taking my phone down with me. Then again, I had a ridiculously expensive 14-megapixel underwater camera.

"We'll take them back to Marathon, drop them at the Fishermen's Hospital, let the docs there give them a full once-over."

"Okay. Hey, Cole, thanks for filling me in."

He snorted. "If I didn't, you'd have called *me* in an hour to bug me."

"Yeah, yeah." I tried and failed to sound offended. Cole knew me too well. "You ever gonna get your tight ass to Mayor Fred's?"

"Call me when they hire a blues band. Bye."

The dive went, you'll pardon the expression, swimmingly. My martial artists had a grand old time swimming around the reefs, the pickle barrels, and the pillar corals. They also frolicked with the blue angel fish and watched the spiny lobsters crawl on the barrels. I learned about all these things from the breathless descriptions provided by Bel's husband, aided by the pictures from Bel's tablet (nicely covered in a waterproof casing she bought at Seaclipse). Bel promised to e-mail me the link to the pictures when she uploaded them.

That night, as was my wont, I wandered over to Mayor Fred's Saloon. I lived and also worked part-time at the Bottroff House Bed and Breakfast, located on Eaton Street, just off Duval in Old Town. Mayor Fred's was a couple of blocks away on Greene Street, built around a big ficus tree (tourist web sites will tell you that it was Key West's hanging tree in the nineteenth century; they won't tell you that it's also a root of Yggdrasil, the world tree of Norse myth). I was always there to see my friends in the band 1812 play Thursday through Sunday. Of course, it was Wednesday, so the bar was less crowded, and also the music was provided, not by a four-piece band on the main stage in the back, but by an acoustic act over near the entrance.

I didn't recognize the person playing guitar, but I remembered

Ihor, the bartender, telling me that the two guys with beards whose names I could never remember got a gig at a place up in Key Largo. The new guy was a painfully thin, absurdly pale, tall guy with a hooked nose and long, stringy brown hair. He also had a lovely voice—he was singing "Scarborough Fair" and doing it justice—and he played his battered old Yamaha acoustic guitar quite skillfully. The guitar had stickers from various cities on it, making it look like a tourist's suitcase from 1957.

I did recognize one of the people at the bar, though: Larry, who was the textbook definition of "regular." Every single day, from the moment Mayor Fred's opened at midday to the second it closed at four a.m., Larry was at that bar, guzzling coffee or a soda. He was the immortal barfly I listed among my acquaintances before, and he got that way by falling in love with a water elemental and then leaving her. As soon as he falls asleep, he'll die—hence the all-caffeine-all-the-time diet—but until he falls asleep, he'll continue to live. He's spent eternity to date at Mayor Fred's, going back to when Hemingway was a regular. I had no idea where he went from four to eleven in the morning, though I figured he must live somewhere. Someday I'd ask.

"What's the word, Cassie?" he asked me as I sat next to him.

I took a deep breath and then let it out in a single burst. "Weird" was the word I finally agreed on.

Larry laughed. I was the first person to answer Larry's rather old-fashioned greeting with an actual word, and it had become our thing. "I'd ask what's weird in your life, but I'm not convinced we'll have enough time for that."

"Yeah, well. I had a doozy on the afternoon dive."

After I told Larry the story of Al Martinez and *Soleado*, he got a faraway look in his eyes. "Wow. That takes me back."

This was interesting. "Back to what?"

He waved a hand around. "About a hundred years, give or take." He patted the pocket of his shirt to make sure his pack of cigarettes was in it. "C'mon outside, I need to smoke."

Florida state law actually allowed smoking in bars, but you still couldn't smoke in Mayor Fred's. Ihor, who was both the night bartender and the general manager, had asthma and reacted very badly to second-hand smoke, so he had to ban smoking in order to not collapse in a wheezing heap while doing his job. To Larry's credit, he remained loyal to Mayor Fred's even after the smoking ban went into effect and stuck around, rather than patronize one of the other gajillion bars on the island that would let him suck nicotine where he sat. Of course, that didn't stop him from complaining about it all the time...

I followed him out under the giant fish over the main entrance to the Greene Street sidewalk where he lit up. "Back around—oh, Jesus, Mary, and Joseph, I can't remember the damn dates, exactly, but it was definitely in the twenties, because I do remember that Harding was president. In any case, I used to spend my leisure hours at an exclusive cigar club down on Flagler. There was a fella named Ruben." He chuckled. "Ruben the Cuban, we called him. He sailed up from Havana and opened up one of the cigar factories. He and I would play cribbage over brandy and cigars."

Holding up a hand, I asked, "Wait, brandy? I thought Harding was president during Prohibition."

Larry just chuckled. "Letter of the law, sure, booze was illegal, but around here that didn't mean a hill'a beans. Treasury Department never really got down this far south, and when they did, they took the railroad, so we knew they were coming." At my confused look, he added, "Tickets had a note on them that said they were employees of the federal government, so if one boarded a train to Key West, the conductor would get on the wire and warn all the speaks to hide the booze."

"Didn't realize you were such an outlaw."

"Drinkin' brandy with my friend didn't make me an outlaw. It just made me another person on the island." He shook his head. "Now you've turned my head around with all this foolishness. What were we talking about?"

"Ruben the Cuban," I prompted.

"Right, so Ruben loved to fish, and kept needling me to come along with him. After what happened with Anne, I wasn't all that tickled to go out to sea, but he finally wore me down by making a wager out of it." Anne was the name his water fae ex used when she was in human form. He went on. "If I lost at cribbage, I'd fish with him. If I won, he'd give me a box of his factory's finest."

I smiled. "I take it you lost, or there wouldn't be a story."

He looked up at me as he took a puff. "You know that smart mouth of yours is gonna get you in Dutch one of these days."

"I think it's cute that you believe it hasn't already. So what happened on the fishing trip?"

Taking a longer drag on his cigarette, he inhaled, paused, and exhaled a puff of smoke before finally answering me. "All right, I don't wanna be unkind to Ruben, rest his soul, but that was one of the most boring afternoons of my life."

"Given how long your life has been, that's saying something."

"You said it." He shook his head. "After we whiled away most of the day without a single bite, we finally hauled anchor and went back home—and that's when we saw it. At first, we thought it was a sea lion, at least until, as God is my witness, I saw a woman's head. Looked like she was in trouble, so I dove into the water with one of the cork vests."

"No life-preserver?" I asked in surprise. We had ten inflatable donuts on each of the dive-shop boats.

"Not like what you're thinking—those got invented later. Back then, we just had a couple cork vests, and I swam out to put one on the lady so we could rescue her. Except she didn't need rescuing. She swam under me and came onto Ruben's boat. I was about fifty yards away when I realized she'd snuck past me, so I turned around to double back. I only caught a few glimpses, but—well, it sure as shootin' looked like a mermaid. Woman's head, long tail, and the body was scaly and strange. Reminded me a little of Anne's true form, to be honest—only got a gander of her like that once, but it was a doozy."

I nodded. As a Dís, I'm immune to disguises of any kind, so I *only* saw Larry's ex in her true, seaweed-encrusted, yucky form. He was lucky to only get the one gander.

"I did catch a glimpse of something peculiar. It was beautiful that day, sky blue as a marble, and not a cloud to be seen. But for a few minutes, the sky changed, went all green. Now, I spent some time in Kansas back in the day, and I've seen the sky turn that color right before a twister. But down here in Florida? Never seen the like, and never so sudden." He took a final puff, then dropped the cigarette onto the sidewalk and stepped on it. "By the time I got to the boat, though, the sky was normal and she was gone. And Ruben, he was just *sitting* there, carrying on to the nines about his brother back home in Cuba and how he wasn't gonna see him ever again. He wouldn't move, he barely blinked, he just sat around like a lump, and every time I tried to talk to him, he was just a broken record about his brother."

This was all sounding annoyingly familiar. Also, the tornado warning Cole told me about was sounding less far-fetched all of a sudden. "Then what happened?"

"I managed to steer the boat back to shore, but it wasn't easy since I hadn't been on a boat in decades. Ruben wasn't ever the same after that. Eventually, he became more himself, but we only spoke a few more times here and there. He lost interest in the club, in cribbage, in drinking, and eventually even in work. He sold the factory, moved back to Havana, and I never saw him again."

His cigarette done, Larry headed back inside under the giant fish. I followed him, and as I entered, I heard the guitar player start his next song with the words:

"One Friday morn as we'd set sail
And our ship not far from land
We there did espy a fair mermaid
With a comb and a glass in her hand…"

I did a double take as I was walking toward the bar, and stopped suddenly. Unfortunately, a tourist was walking toward the restroom from the bar, and crashed right into me, spilling his beer. I apologized and offered to buy him a new one, but he muttered that it was okay and kept going to the men's room.

As I sat down at the bar, where a pint of beer was waiting for me (it's good to be a regular), I caught the rest of the song, and was even more freaked out.

"Then up spoke the captain of our gallant ship
Who at once did our peril see
I have married a wife in fair London town,
And tonight she'll a widow be.
And then up spoke the little cabin boy,
And a fair-haired boy was he.
I've a father and a mother in fair Portsmouth town,
And this night she will weep for me."

I wound up gulping down two-thirds of the pint at once.

After he finished the song, he said, "And now I take a pause. If you enjoyed what you heard, please make your pleasure known." With that, he held up the tip jar on the stool in front

KEITH R. A. DeCANDIDO

of him. Surprisingly, he had no CDs for sale, no cards listing his website, or anything like that.

I approached him as he put his Yamaha in its case. "What was that last song?"

"It's called 'The Wrecked Ship.' Based on an old sea shanty, I think. Always loved that one."

"Yeah."

A few days passed, and I didn't hear anything new about mermaids or boats going missing or tornado warnings or people muttering about the people they left back home. I *did* hear that Al Martinez quit Azucar to move back to Tampa. The owner of Azucar told me that right before he tried to poach me from Seaclipse, a request that I rejected, though it was flattering. If nothing else, it gave me leverage to bug my bosses for a raise.

Didn't know what happened to the four tourists who jammed into the galley with Al, but a little Google-fu revealed more about Ruben the Cuban. His real name was Ruben Hernandez Jr., owner of the prosaically named Hernandez Cigar Factory on Front Street. He sold it in 1922, when Warren Harding really was president, and he moved back to Cuba. The new owners of the factory kept the name, until it was badly damaged by the Labor Day Hurricane in 1935—same one that took out the railroad, actually—and it shut down for good.

Unsurprisingly, I found nothing online that mentioned that Hernandez saw a mermaid. Still, the details I could find matched Larry's story.

I also did a bit of research into mermaid legends, though there was a lot of stuff from a lot of different regions, and not much to match what I'd heard beyond the song the guy at Mayor Fred's did. I was amused to read that Christopher Columbus made references to seeing mermaids in his journals written during his infamous sea voyage of 1492, though some modern folk assume that he and his crew really saw manatees or rays and were just *really* hard up for sexual companionship.

None of my dives took me anywhere near Pickles Reef until the following Monday when the South Dakota Seafarers came back to the Keys. The SDS were a bunch of retirees who got together to do various water-related things, and every three months or so, a group of them came down here. This quarter, I got five of them, and they had their hearts set on diving the wreck of the *Duane*, a Coastie ship that was deliberately sunk back in the eighties to create an artificial reef. Wreck divers *love* the *Duane*, so I usually wind up going there at least twice a month.

We headed there in *Chico* this time, on a partly cloudy day with decent winds. Not enough to make the water choppy, thankfully.

Then the sky turned green.

For a second, I thought I imagined it. The sky just went from blue and white to an emerald-green instantly. And then it changed back just as fast.

Before I even had time to process this—or figure out how to answer the inevitable questions from a quintet of senior citizens as to what the hell was going on—I saw a hundred-and-twenty-five-foot gaff-rigged schooner hauling ass across our path. They were at full sail and pootling along at eight knots or so. Frowning, I double checked the charts and realized that they were heading straight for a shallow reef, and if they didn't change course in about thirty seconds, they were going to crash right into it.

Then I caught sight of the logo on the side, and realized it was the *Lilly*, a local schooner that did intimate little cruises for small parties in and around the Bahamas and the Keys. Her captain was Meg Michaels, and she wasn't usually batshit crazy. In fact, the last time I'd talked to her was about a month ago when she came back from a triumphant second-place finish in the Great Chesapeake Bay Schooner Race, and a bunch of us, including all twelve of her crew, got *seriously* drunk at Mayor Fred's to celebrate.

I snagged the radio. "*Chico* calling Schooner *Lilly*. Come about, you're gonna hit a reef. Meg? It's Cassie, you there?" I shook my head. "Fuck!" I hit the throttle, even though I knew I wasn't gonna make it in time.

I always used to make fun of TV shows and movies where they'd go into slow motion when something bad happens. After watching *Lilly* slam into the reef, I stopped doing that. It took maybe a second and a half for it to go from going full-bore through the ocean, to jutting at an angle up out of the water with a big-ass hole in the hull, but watching it felt like at least a full minute.

After sending out a general distress call, which would bring

Cole and his buddies out here, as well as any other boats in the area, I set course for what was now a wreck.

Just like with *Soleado*, I pulled alongside *Lilly*, though I was careful to take it slow. At twenty-nine feet, *Chico* was able to handle the reef better than a schooner four times its length, but I didn't want to take any risks.

I tied us to *Lilly*'s transom, which was the least damaged part of her, and then hopped on board.

Just like with *Soleado*, the crew was all bunched belowdecks, this time in the captain's cabin. (Which told me right there that supernatural forces were at work. Meg didn't let *anyone* in her cabin for any reason. In related news, the place was a mess and smelled kinda funky.) I got the same litany of family members they thought they'd never see again, from Meg's brother in Boston, to the chief mate's children in Norfolk, to the cook's husband and kids in New York, to the engineer's parents in San Francisco, and so on—just like *Soleado*, and just like that song.

Cole showed up soon enough, as did two other boats. He regarded me with concern. "This is some very bizarre stuff happening, Cassie."

"You ain't kiddin'."

That night, I returned to the Bottroff House, where I shared my room with the ghost of the wrecker captain who originally built the place, Captain Jeremiah Bottroff. As a Dís, I was the only person who could see or hear the captain, which meant I pretty much got stuck with his company, since I've been his only regular source of conversation for the past century and a half.

"I got to see how your job used to be today," I said as I climbed into bed.

"And how's that, exactly?" Bottroff asked.

I told him about *Lilly*—as well as *Soleado*, and I threw in Larry's fish story while I was at it—which prompted a derisive snort from Bottroff.

"If you didn't tow the vessel back to shore, if you didn't claim salvage of a percentage of its cargo in exchange for rescuing them, then what you did was nothing like my own travails as a wrecker." Back in the nineteenth century, wreckers like Bottroff would rescue boats that crashed on reefs and then do all that stuff he just said. When I first got here, I thought that meant he was a pirate, but it was actually all completely legal, and also seriously regulated. The practice faded away as boat construction improved to the point where those kinds of wrecks weren't everyday occurrences.

"Yeah, the Coasties handled the really fun parts."

"Actually," Bottroff said, "your story of the vessel *Soleado* does have a ring of familiarity to it, as does your immortal friend's tale of woe. I, too, encountered a vessel that claimed to have seen mermaids. They, too, babbled about their homes and family. At the time I dismissed them as madmen, but in light of what I've seen in the days since my death..."

"So what happened?"

"In truth, I only recall the incident, not due to the fatuous ramblings of the passengers and crew, but because I was forbidden from claiming salvage. The boat did not actually come upon a reef, nor was it damaged in any way. Rather it was adrift, and while we did indeed tow them back to shore, the judge denied our salvage claim. As you can imagine, my boys and I were rather upset."

That night, I dreamed of a mermaid swimming around one of Seaclipse's boats, with me and Larry and the guitar player on it, and I started wishing I could see my parents back in La Jolla again. Since I still hadn't seen the thing, my brain decided to make the mermaid look like the Disney character Ariel from *The Little Mermaid*.

The next day, I was working at the B&B all day, with no dives to run, and that night I headed to the open mic at Mayor Fred's. Larry was there, of course, as was Ginny. The drummer in 1812, as well as being a Norse god and the ex-wife of the trickster Loki, Ginny had been encouraged by the rest of the band to do some singing in addition to her excellent drum work. She wanted to try it at the open mic first, and if she was comfortable with it, she'd sing with the band onstage. Their already-impressive repertoire of covers (and harmonies) would be increased greatly by adding a fourth voice to the mix.

Because Ginny was there, a third familiar face sat at the bar: Loki, who was trying (and so far, to my delight, failing) to win

Ginny back.

Loki greeted me with the supercilious smile he always used. "Larry informs me that you encountered a *havsrå*."

I blinked. Then I remembered my crash course in Norse myth that I imposed upon myself after learning I was a Dís eight months ago. "Right, that's what you guys called mermaids."

"In a manner of speaking. In truth, the only reason *havsrå* have been seen in Midgard or Asgard is because of a little joke I played on Thor once. You see, he had just married Sif, even though I kept telling her my cousin would have sexual congress with virtually any female he could get his hands on. To prove his lack of faithfulness, I summoned a *havsrå* from another of the Nine Worlds, and Thor did indeed attempt to ravish her."

I let out a long breath. "Let me guess, the sky is emerald-green on that particular world?"

"I believe so, yes." Loki grinned. "Sadly, in the end, no one was happy. The *havsrå* wished only to go home, Sif was furious at me for starting it all, and as for Thor, he faced certain—logistical difficulties."

I chuckled and shook my head. "Couldn't fit Tab A into Slot B?"

"Well, a *havsrå* has no, ah, 'Slot B' as such. Sif forced me to send the creature back, and I did. I suppose it's possible others of her kind have slipped between the worlds and arrived here."

"Just to board ships and make them act weird? It doesn't make sense."

Ginny was walking up to the mic now, and started singing an *a cappella* song called "Seven Bridges Road," which pretty much ended the conversation. Enraptured, Loki watched her sing the song in a lovely alto, and he clapped the loudest when she was done.

To be fair, I clapped the second loudest. She absolutely nailed it. When she came back to the bar to hearty congratulations from me, Larry, Loki, and the entire rest of the bar, I asked her, "Why didn't you sing before?"

"I must confess, Cassie, that, at this moment, I cannot imagine why."

Loki smiled. "I always knew you had a voice that could move the heavens themselves, Sigyn."

"Thank you."

I shook my head. On the one hand, Loki was a prime asshole. On the other hand, he really did love Ginny.

Two days later, I was in *Harpo*, taking three sisters back from a dive near some lovely coral, when I saw a sea lion swim by the boat. Scared the hell out of me at first, but I got a good look at it, and it was an actual sea lion. I found myself remembering the jokes about sea lions being mermaid dogs.

Just after I caught my breath and recovered, I saw another sea lion tail—but it was green. And then the head popped out, and it looked kind of like a person. The face was more or less feminine, with hair that extended down past her shoulders, but looking a lot like a pelt.

The tail was definitely that of a sea creature, and the head looked like a woman with funny hair, although her eyes were wide enough to qualify as an anime character; she didn't have a nose so much as two slits above her upper lip, and her lips were huge and full. But the weird part was her body. She had a flexible torso that didn't look like a sea lion or a woman—no boobs, no obvious thorax, just a stretch of skin and bone that linked the head to the tail. Two arms grew out of that torso, with no elbows, but ending with three-fingered hands, complete with opposable thumbs.

I also realized I couldn't see her skin directly. It was wet and matted and short, but her entire body was covered with the green pelt, making her appear a tiny bit like a green polar bear.

She was holding something in one hand that looked like a heavily serrated blade, and a glass ball in the other. I shook my head—there's your glass and comb from the song.

"Wow, she's beautiful." That was one of the sisters, who obviously had a different definition of "beautiful" than mine. Then again, the creature might've been using a glamour to appear more attractive to whoever's looking at her. After all, most of the mermaid stories, from Columbus to Captain Bottroff to Larry to the Walt Disney Company, have them looking all pretty, and if they saw what I was seeing, they wouldn't think that.

Anyhow, the mermaid—or whatever—burst through the surface just like a sea lion and flopped onto the deck of *Harpo*.

KEITH R. A. DECANDIDO

Then she just stared at us.

The sky turned emerald green—the same color as the mermaid's pelt.

The three sisters ran belowdecks and crammed themselves into the head.

I didn't move.

I felt...something in my head. A weird longing... and an overwhelming sense of wanting to be back in La Jolla.

No, that wasn't it. The images in my head were of the house I grew up in outside San Diego, but I wasn't thinking of the house specifically.

I was thinking about home.

I need to go home.

That wasn't me thinking that, even though the thought was in my head.

After a minute, I realized it was the mermaid who wanted to go home.

Fuck me.

"How can I get you home?"

You understand me? Finally, someone who understands me!

"I guess I do, yeah."

Are you of the Aesir?

I snorted. That was what Odin, Thor, Loki, and the other Norse gods liked to call themselves. "Sorta."

Their trickster kidnapped our sister once, and since then, the boundaries between the worlds have weakened. Sometimes we fall into this world and must find our way home to our sisters. I miss them so!

She slithered toward me on the deck, and I saved her some trouble by moving toward her, and as I approached, she held up the glass ball.

This talisman may return me home, but they do not function.

"May I?"

Of course.

I took the ball, but I had no idea what it was, really, or what it did. And me holding it had no effect on it. Sometimes, when I touched something, it acted weird. But not this time. Have I mentioned I didn't get an instruction manual?

How-some-ever, I knew someone who could help.

"My name is Cassie. I'm one of the Dísir. I'm—acquainted

with the trickster who kidnapped your sister back in the day, and I can learn from him how to get you home. Can you meet me back here later tonight—say in six hours?"

Very well. And thank you, Dís.

"My pleasure." I handed her the ball back.

The mermaid—or, I guess, *havsrå*—took it and then dove back over the side of the boat. I ran down to the head, where the three women were just sitting there.

"My husband's back home in Philadelphia. I'll never see him again."

"My daughter's back home in Perth Amboy. I'll never see her again."

"My wife's back home in Tarrytown. I'll never see her again."

I sighed. I knew I forgot to ask the *havsrå* something.

That night, I went to Mayor Fred's, where 1812 was playing with the full band, including Ginny on drums, which meant Loki was in the audience. I walked in, grabbed his ear, and dragged him out onto Greene Street.

"Ow! What are you *doing*, little Dís?" He only called me that when he wanted to piss me off, but he'd already done that more than he realized.

"In April, when it snowed and the world was almost destroyed, that was your fault. Last month when the ghosts on the island got super-active and everyone could see and hear them, and one of them killed people, that was your fault. And now *havsrå* are causing shipwrecks and have been for centuries. Guess what? Your fault *again*. What the fuck is *wrong* with you?"

"How is this *my* fault, exactly?" he asked archly.

I told him what the *havsrå* told me.

His voice much more subdued with all the high dudgeon gone, he said, "Ah, I see. Sadly, Cassie, I cannot help you. While the spell itself is rather simple, it takes great power to bridge the gap between worlds to send the *havsrå* home. I am but a shadow of my former self. Even when the peoples of northern Europe worshipped the Aesir as gods, and my power was at its absolute height, it was difficult for me to manage it. Now, there is no chance of it."

"She has two talismans—a glass ball and a multi-bladed

knife of some kind."

"I know not what the knife would do, but the glass ball is likely an orb, which can focus magic very much the way a lens focuses light. That will merely direct the spell, not create it."

"Fine, you said the spell was simple. Teach it to me. I know I've got the mojo." I grinned. "How do you think I stopped *you*?"

Raising a blond eyebrow, he then asked, "And what reason do I have to do you this kindness?"

I blinked. "I beg your pardon?"

"What boon shall you grant me in exchange for doing you this service?"

For a moment, I just stared at him. "My parents have a word for what you just did. It's *chutzpah*. And if you really want a boon, how about this? I won't have to tell Ginny that you were a total douchenozzle when I asked you to help me out. On the other hand, if you do help me, I could tell the woman you're trying to win back that you selflessly helped me get a *havsrå* back home."

He seemed to consider it, but I knew him well enough at this point to know damn well that he wouldn't do anything to jeopardize his chances with softening Ginny toward him. "Very well. Shall we retire to your dwelling?"

I sighed. The notion of Loki in my room did not appeal, but the *havsrå* needed to get home before somebody got hurt. So we went back to the Bottroff House and, over the strenuous objections of the captain, had a spellcasting tutoring session. The language of the spell was in the same unrecognizable tongue as the spell I used to stop Loki in April, which helped me pick up the cadence faster.

Once we were done, and I was sure I had the spell's words and proper pronunciation memorized, Loki said, "Excellent. Good luck, Cassie."

"Oh, I'm gonna have more than luck. You're coming with me."

"But—"

"But me no buts, butthead. I'm not taking any chances, and I need backup, even if it's just—" I shook my head, laughing at the irony even as I said it. "For moral support."

Loki grinned. "Not my usual type of support, I must say."

We drove out to Stock Island. I had already convinced my bosses at Seaclipse to let me take one of the boats out on my own, on the condition that I'd pay for the gas used on the trip. Luckily, there were only enough evening-dive signups for one boat, so they had two to spare.

Loki and I went out in *Groucho*. He looked really nauseated as we went, and by the time we reached the rendezvous spot, he was almost as green as the *havsrå*.

Speaking of whom, she was waiting for us in the same place as planned. She once again flopped onto the deck.

I am glad you returned, Dís. I was not sure you would. Our experiences with the Aesir are not ones that engender trust.

She was looking right at Loki. So was I. "You know who this is?" True, I'd said that I'd be consulting Loki, but he was a shapechanger, and I doubt he looked the same now as he did when he kidnapped her sister in order to tweak Thor and Sif.

We all are well aware of the trickster who ripped our sister from us.

"My apologies, sweet lady." Loki bowed and almost came close to sounding like he was trying to be sincere. "I was young and foolish, and was poor at thinking through the consequences of my actions."

"And you're using the past tense, why, exactly?"

Now Loki gave me a look. "Shall we begin?"

The *havsrå* handed me the orb. *You will need this.*

"Thank you." I took the orb from her and then started to chant the familiar words in the unfamiliar language. As I spoke, I felt something tug at my heart, and the orb started to glow from within.

The sky turned green, and a small whirlpool started forming in the water just off our port bow.

Thank you, Cassie of the Dísir. You have the eternal gratitude of the havsrå *for what you have done today.*

Then she turned to Loki and held up the knife that sea shanty writers had mistaken for a comb.

And thank you also for allowing us to at last have our vengeance.

With that, she slashed Loki's throat with the blades. Blood started spurting all over the deck, and Loki fell to his knees, a look of total surprise on his face. I grabbed him and eased him down onto the deck.

KEITH R. A. DeCANDIDO

Turning to the *havsrå*, I cried, "What the *fuck*?"

Since the day our sister was returned to us from Asgard after being wretchedly ill-treated by the Aesir, we have travelled with two items in our possession. These were to be used if we fell through one of the many portals between worlds that this trickster created for his sport and for our agony. The orb could be used to return us home, though it does not always function as it should. The blade was to be used to avenge our sister for her mistreatment at this foul creature's hands, should we ever be fortunate enough to cross his path once again. Good-bye, Cassie of the Dísir. Fare you well. And good-bye Loki of the Aesir. Fare you poorly.

And then she dove over the railing and into the whirlpool, which closed up behind her, the water becoming still once again.

Loki stared upward. The sun was starting to set, painting the sky a spectacular orange and purple.

His voice a gurgling croak, he said, "Sigyn is—is back in Key West. I'll never see her beautiful face again."

Then he just faded away. Seriously, he went transparent and then disappeared. Even the blood he got all over *Groucho*'s deck was gone (which, if nothing else, meant I wouldn't be stuck cleaning it up). Gods don't die the way we do—if they even really die at all.

But right now, Loki was gone. How the fuck was I gonna explain this to Ginny?

I sat completely alone on the deck, the orb rolling around next to me as *Groucho* bounced with the tide.

Whilst the raging seas do roar,
And the lofty winds do blow,
And we poor seamen do lie on the top
Whilst the landmen lies below.

On....The Mermaid

Child lists six versions of Ballad 289 while the Roud Folksong Index lists two hundred and sixty-two versions of #124, The Mermaid. When the crew of a ship on the ocean spies a mermaid, they know they are in trouble—mermaids were a portent of disaster. Even seeing one with a mirror and comb didn't forestall their troubles. In some versions, the Captain, Mate and Boatswain all mourn that soon their wives will be widows while the cabin boy bemoans his parents' grief. Whether the ship goes around three times in some versions or was en route to Greenland in another, they all testify to how important shipping was and how futile it was to fight the power of the sea. (1)

As shown on the YouTube uploads, this is a popular ballad with amateur singers. Others such as Martin Carthy, Celtic Mayhem, The Pirates Of St. Piran, Celtic Stew, and The Sharecroppers have also recorded The Mermaid.

1) Child, Francis James. The English and Scottish Popular Ballads Vol. V. Mineola: Dover, 2003.

MAKING MUSIC

BY
KELLEY ARMSTRONG

Izzy sat in front of her computer, headphones on, eyes closed, listening to the latest top five rock songs, looping them over and over, struggling to find meaning in the lyrics. To find lyricism, poetry. Hell, at this point she'd settle for a clever rhyming couplet. She'd sampled the top country hits, but that wasn't really her forte. She loved good old rock-and-roll, not surprising, given that if she'd been a boy, her father had planned to name her Ozzy. An old-school roadie for a father. And an English lit professor for a mom. That particular mix was partly what landed her in this very place, at this desk, so deeply engrossed in her task that sweat had broken out along her hairline.

When the phone rang, she jumped, her headphones tumbling off, almost taking one dangling earring with them. She winced as she disentangled the earring with one hand and lifted her phone with the other.

"I have news," her agent trilled, somehow managing to get three syllables out of the last word.

"Let me guess," Izzy said. "There's a newly formed punk group out of Nowhere, Missouri, that wants to give me amazing exposure by covering 'The Unquiet Grave' free of charge." She paused. "No, wait. They're asking me to pay them, right?"

Monica sighed. "You are such a pessimist, Iz."

"No, I've just had that generous offer too many times. Sometimes brought to me by my agent, no less."

She swore she heard Monica's lacquered pageboy crinkle as she bristled. "That was a successful punk rock group from Kansas

City. It would have been good exposure . . . before Grave. You are now a bona fide songwriting star, my girl. I head them off at the pass if there isn't money attached. Significant money."

Izzy eyed the bills stacked on her desk. "Actually, if there's any money attached, I'd like to hear—"

"Significant. Otherwise, you look desperate."

True, except for the fact that she was desperate. "The Unquiet Grave" was two years old now, and she was the writer, not the performer. It hadn't exactly made her rich.

"Do you want to hear my news?" One syllable for news now. Apparently, Izzy had not displayed the proper degree of gratitude.

"Sure."

"A major recording artist heard the NPR retrospective of your work and has contacted me directly. Directly. Not through his agent. Not through his manager. He wishes to speak to you about writing a large amount of his next album."

"Uh-huh."

The line echoed in silence. Then Monica said, "Did you hear me, Iz?"

"I did. That's why I said 'uh-huh.' I'm just waiting for a name attached to that 'major recording artist.'"

"I'm not at liberty to say."

Izzy shifted the phone to her other ear. "What?"

"He'd like me to keep his name out of it until you two meet in New York tomorrow—"

"New York? I'm expected to meet someone in New York tomorrow, at my expense, I presume, without even getting a name? Hell, I wouldn't drop everything and fly out for Bruce Springsteen."

"I should hope not. Have you seen the sales on his last album? I swear, girl, you are the oldest twenty-nine-year-old I have ever met. I'm actually glad I can't give his name because you'd probably say 'huh?' despite the fact his last three albums went plat-i-num."

"Give me a try."

Monica snorted. "Not likely. I made a deal. As for flying your ass out there, he's comping the ticket. First class. Have you ever even flown first class, Iz?"

"Sure, I got an upgrade once."

"Pack your bag. Gather your portfolio. You are going to New York at the crack of dawn, and when you find out who brought you there, just remember, I like Bollinger. Cristal is for thugs."

Izzy sat on the bank of Bank Rock Bay in Central Park, listening to the pound of feet jogging across the Oak Bridge. She closed her eyes and imagined them as drumbeats. There was music there, as there was everywhere. One only had to find it. She knew that better than anyone.

She fingered her portfolio of sheet music. Old-fashioned, Monica would sniff, but Izzy found music in the medium, in the crackle of paper, in the hand-scratched black lines. She'd brought an iPod, too, with recordings of her latest songs, but she preferred the sheets. An old-fashioned medium for an old-fashioned art. The crafting of music from poetry.

Even in rock, there was a place for poetry. For beauty. For balladry. She created both—turning old ballads into rousing rock anthems. It was, as one might expect, a very narrow specialty. Despite this, critically acclaimed artists weren't exactly clamoring to work with her. Even Whiskey Roar—who'd seen their first gold album based largely on the success of her re-imagining of "The Unquiet Grave"—had only contacted her once more for a song, buried deep on their second album, as if an act of charity.

"'Tis down in yonder garden green,

Love, where we used to walk.

The finest flower that ere was seen ...'"

When Izzy heard the words, she thought she was still lost in her thoughts. Then she realized they were real and she jerked upright.

"Just don't ask me to recite more." The man's figure was almost hidden in the dark shade as he walked toward her. "That's the only part I memorized and only to impress you."

"But that stanza isn't in my song."

"Which makes it even more impressive, right?"

He stepped into the sun. A slender man in his mid-thirties. Dark hair falling into his eyes. A boyish grin. Glittering blue eyes. He was dressed like any other park-goer—in jeans, a T-shirt, and old sneakers—but the moment she saw him, her jaw dropped.

Shit. Holy fucking shit.

She made a mental note to send Monica her Bollinger, whether this meeting panned out or not. For once, her agent had earned it.

"Beau Wallace," she said.

"That's what my driver's license says. Or so I think. Haven't used it in a few years."

Before she could stand, he plunked himself down on the bank beside her without so much as a fastidious glance at the grass and dirt.

Beau Wallace. Monica might lament her client's old-school tastes, but Izzy sure as hell knew who this was. Former boy-band crooner turned mega-selling solo star. If she was being perfectly honest, she might admit to a Beau Wallace poster in her bedroom when she was twelve. These days, he got a little too much airplay on light-rock stations, but she still had a few of his hits on her playlist.

"I want to branch out," he said, as if reading her mind. "As flattering as it is to top the easy-listening charts, after a while" — he lowered his voice conspiratorially—"it's not so flattering, if you know what I mean. I want to go harder, roughen my edge. Maybe I'm kidding myself to think I have an edge to roughen but . . ." He shrugged. "I want to try."

"Sure." A lame answer, but it was all she could manage, her inner adolescent shrieking, "I'm talking to Beau Wallace!"

He glanced toward the path. A woman had appeared there. About Izzy's age, pretty but unsmiling, with a dark ponytail and darker shades. Dressed, like Beau, in jeans and sneakers, but wearing a denim jacket despite the warm late spring day.

"No, not a stalker fan," Beau said, nodding to the woman. He raised his voice. "Not a fan at all, are you, Jill?"

"I like your work just fine, sir." She tilted her head. "Some of it anyway."

Beau laughed, and though the woman—Jill—didn't crack a smile, Izzy got the feeling this was an old joke between them.

"Jill is my bodyguard," he said. "But right now, I don't think it needs guarding. Go amuse yourself, Jilly. Give me an hour."

The woman hesitated, but at a look from Beau, she dropped her chin in a nod and strode off.

"As I was saying," Beau continued, "I want a change and a challenge. But I don't want to forget my roots, either. I'm a balladeer, and that might chafe, but ballads have been good to me. What I want, then, is to acknowledge my roots and tweak them. If you know what I mean."

She did, better than he could imagine, but she only said, "You want a real ballad. With a heavy metal beat."

Another laugh, as easy as the one he'd given Jill. "Well, I wouldn't go that far. Heavy metal isn't quite my scene or my audience. But I want rock. Solid rock."

"Old school."

"Exactly. More AC/DC, less Iron Maiden. More Zeppelin, less Sabbath. Can you do that?"

Izzy smiled. "With a little help from you, I sure can."

Most creative types were flakes. Flakes with money were worse. They'd think nothing of flying her out, wining and dining her, making vague pronouncements about their hopes and dreams, telling her how much they loved-loved-loved her work and were dying to collaborate with her...and then never contacting her again, their whims having drifted elsewhere, like a leaf floating downstream.

Beau Wallace was not one of those guys. He knew exactly what he wanted, and the minute she agreed to discuss it, he set to work. He'd brought a list of his favorite ballads, not only in order of preference but identifying the elements that spoke to him. They sat on that bank until Izzy's butt numbed. Jill came by half a dozen times, only to be waved away by Beau, too intent on their discussion to spare a word for her. The bodyguard didn't seem to mind. She brought coffees at the midway mark and then continued doing whatever she'd been doing, periodically checking in.

Then, after they were done talking business, he relaxed, seeming content to linger, looking out at the water and chatting. Chatting about her no less. Where did she get her interest in ballads? Which were her favorites? Had she ever considered folk music? They'd laughed about that. Folk was the obvious choice for ballads, but neither of them had any interest in it.

Soon the sun was dropping, the light playing on the water,

and Izzy commented on that.

"It looks like music," she said.

He glanced over quizzically. "It does?"

She pointed out the sun's reflection on the ripples and started singing the notes as the sun bobbed between the ripple "lines."

Beau grinned. "Okay, I get it. Not a bad tune either. A little slow though. The wind needs to pick up."

He did get it. Few of his kind did.

She smiled. "It'll pick up tonight. And I bet the moon works just as well."

His grin turned wolfish. "Are you saying you want to see the moon on the water with me, Isabella?"

Her cheeks heated. "No, of course not. I just—"

"Damn."

The grin changed, simple boyishness now, putting her at ease again. They talked some more. Before they left, he told her where he was staying—the hotel and the alias. "In case you decide you do want to see the moon on the water." Another grin, one that said he was just kidding...unless she'd rather he wasn't. She'd blushed, said good night, and hurried off.

Izzy watched the moon play on the water. The bank in Central Park again, but not near the Oak Bridge. That was a little too public, even at this time of night.

She'd called Beau at his hotel just past midnight. Told him she had a song for him—the perfect song—and she wanted to show it to him in the perfect location—where they'd discussed it that morning. A bullshit story, of course, but he'd been the one to nudge-nudge-wink-wink about the moon on the water, so the moment she suggested it, he likely figured he was getting a rumble in the Ramble and hopped to it.

He was a bit of a fool, really, which was disappointing. All humans were, of course. Herself included, having joined their ranks nearly thirty years ago, after her rebirth. A regrettable but necessary transition. The world was no longer a safe place for fae. In the modern, wired-in world, people noticed when you didn't age. So she'd undergone the process of death and resurrection, brought back as a babe and exchanged with a human one, becoming human herself by feeding on her new mother's milk.

Some parts of her fae self remained, primarily her love of music. No, more than love. It was the stuff of life. She consumed it and was, in turn, consumed by it. Which led to a problem with only one solution.

Beau Wallace appeared at the stroke of two, like a shining faery prince. There was some fae blood in him—she'd seen that when he'd spoken of his music, and she could see it now, shimmering from his skin in the moonlight. She still felt that girlish flutter inside, seeing in the flesh the face that had once adorned her wall. She was, after all, human now. Mostly.

"So you have a song for me?" he said as he strolled to the bank.

"No, you have one for me."

His grin faltered for perhaps the first time since they'd met. She stepped forward and looked him in the eyes, calling forth every bit of fae charm she still possessed.

"You have a song for me," she said. "The sweetest, purest song I have ever heard." She took another step, her gaze fixed on his. "I need your song, Beau. I need it the way you need air to breathe. Your song feeds mine, and without mine, I would wither and die for wanting. I've taken seven songs before yours. Seven wonderful songs from seven wonderful men, and they live on, through me, through my music. That's what you want, isn't it? To live forever? Through music?"

Her lips went to his. It was easy. Always so easy. They looked into her eyes and they heard her words and they breathed their song—with their life—into her and—

He yanked back from the kiss. "What the hell?"

She reached for him, but he staggered out of her reach, his face screwed up. "No, seriously, what the fucking hell are you on, Isabella?"

Okay, maybe not so easy this time. Damn it. Those few drops of fae blood seemed to inoculate him to her charms.

She dropped her face into her hands. "Oh my God. I'm so embarrassed. You're right. I took something this guy offered me earlier, and I don't usually do that and . . ." She broke off on a sob.

"Okay, okay," he said. "Let's just get you out of here."

She cried louder, waiting for him to come over and comfort her.

"Enough of that," he said, and there was no sympathy in his voice, only annoyance. "Let's get you a cab. We'll—"

She sprang. She caught him by the throat, hands wrapping around it, cutting off his gasp. She pressed her lips to his again, kissing him and drawing out his—

He punched her in the stomach. Hard. She didn't let go, but squeezed his throat tighter, pulling out his breath with her kiss while choking it out with her hands. He went slack, finally giving in to her charm, kissing her back even, reluctantly at first, then picking up, kissing her hard, feeding her his song, his hands rising to wrap in her hair and—

He wrenched her away from him. She kept her grip, iron-tight, on his neck. When he opened his mouth to speak, she squeezed harder. Then his hands were around her neck.

"Let go," he wheezed. "Let go or—"

She kissed him again and when their lips touched, he flung her back, her grip tightening fast and hard as he began to struggle violently. He kicked, knocking her legs from under her, but she kept her grip and they went down, her on top of him, their hands still wrapped around each other's necks. Hers slipped just enough for him to gasp a few words.

"Stop. Damn it, I don't want to hurt—"

"Then don't," she managed. "Stop struggling. Let go. It'll be over soon."

He kicked at her again, and kept kicking, kneeing, scrabbling. She'd be a battered mess when this was over, but it would be over. She had the advantage of a little not-quite-human strength. Yet somehow it wasn't enough. The moment she loosened her grip, he found a better hold, pressing hard, gasping for her to stop, just stop, damn it, let go and he would, too. Only she couldn't. She was close—so damned close—and she needed this, needed it like she'd never needed anything before. This was music. He was music. Pure music. She could feel wisps of his song filling her, and she had to have it all, had to . . .

The world seemed to spin. He released her fast, grabbing her as she fell, his lips going to hers now, trying to breathe his life into her. Trying to bring her back, despite all she'd done to him. There was music in that. In that final act of kindness. Of goodness. She heard it, even as her life seeped away. The strains of death's music, so clear and perfect, and she breathed it into him. Her music, for him. Perhaps an apology. Perhaps, simply, because she did not need it anymore and because he could use it, and she could live on, in that small way, through him.

She gave it to him and she listened to those final strains and then . . .

Silence.

Ever since Beau's first hit single with the band, he'd been warned about parasites. "Folks will always be looking to take advantage of your talent, son. They don't have any of their own, so they'll steal yours." Which was true. It had happened many times. He looked down at Izzy's body. Just never quite so literally.

He had no fucking idea what just happened. Drugs, he could say—and would, when the police arrived, though he had a feeling they wouldn't find any in her system. He was just very, very happy that one of those early mentors had warned him to tape business conversations. He'd always heeded that advice—even tonight, because he had come here for business.

He'd had no intention of screwing around with Izzy. Jill would have his balls for breakfast if he cheated on her. Not that he would have anyway. He'd flirted with Izzy because, well, there were certain expectations that went with this career and he felt obligated to deliver. He would have just flirted and teased his way out of it as he always did. That, he expected. This...

He looked at her body again. Shit.

Footsteps pounded down the path. It was Jill, a damp coffee stain on her faded denim jacket, as if she'd literally dropped her cup when he texted.

"Apparently, she wanted more than a cuddle in the woods," he called as she ran over. Still feeling shaky, he rubbed the back of his neck with an unsteady hand. "Tried to strangle me. There was nothing I could do. She wouldn't stop, so I had to stop her, and I couldn't bring her back."

Jill stopped short and stared at him. "You stopped her?"

He chuckled, wincing as his throat hurt. "I'm a modern guy. I can take care of myself." He fingered the rising bruises on his throat. "Pretty much." He winced again and coughed softly. "But the next time I say I don't need you to stick close..."

"Ignore you?"

"Please."

Jill gave him a hug, quick and fierce. Then she placed the call. As she did, Beau stared down at Isabella. Why? Goddamn it, why?

For the music.

The answer seemed to whisper to him on the breeze and he looked out at the distant water, the moon playing on the ripples. Playing a song. Before, when he'd told her he could see it, he'd been lying. Humoring her. Now, he saw it. A song playing for Isabella. A tragic and terrible and haunting song, like all the best ballads.

He reached for his phone to record the tune. Then he stopped, rummaged in his jacket, pulled out a scrap of paper and a pen he carried for impromptu autographs. And he began to write.

On...Lady Isabel and the Elf Knight

Child wrote that Ballad 4 (Roud #21) might be the most circulated of all ballads. It's found in Southern as well as Northern Europe, the Netherlands, Poland, Germany, and the Scandinavian countries. There are many versions throughout North America as well. The earliest version Child lists is from 1560.

This ballad is wonderfully refreshing since in most versions Lady Isabel (referred in other variants as May, the King's daughter, Pretty Polly, etc.) gets herself out of trouble. The first ballad Child describes begins when an Elf knight blows his horn and inspires love-longing in Lady Isabel. He appears and convinces her to ride with him to the green wood. In the wood, he tells her to get down, she's come to the place where she's going to die. He's already killed seven kings' daughters here and she'll be the eighth. She convinces him to sit and put his head on her knee, then lulls him to sleep with a charm, ties him up with his own sword belt, and stabs him with his dagger, saying "If seven kings' daughters you have slain, lie here a husband to them all."

In another version, the elf knight brings her to a body of water with the same intent, but she drowns him. In some versions he tells her he will cut off her head. She suggests he take his coat off so her blood won't spurt all over it. As he does she cuts off his head. The Dutch version takes this further—she brings the head back with her to her father's house. There they celebrate by having a feast and put the head in the middle of the table. (1)

1) Child, Francis James. The English and Scottish Popular Ballads Vol. 1. Mineola: Dover, 2003.

TAM LANE

BY
LISA MORTON

T he old newspaper building was haunted.
At least that was what Janet had always heard about May
O'Greene's extraordinary 1910 masterpiece. Tucked in
a forgotten corner of downtown L.A., wedged in somewhere
between the Garment District and the endless cheap appliance
stores, it had stood for over a century, long after the *Daily Examiner*
had folded and the structure's original purpose had vanished.
Three stories tall and occupying most of a block, its once glittering
turrets and graceful, swirling archways were grimed over with
decades of accumulated urban grit and neglect.

Still, it stood out enough that, as a youngster driving past it
with her father, Janet had asked him about it. "I'll buy it for you
one of these days," he'd told her.

With her father, that was no joke. Edward Carterhaugh III
probably owned more of Los Angeles than any other mogul; he
bought and sold properties, redeveloped and repurposed and
renovated and demolished and rebuilt. The Carterhaughs' own
home was a classic Greene and Greene craftsmen house; as a
child growing up in it, Janet had gotten used to seeing strangers
peering in through the fence, taking photos.

It was almost remarkable that eight years passed between
the time eleven-year-old Janet had asked about May O'Greene's
monument to journalism and her father's acquisition of same.
During that time, Janet had developed an obsession for architecture
that had transformed into a career choice. Now in the second year
of her major, she had favorites (Gehry, Paul Williams), but none

she admired so much as May O'Greene.

When her father mentioned at dinner one hot August night that his offer on the old *Daily Examiner* building had been accepted, Janet's eyes had widened and Carterhaugh laughed. "I thought that might pique your interest."

"I've always wanted to get into that building."

Edward wiped his mouth with a napkin, took another sip of his dirty martini, and said (with a slight smirk), "They say it's haunted, you know."

Janet returned his smile. "All the better."

Their housekeeper, Maria, placed plates before them. She squinted at Janet. "You don't eat enough. Too thin." It was an old joke between them. Maria had been with the family for a dozen years—she lived in a bedroom just off the kitchen—and Janet loved her like an aunt.

"It'll be your fault when I weigh three-hundred pounds," Janet said. Maria smiled and returned to the kitchen.

Edward picked up a knife and fork, resuming the conversation as he cut into his rare steak. "There's a film crew shooting on the ground floor right now—it's been used mainly for movies over the last thirty years, I guess, but only the first floor. The two upper floors are pretty useless."

"I want to see it."

Edward nodded. "I'll have Amy call in a pass for you tomorrow." He paused, a forkful of Maria's good beef halfway to his mouth, then lowered it and added, "I'm thinking of converting it to office lofts. Might be a great first job for a young architect…"

"Are you serious?"

He nodded. "You're welcome. Just don't embarrass me."

Janet knew this was probably where she should have risen and hugged him; that was how the scene would have gone in a movie, or even a lot of real households. But there'd been tension between them since Mother had died four years ago. It had been a miserable death—a month-long coma following too many years of too many prescription drugs, until finally the coma had ended in seizures and a lonely passing in a hospital bed. Janet secretly blamed her father for her mother's dependence on self-medication, and she'd wondered if he didn't feel the same about her.

At least he's trying. Of course he probably just knows I'll be the cheapest architect he can get.

Whatever the circumstances—whatever unearned privilege, whatever paternal guilt—Janet was still happy, the next day, to walk into the grand *Daily Examiner* building. She'd spent the rest of that night reading up again on May O'Greene's history. The *Examiner* had been her last major work; it had taken her nearly ten years as she'd overseen every detail, every tiny bit of tile and ornament and fixture. Many critics felt the *Examiner* lacked the sheer spectacle of some of May's earlier work, especially her Santa Monica amusement park Sealight, which had been completed in 1898 and torn down in 1942, its wood and metal used in the creation of war machinery instead. Sealight had been called "a fairy palace." The *Examiner* had been dismissed as "a wealthy Indian's brothel." It combined art nouveau and Orientalism in ways that hadn't always pleased architecture buffs; Janet, however, found it sensuous (as she thought O'Greene had likely intended). O'Greene's reputation should have been as great as Williams's, or certainly Julia Morgan's, but Janet doubted if most of the film crews that shot in its ground floor recognized the brilliance they stood within.

The guard at the building's entrance found her name on a list and admitted her. It was an uninteresting side entrance. Once inside, Janet found herself jostled by frantic assistant directors and grips hauling apple crates and coils of cable. She passed a row of glassed-in offices where she glimpsed cameras and actors (dressed in white lab coats). A few of the crewmembers eyed her curiously, but something about her—some indefinable aura of confidence, status—kept them from approaching her.

She moved past the crew, and the hallway she was in emptied out into the *Examiner*'s front lobby. She stopped and gazed around, stunned; here, she could finally commune with O'Greene's glorious designs. The spacious interior went up three stories to skylights; curving flights of stairs flanked either side. Rich, original tile in burnished earth tones graced the floor; dual Moroccan-style turrets framed the carved oak front doors, locked for decades against the Los Angeles streets. The handrails on the stairs were rich mahogany, rubbed to a deep, nearly decadent finish from a century of use.

Janet stood unmoving, breathing it in. The sunlight that penetrated through the skylights and turrets was filtered by heavy dust (this building had never been designed for air conditioning); behind her, the sounds of the film crew had sunk to a constant low thrum.

It was easy to believe this palace was haunted.

Janet remembered, then, why she was here. Her father wanted her to lay waste to this space, to turn its offices and storage areas into the large single-room apartments he liked to refer to as "artists' lofts."

For a second the idea sickened her. She hated the job. She hated her father. It was a sacrilege.

But then she reconsidered. She could, after all, keep the lobby; it was functional as well as beautiful. It would provide pleasure to those tenants ("artists," she reminded herself) with enough soul to appreciate its art.

She was sweating as she climbed the stairs to the second floor; it was August in Southern California, and she was in a building that kept only part of its ground floor acceptably cooled. Here, on the second floor, the temperature rose sharply. Janet picked her way through ancient offices, most empty, a few strewn with trash. In one back room she found the remains of a party—a bag full of empty bottles of cheap red wine and a used condom. It was hard to tell how long they'd been there. She began to feel better about rededicating the *Examiner* to a purposeful existence.

A twisting back staircase led her up to a third floor that had plainly seen even fewer visitors in recent years. From her online study of the *Examiner,* she knew the third floor had once housed the executive offices; May O'Greene herself had even had a suite up here. Motes glittered in the air, turned opalescent by afternoon sunlight. Later, Janet would come back with a camera and tablet computer and begin planning; today was purely exploratory.

The heat on the third floor was stifling. Janet was wiping sweat from her brow when she poked her head into a room...and gasped.

She looked into a sitting room that could have stepped out of a silent film. Low tables, chairs, writing desk, vintage sofa, and cabinets all squatted, as clean as the items in a showroom. On the desk were a shaded lamp, a blotter, pens, and an elaborate

Art Deco paperweight. On one gorgeous teak end table was something that looked for all the world like an original Tiffany lamp. Even Janet, who'd grown up with wealth, wondered what the lamp alone was worth.

She stepped into the space, running her fingers lightly along the fixtures, astonished by the lack of apparent age. Surely they were all reproductions, but…why? Who would install all of this in an unused office on the third floor of a nearly-abandoned building? Some eccentric film exec, maybe? She nearly pulled out her cell phone and called her father's office to ask if they'd forgotten to tell her that part of the third floor was rented out, but somehow she knew the answer would be "no," followed by questions she didn't want to deal with.

Was it possible that this room was just miraculously forgotten and preserved, a happy accident of time and environmental circumstance?

Janet reached the desk and picked up one of the items she found there. It was an antique fountain pen with a silver, scaled finish like a metallic lizard. Curious, she pulled the cap off and ran the nib across a sheet of cream-colored paper; it produced a clear, perfect dark line. Janet often made preliminary sketches in pen before rendering them in software; she somehow felt more connection to her work when she used ink instead of pixels. The idea of sketching out her designs for the *Examiner*'s new artists' lofts in a pen she'd taken from it appealed to her, and so she replaced the cap and was lowering the pen into her purse when a voice sounded behind her.

"That's not yours."

Janet jumped and turned, trying to find the source of the words. It was a young man, seated in what looked like a genuine Louis XVI settee. White light streamed in through Venetian blinds behind the man, rendering him into a striped silhouette.

Janet struggled to make him out as her heart pounded. How could she not have seen him there before? Startled, nervous, she held the pen up, jiggling it. "Oh, I'm so sorry—is this yours?"

"Yes." The man rose now and stepped forward, and when his face caught the light, Janet nearly gasped.

He was the most beautiful man she'd ever seen. Light brown skin, glossy black hair that fell onto his forehead in charmingly unruly locks, golden eyes whose shape hinted at an Asian parent, dazzling white teeth that Janet didn't even think were capped. He was dressed in an oxford shirt that defined his sculpted, hard surfaces, and simple khaki pants.

There was also something familiar about him, something that tugged at the back of her mind, tickling. She caught herself before she used the hackneyed, "Have we met before?" Instead, she said, "I...didn't expect to find anyone up here."

"Well, I don't get many visitors. But the ones that I do are..." He reached out to take the pen from her, and when his fingertips brushed over her skin, Janet shivered—they were impossibly cold, icy. "...always *special*."

He stood there staring at her, a look that caused Janet's pulse to race.

Trying to cover her nervousness, she asked, "Just what *are* you doing here?"

"This place is mine."

Janet laughed, then said, "I'm sorry to disillusion you, but it's not. My father just bought it. It's in escrow already. We'll be turning it into artists' lofts."

"'We?'"

"Yes. I'm an architect." She felt like a fraud saying that, in this place, but it was too late to take it back.

"Like May O'Greene?"

"Yes," Janet said, before blurting out, "I mean, no! May O'Greene was a genius. I take it you're a fan...?"

The look that crossed his perfect face then was unexpected, full of fear and regret. "I can't really say I am."

"Oh...then, what...?"

Abruptly, he grinned again, apparently anxious to move past the mention of the architect. "My name's Tam—Tam Lane. And you are...?"

"Janet Carterhaugh," she said.

She placed her hand in his...and lost herself. His skin was chilled, but the sensation of it on hers ignited fire. He squeezed her hand, lightly, and it was enough to leave her weak-kneed and desperate. Janet was hardly virginal—her own aristocratic beauty had made many boys seek a place in her bed (when her father wasn't home), and she'd given it to a few of them—but she'd never experienced a need so all-devouring that it made her forget where, who, what she was.

"Tam," she breathed out.

"You know," he said, stepping closer to her (and that action alone flooded her with fresh arousal), "I did catch you trying to steal from me. I think I'm owed something."

"I already apologized."

He placed two fingers beneath her chin and tilted it up. "That's not what I had in mind."

He took his payment as a kiss. Janet returned it; even as she did so, feverishly, some small part of her whispered, *Something's wrong here...walk away. No—RUN.*

But she didn't listen to that part. All she heard were the soft, moist sounds of their lips and tongues, her own breath, his.

When, several moments later, he lowered her to the velvet couch as his fingers sought her buttons, she let him.

§

After, as they lay together, unclothed, her bathed in sweat, his skin only slightly warmed, she turned to him and asked, "Why do I feel like I know you?"

He answered, "I confess. In a former life, I was an actor. I starred in a television series called *Thorn in the Roses* –"

Janet cut him off. "Oh my God—I used to watch that show every week! It ran for—what, four years?"

"Five."

Pictures came together in Janet's mind, like two etched images lining up to form a moiré pattern. A beautiful boy, with dark skin and eyes the color of certain clouds at sunset. Every girl she'd known had had a crush on the star...Tommy Lynn, she remembered.

Tam Lane.

"But your name..." Janet said.

"The network made me change it."

"You were so young on that show..."

He nodded. "I was only sixteen when it ended."

"And what did you do then? I don't remember any movies, or..."

His expression darkened, and Janet instantly rued the question; she would, in fact, have rued anything that caused distress to crease that face. "I...well, I'll tell you some other time."

The last ray of light faded; the room plunged into shadow. For a second, Janet had the unsettling thought that all the other furniture had vanished, that the couch beneath her felt old and sprung...but then her eyes adjusted, she made out the shapes of the desk and tables and chairs, and velvet caressed her where Tam didn't. "I should be getting home," she said.

Tam said nothing.

Janet untangled herself from him, feeling suddenly modest as she sat up, gathering her discarded clothes. She dressed in silence and then turned to look down upon him. In the room's semi-darkness he looked unreal, like an out-of-focus photograph, or fog.

"Come with me," she said, even though she knew Daddy would throw a fit if she walked in with a man.

"I can't," he said.

"Oh." The thought struck her: She'd just had unprotected sex with a man she didn't know. She nearly turned and ran, so strong was her urge to be home, safe, away from...*whatever was so wrong here.*

She had nearly reached the doorway when he called after her, "Wait."

She turned, saw him rise and walk to the desk, where he picked something up. Even in the room's darkness, growing stronger with each passing minute, his beauty—freed from clothing now—shone, paralyzing her.

"Here." He held something out to her, and, numb, she reached a hand up. He placed the object in her palm. "Your pen."

"Will I see you again?"

"I truthfully don't know."

The last of the day vanished. Janet stumbled out, feeling her way blindly along the walls, shivering as her fingers scraped away chips of paint; something sticky clung to her like a poisonous spider's web. The floorboards groaned beneath her; she felt their rot and wondered if they'd hold her. The silence was otherwise complete.

Janet forced herself to remain calm, to find her exit. She had a good memory for layout and located the staircase; she stumbled twice negotiating its creaking turns in the dark, but soon she was on the ground floor, filing out with the last of the film crew. Some of them cast side glances at her, and Janet wondered what they saw: A disheveled woman with a shell-shocked look, perhaps?

When she reached the sanctuary of her car, she cried.

After ten minutes she stopped. She wondered, with a turn so complete she couldn't begin to understand, why she'd been sobbing.

She started the car and drove home.

§

On the way, she stopped at a pharmacy and bought two items: A bottle of juice, and a pill that would prevent pregnancy.

She swallowed the pill with the juice and disposed of the box in the drug store parking lot.

When she got home, she took a forty-minute shower, let Maria feed her, then fell into bed. Her sleep was black, dreamless.

§

The next day she asked her father's secretary, Amy, to find out if anyone was renting part of the *Examiner*'s third floor. Amy checked. The answer, of course, was no.

She Googled Tommy Lane. It turned out that his show, *Thorn in the Roses*, had been canceled because he'd disappeared, not the other way around. His parents claimed they knew where he was and that he was in good hands. Speculation was that he'd run afoul of drugs, been shipped off to a very quiet rehab somewhere. After a time, mentions of him stopped altogether.

Amy arranged a permanent pass into the building; after all, she was now lead architect. The next day she returned to the *Examiner*, her heart in her throat as she climbed the spiral staircase to the third floor. She was shaking by the time she reached Tam's corner; she half-expected to look in and see nothing at all, no furnishings, not even a trace.

The furnishings were still there. But Tam was not.

She called his name. She sat on the couch, quivering as she

remembered the feel of his icy fingertips on her shoulders, her breasts, between her legs. She jumped to her feet, trying to ward off arousal, calling again, again. "Tam! Are you here? Tam?"

He didn't appear.

As night fell, she left.

Over the next month, she visited the room as often as she could, working her trips in around classes. When a good-looking PoliSci major named Matt asked her out, she politely declined. The next day she sat on the velvet cushions in Tam's room and talked to thin air. She told him about Matt. She told him she'd turned down the invitation.

She told him she wanted him.

He didn't appear.

A month passed, and the memory of their lovemaking became more precious to her, not less. August spilled into September, and one morning Janet woke up sick. As she knelt over the toilet, one hand instinctively clutched at her belly. It was too soon, of course, to show anything there but she knew.

October arrived, and the sickness continued. Janet tried to be quiet, but she'd never been able to hide anything from Maria. "You sick a lot lately," the housekeeper said, looking away.

Janet had no answer.

Maria came out of the bathroom with a load of towels for the laundry. She stopped before Janet. "You know you're like family to me, Miss Janet..."

"Of course. You, too."

"So you'd tell Maria if anything was wrong? If you needed help?"

Janet's throat was dry, her tongue useless.

Maria kissed her gently on a cheek and left the room.

§

A day later, Janet sat on the couch in Tam's room and cried. "Tam, goddamnit, I really need to see you. I...I think I'm..."

She couldn't say the words, not to empty air. And emptiness was all there was.

§

A home pregnancy test confirmed what she already knew. It shouldn't have been possible, but it had happened.

She finally gave up going back to Tam's room. She grew distracted and missed classes. She wondered what Maria's offer for help meant. She was afraid of the answer.

The boy at school, Matt, asked her out again, this time to a Halloween party. Was it really October already? She politely declined. As she walked away from him, she laughed.

Halloween party? Sure...I could go as Stupid Pregnant Girl. I won't even need a costume.

One morning she awoke to a knock on her bedroom door. She was sprawled on her bed, looking at old pictures of a handsome, young television star named Tommy Lane on her tablet. "Yes?"

The door opened and her father entered. Janet thumbed a tab on the screen to switch to another website, then set the computer aside. "Oh, hi, Daddy."

"Hi, sweetie. Listen, I've got some bad news. The *Examiner* failed inspection, and I mean as in epic fail."

Dread crashed down on Janet, nearly suffocating her. "So what does that mean?"

"I'm sorry, I know you've put a lot of work into this, and I really liked your ideas, but...the lofts aren't gonna happen. The building's just too far gone—it would cost more to bring it up to code than it's worth."

"So...?"

"It's going to have to come down."

"When?"

"Demolition starts tomorrow—"

"You can't!" Janet leapt from the bed, face flushed, fingers clawed.

"There's really no choice."

Of course there's a choice, she wanted to say. *Spend the money to bring it up to code. Honor the building.*

Love your daughter more than business.

Instead, Janet pleaded, "Can't you at least postpone it?"

"Why? What difference will that make? There's nothing left to get out of that building, Janet."

Janet strode past him, pausing only long enough to grab a

jacket. "Yes, there is."

He reached out as she ran by. "Don't go down there—"

But she was gone.

§

The side door she always used was secured with a heavy chain that had been added since the last time she'd been here three days ago. She wouldn't be getting in that way.

But she knew the *Examiner* now; it had become an old and dear friend. She knew its secrets, the hidden ways in and out. She knew about the rickety door next to a loading dock in the back that gave easily when she applied pressure.

The ground floor was dark, but she'd brought a mag lite. She turned it on, heading for a back stairwell.

She shivered.

It wasn't cold; October in L.A. never was. But something in the *Examiner* had changed. It was no longer the friend she'd come to know intimately. It felt charged with fear, electrified with dread.

It felt haunted.

Janet remembered what day it was and forced herself to smile. *Right…it's Halloween and I'm in a haunted house. All I'm missing is a jack-o'-lantern full of candy.* But the thought didn't cheer her; it didn't dispel the *Examiner*'s newly acquired aura.

She was relieved when she reached the third floor and sunlight spilled in through a few windows, wan but enough to reassure her that there was a world outside where kids were putting on costumes, laughing, looking forward to their night of mock terrors.

Tam's room looked the same. She knew crews had toured every room in the *Examiner*, and she wondered what they'd seen here. A Tiffany lamp? Antique fountain pens? She guessed not.

"Tam…goddamnit, Tam, you need to hear me! The building's coming down tomorrow!"

Nothing.

She paced the carpeted floor of his room, desperate. She'd called him once before, hadn't she? She tried to recall exactly what she'd done on that sweltering August afternoon. Of course she'd tried this before, dozens of times, but she had to try again. She'd come in...she'd gaped...she'd admired the lamp...she'd picked up a pen...

The pen.

It had to be the pen. But she'd tried this before, on so many other days. She'd picked up one of the other pens (there were still half-a-dozen on the desk), even waved it around...but nothing. No Tam.

There had to be something else—

Wait—I tried to steal it.

Janet grabbed one of the pens and shoved it into a pocket of her jacket.

"I've been waiting for you to figure that out."

She turned as Tam rushed forward to embrace her. "God, Tam, I've got so much to tell you..." she began, her voice husky, but she broke off as his mouth found hers. They were ravenous for each other, and need to speak gave way to other, more urgent desires. She fell back over the desk, he moved between her legs, and two months of separation vanished.

It was over quickly, and then Janet's rush of words came out. "Tam, you have to leave here, tonight. My father's tearing the *Examiner* down tomorrow and I can't stop him—"

He put two fingers to her lips, gently. "Just slow down..."

She looked into his eyes, and she saw compassion, a hint of mischief, love...and a trapped animal. She lifted herself from the rough wood of the desk, pulled clothing back into place. "I'm sorry. It's just that I have so many questions, and with the baby and all –"

"Baby?"

The ability to make coherent words left her. She looked at him uncertainly. Would he mock her? Question if it was his? Dismiss her?

Instead, he pulled her to him. "Janet...my Janet..."

She let him hold her for a few seconds before pulling away. "Tam...what exactly *are* you? Why are you here?"

Tam sighed, a slight expression but enough that she felt his breath on her skin. "I'm something both more and less than human. Remember that show, *Thorn in the Roses*? We shot the last episode here. I was a stupid kid, sixteen. I got bored once while I waited for the cameras to set up, and I wandered off to the third floor. This was where I met *her*."

"Who?"

"Who else? May O'Greene."

Janet's mind raced back to the biography she'd read months ago. "But...May O'Greene died in something like 1912, not long after she finished the *Examiner*."

Tam shook his lovely head. "No. She can't die, because she's not human."

"What...what is she?"

"She's had many names. Titania... Oona... Mab... Maeve... May... Queen of the Fairies."

Janet couldn't suppress a sharp laugh. "Fairies? Now I'm supposed to believe in fairies?"

Tam took her hands, kissed her fingers (sending another ripple through her), and said, "Nowadays people would call us ghosts. We're the ones who live on the outside...or, maybe more accurately, tucked into the edges of your reality. We never die, but we don't really live, either."

"But you...?"

"Ahh, yes...the boy who wandered away from the film crew. Well, it was a Halloween—like today—and May came through the veil between the worlds and took me back with her. She laid magicks on me first and then on my parents, so they lied about knowing where I was. And she kept me prisoner, or rather— *collected*, a pretty trinket she can look at when she's bored."

"But if the hotel is torn down..."

Tam's look contained almost inexpressible weariness. "I'll go with it."

"How do we get you out of here, then?"

"There's one way, but..."

He turned away from her, and Janet walked to his front, forcing him to look at her. "I don't care. What do we do?"

"Do you know about Halloween? I mean, it's real meaning beyond silly costumes and pumpkins? It's the night when fall becomes winter, when sun's life turns to night's death, when the veil between worlds is thinnest. You sense it, don't you?"

May thought about the walk from the first floor, how she could almost feel a vibration in the air itself. "Yes."

"At midnight, that veil will be the thinnest and you might be able to pull me through, but May will try to stop you."

"Stop me? How?"

"By tricking you. She'll tell you that you can have me...if you can hold me. Then she'll try to frighten you into letting go. She'll change me three times, and each transformation will be worse than the last."

Janet's hands moved to his face, his cold skin. "I don't care. If I get you out..."

He encircled her wrists with his hands. "You can. But don't make the mistake of underestimating her, Janet. It will be the hardest thing you've ever done. Just remember: *Don't let go*. When I return to my true form, wrap me in your jacket and it'll be over."

She nodded, too overwhelmed to speak. He smiled warmly at her. "You can do this."

She wished she shared his confidence.

§

They spent the rest of that day talking, holding each other. Tam asked her questions about what had happened in the ten years that he'd been May's prisoner. Janet talked about her life, her plans, how she both loved and hated her father.

As the sun set, the Tiffany lamp glowed softly, casting the room in the soft shades of its colored glass squares. The light would have been pleasant under any other circumstance, but as the time drew closer to midnight, the oppressive atmosphere intensified. Janet felt it like a low frequency hum in her midsection, setting her on edge, making her want to flee.

But she didn't. She stayed with Tam as he spoke to her, soothing her, telling her that May had treated him well (for a prisoner), and that he believed she loved him.

"Who wouldn't?" Janet asked.

Janet glanced at her phone, and saw the time was just after 8 p.m. "Four hours to go," she said, setting the phone up where she could see it.

She glanced out the window, and her heart skipped a beat as she saw eyes looking in at her. Yellow eyes that didn't blink, that weren't shaped like any animal she could name.

"Tam!"

He followed her wide gaze before pulling her close. "It's starting. The veil is lifting."

"But it's too early, it's only—" She looked at the phone.

It read 11:58.

"That's not possible. It was just eight o'clock—"

The building began to rumble as if a small earthquake were happening. The Tiffany lamp blinked out so that the only light in the room came from the glowing eyes of whatever watched them from outside. Janet clutched at Tam, her breath quickening; the temperature plummeted, and steam puffed from her with each exhalation.

The other side of the room began to glow, softly, a bluish light that might once have been seen above a dank graveyard or in the heart of a darting will-o'-the-wisp.

"Tam...?"

"It's her."

Something moved in front of the glow—a feminine shape. Tall, dressed in some sort of full-length dress or gown, hair flowing... "Well, now, Tam, what's this?" asked a husky feminine voice, with a hint of old world accent.

The glow moved to reveal her face, and Janet gaped—the photo of May O'Greene she'd found hadn't begun to capture her extraordinary face. Her features were too sharp—almost feral— to be truly beautiful, but her eyes glinted with both youthful passion and the madness of great age.

Janet saw that even Tam was unnerved by May. "This is Janet, and we're leaving."

May laughed, a sound that was every Halloween witch's shriek mixed together. "Oh, dear Tam, are we actually going to do this?"

Tam ignored her and turned to Janet. "Are you ready?"

She nodded and put her arms around him. He whispered into her ear, "Remember—*don't let go.*"

Whatever Janet expected—a snake, a giant spider, a flame that might scald her—she didn't anticipate Tam trying to pull away from her.

Except it wasn't Tam's voice that said, "What the...? Janet? Where am I?"

She pulled back as far as she could without releasing him, and saw: a college boy who'd asked her out. "Matt...?"

Even in the dim light, she made out the terror on his face. Her first instinct was to release him, tell him to run, this wasn't his fight... "*No.*" She held him tighter.

May said, "That's one..."

Janet closed her eyes. Maybe if she just kept them shut, if she didn't look at whatever came next...

"Janet, look at me," said her father.

Her eyes snapped open involuntarily, and Janet gasped and shrank back at what she saw. It was her father, but his features had altered, become savage, almost demonic. He leered at her and pulled her to him; she felt the bulge in his crotch and cried out wordlessly. "There's been nobody but you since your mother died," he said, and he ran his tongue down her cheek.

Janet willed her knees to hold her up, her arms to keep their circle around him. *It's a phantom...It's not my father...*

"You've disappointed me in so many ways," he said, and she hated the tear that she felt trace down her cheek, "but you could still make it right, if you're good to me..."

He ground against her. She swallowed back a scream, turned her head, but finally forced out, "I won't let go!"

"Oh, really, child?" May asked. "How about now?"

Her father's face melted away, the figure in her arms grew smaller, more compact, until Janet saw that she held—

Herself.

She stared in confusion. It was like looking into a mirror, except she felt the body solidly in her arms—*her* body. How was this supposed to scare her? It was strange, yes, but hardly fearful enough to make her relinquish her hold—

The face began to shift. To *age*.

Twenty...twenty-one, an adult now, and doubt etched itself in her features...twenty-three, twenty-six, and she saw anxiety, premature lines...twenty-eight, thirty, thirty-three, and failure was deeply graven, the eyes half-lidded and sunken, the mouth turning down forever...

Janet sobbed as she realized—this could be her life with Tam. Joyless and careworn, burdened with a child at too early an age—

Thirty-eight, forty, forty-five...

LISA MORTON

She looked like her mother. Her unfocused eyes and sallow cheeks were testament to prescription drug abuse, and she knew she'd be dead soon, dead like her mother, worn away by life...

But she could have life back if she let go. The next thirty years didn't have to go like this.

Let go...

"Noo!" It was a shout of desperation, but it worked. It roused her to realization: *a trick.*

She tightened her grip.

And she felt bare, warm skin beneath. She held Tam again. He looked drained, barely conscious. Janet reached one arm to the desk, found the jacket she'd placed there, and draped it around him. He fell against her. She lowered him to the floor, kneeling with him, keeping the jacket in place.

May O'Greene didn't shriek or storm. Instead she sobbed.

"You've won him, girl," she managed between cries. "Be good to him."

She blinked out. The world changed. The eyes at the windows were gone, the lovely furnishings vanished, the smothering sense of wrongness replaced by the ordinary air of a world that held a future for her again.

"Is it over?" Tam muttered, trying to re-gather energy he hadn't possessed in ten years.

"It's over," Janet said as she bent to kiss his head.

Or, she thought as she felt a lifetime's worth of happiness wash over her, *it's just beginning.*

On...Tam Lin

The ballad of Tam Lin resonates throughout our culture. It's the 39th Child ballad (Roud #35) - a "transformation story." Tam Lin is a lusty young man, loved by the ladies, human and fairy. When Janet (or Margaret or Jenny) finds she is pregnant by Tam Lin, she goes to pick an herb that will cause her to abort. There Tam Lin himself appears and explains that he has been taken by the fairies and is going to be given to hell that Halloween as a tithe. He tells her to wait by the road until the fairy procession rides by. She must then pull him off his horse and hold him, no matter what he transforms into. Janet is brave enough to hold on as Tam Lin transforms into a myriad of creatures. Some listed include an adder, a bear, a lion, a toad, an eel, or a black dog—creatures no one would want their arms around. In some versions he then becomes his normal comely self, in others he must be submerged in either milk or water to become human. Many versions end with the fairy Queen saying if she had known Tam Lin would be taken from her, she would have replaced his heart with a stone or stored his heart in a tree. (1)

Janet does much better than a husband in a similar story, but with the roles reversed. When he tries to save his wife in the same way, he lets her go in fright, thus condemning himself to current and eternal unhappiness. (2)

The Ballad of Tam Lin has inspired many writers including Susan Cooper, Diana Wynne Jones, Charles Vess, and Holly Black. Musicians love the ballad and a small selection includes The Decemberists, Enter The Haggis, Fairport Convention, and Frankie Armstrong.

1) Child, Francis James. The English and Scottish Popular Ballads Vol. 1. Mineola: Dover, 2003.

2) Child, Francis James. The English and Scottish Popular Ballads Vol. 1. Mineola: Dover, 2003.

John Barleycorn Must Die

By
Marsheila Rockwell and Jeffrey J. Mariotte

The sign read "Bacchanal Brewing—Ale Fit for the Gods," and not only was it the last place in town I wanted to be, it was also the last story in all of this news-challenged state that I wanted to be covering. And considering my other choices were batteries made from cowpies and allegations of fraud at the local dog show, that was saying something.

This piece would have been a natural for Paul Hendricks, who worshipped microbrew as if those aforementioned gods had wafted down from paradise to personally hand-deliver it to us lowly mortals. So of course Paul was out with a flu that came out of nowhere, hit him hard, and looked like it would keep him down for the count. Which meant Jayne had assigned the story to me, and it was about as welcome as a punch in the kidneys.

Send a dry drunk, an alcoholic with fourteen years, nine months, and twenty-two days of sobriety under his belt, into an up-and-coming microbrewery. What could possibly go wrong, right?

I checked my notes again, not wanting to turn the car off and step out onto the newly paved and striped asphalt. Not that I needed the refresher—I'd committed the words to memory when I had first written them down, and the neat block letters weren't suddenly going to divulge any information about the place or its owners that I didn't already know. Still, it gave me a chance to steady my nerves and a few more minutes to wait for a text from my sponsor—something I wasn't sure I had the guts to enter the brewery without.

Bacchanal was owned by three women who'd gone to college together at Southern Montana State—Anna Reeves, the business major; Carrie Reeves, her sister and the trio's public relations guru (though I wasn't clear on what exactly her major at SMSU had been, or if she'd even had one—she didn't appear to have graduated); and Honey Harrelson, the nerdy one with degrees in both botany and agricultural engineering.

Both Anna and Honey had graduated last year, Honey with honors. Honey's picture was a fixture in the *Big Sky Standard* (or the *BS Standard*, as those of us who had to work there liked to call it), for everything from winning scholarships to charity work around town. In the space of a year, she and the Reeves sisters had gotten Bacchanal up and running with money from . . . well, that wasn't exactly clear. Definitely one of the things I was going to try to discover in the course of our interview.

As I was flipping through the articles on Honey—a pretty blonde with big green eyes and a Marilyn Monroe figure—my smartphone chimed.

Finally.

"Sorry, John, been AFK. No way 2 get there 2day. Reschedule?"

Damn it.

"No," I typed back quickly. "This is the only day the owners would agree to." I hated the lazy shortcuts texters used and refused to indulge in their wholesale slaughter of the English language. Not that any of the five people I exchanged texts with ever noticed.

"U can do this. Just another interview. Treat it that way."

Easier said than done.

When I didn't immediately reply, Eddie—who'd just earned his twenty-five year chip—sent a quick torrent of follow-up texts, making my phone sound like a doorbell being abused by an impatient and probably not very personable salesman.

"U CAN do this, John."

"I got faith in U. Have some in URself."

"But . . . maybe do the interview outside?"

"Good luck!"

With that, I knew he was gone—my only life preserver in what was sure to prove a perilous ocean of pale ale and dark lager sharks. Sighing, I put the phone on vibrate and stuck it in my pocket. I stuffed my notes back into their file folder, pulled the key from the ignition, and with a wordless plea to my higher power, climbed out into the late June heat to meet my demons.

§

The brewery's interior was cool and dim and smelled of dank hops, making my palms sweat and my mouth go dry even as my nose crinkled in response to the sour aroma. How I'd ever found this scent—vaguely reminiscent of cheap weed—to be appealing, let alone tempting, was beyond me. And yet, here I was, swallowing hard for sudden want of it.

The place seemed deserted, and a quick glance at my phone showed that I was a few minutes early, so I turned the flash on and started taking pictures to fill the time. Considering the *Standard* didn't have the budget for more than one full-time photographer—who was busy covering the scandal-plagued dog show, lucky bastard—whatever I got with my phone's camera would have to do.

I'd expected a Greek motif, what with the name and the reference to gods, but there were no marble columns, replica Venus de Milos, or bunches of grapes to be seen. Instead, drying herbs hung from the foyer's low rafters, green candles burned in holders on every available sill and shelf, metal moons in various phases graced the walls, and a pair of wooden-handled brooms hung crossed over the entryway, like props from cheap Halloween costumes.

"They're called 'besoms,'" a soft voice said from behind me as I snapped a photo. Turning, I saw Honey Harrelson standing there, dressed in a black and gold V-necked Bacchanal Brewing T-shirt, jeans, and tennis shoes. A black cord wound its way about her neck and underneath her shirt, so I couldn't see what pendant might be nestled in her generous cleavage, but I found myself jealous of it all the same. A feeling I quickly smothered; an alcoholic getting involved with a woman who owned a brewery could only end badly, no matter who was writing the story. "An old tradition to keep negativity from entering a space."

Didn't stop me, I thought, but didn't say. Instead, I pocketed my phone, pulled out my notebook, and dutifully wrote this tidbit down, wondering what ever happened to my big-city, Pulitzer Prize-winning dreams.

As I did, two other women stepped into the foyer, both brunettes and obviously related, though one was several inches taller and had a cleft in her chin the other lacked. They, too, wore low-cut Bacchanal T-shirts, and if they weren't Monroe-caliber beauties, they still had a way of moving that drew and held the eye. I suddenly didn't have as many questions about how they'd acquired the capital to open this place—a smile and a wink from any of them was probably all it would take for me to empty my wallet on the floor at their feet, though the most they'd be able to buy with the contents would be some real brooms to go with the decorative ones over the door.

"Mr. Woodward," the taller siren said, sticking out a well-manicured hand. "So glad you could join us today for a tour . . . and perhaps a tasting?" I wasn't sure if I imagined the sardonic twist to her grin or not.

As I shook her hand, hoping she wouldn't notice how much sweatier my palm had become at her words, the other woman—Carrie—spoke.

"Don't mind Anne, Mr. Woodward," she said, casting her sibling a warning look. "She thinks because it's her birthday, she can take liberties."

"Oh? Happy birthday," I said, wondering why they'd chosen to schedule an interview on a day when they should be downing their product instead of showing it off.

"Thank you," Anne said, her smile still bordering on mischievous. "We share that, though, don't we?"

"I'm sorry?"

"I was born on the summer solstice, and you were born on the winter. We're both children of the solstice." At my surprised look, her grin widened, and she winked. "We do our homework."

Not very well, I thought, but again didn't say. Though she wasn't the first person to make that mistake. My ex had been into astrology, and made a big deal about how compatible our charts said we were—her an Aquarius and me a Sagittarius. Until she found out that since I'd been born "on the cusp" in Arizona, a place that didn't observe Daylight Savings Time,

I was really one of those hard-headed Capricorns who only wanted to stifle her airy creativity.

It was all bullshit, of course, but if she wanted to blame the stars for our breakup instead of my drinking, I was more than willing to let her.

"Anyway," Carrie said, the glance at her sister sharp enough to cut this time, "while we'd normally offer you the opportunity to taste some of our award-winning brews for your piece, your editor made us aware of your particular . . . sensitivities . . . in that regard, so we'll skip it this time. We'll take you out to the fields instead, so you can see how our products go from barn to bottle without ever leaving town. A fact we're very proud of, and one we believe has greatly contributed to our success."

"That—that'd be fine," I answered, taking her hand in turn, using the movement to cover my surprise at both her bluntness and the fact that it seemed like she'd read my mind. The sooner we could move this show outside and into the light the happier I'd be.

Carrie smiled broadly.

"Excellent," she replied. "Shall we begin?"

§

"The angle Jayne McClure—my editor—wants," I said, "is how three young women, fresh out of school, have managed to create one of the most popular and profitable microbreweries in the state in such a short time. You attribute your success to your locally grown hops or whatever, so explain that to me. That sort of thing. I'm not writing a hit piece. Think of it as free advertising."

"How much do you know about beer, Mr. Woodward?" Honey asked.

"How it tastes," I answered. "How it feels going down." I swallowed, hard. Here, enveloped by the smell of it, those things felt fresh, as if my last drink had been fourteen minutes ago instead of fourteen-plus years.

I also remembered what it did to my head. I remembered the paychecks that had never made it home, the lost days and nights, the time I'd forgotten a laptop in a bar. A laptop owned by the *Boston Globe*, containing the only copy of an investigative piece I was writing on Russian gangs—former Soviet thugs, KGB types—taking over the drug and hooker businesses in the Combat Zone. Those had been the days of my Pulitzer dreams. But the farther away those dreams got, the more I drank, and the more I drank, the faster those dreams raced away. The lost laptop had ended my stint in New England *and* my marriage. When I heard that one of my confidential sources had been found in the Charles River with two bullet holes in the back of his head and his tongue cut out, presumably because in my notes on the laptop his name *hadn't* been confidential, it nearly ended my stint on the planet.

It turned out I couldn't drink enough to kill myself because I always passed out first. Didn't stop me from trying, though—first in Massachusetts, then back in the arid wastelands of my birth, and finally here, in the Nothing-But-Big-Sky State. Still, it was touch-and-go a few times, until I finally hit bottom and a drunk named Eddie Kemp reached down for me, pulled me up, and introduced me to his friend Bill W. Eddie'd had to kick my ass a few times to keep me in line, but eventually, it took.

Yet here I was, inside a brewery, with the aroma digging around under my skin like some kind of invasive parasite.

I realized Honey had been talking the whole time I'd been inside my own head, and I'd been wandering around half-blind as the women showed me their brewing process. I snatched a couple of words from the atmosphere, where they'd hung while I was barely listening—grain mill, rollers, stuck mash, wort. I blinked, and saw that we'd stopped in front of a shiny silver tank with hoses attached here and there, and various gauges and dials on top.

". . . the mash/lauter tun is where we hydrate the grains," Honey said. "We don't want any dry spots in the mash. We wet every bit of it down, to draw out all the sweetness, and mix the grains with the liquor. We say liquor, but at this point, it's just water. Hot water; we go with a steady one-fifty Fahrenheit. We use water temperature to regulate the rate at which the enzymes in the malt convert the starches to sugars. Sweetness is good, but as with most things in life, I've found, it's balance that's critical."

"Can you spell that?" I asked, making my first note since we had left the foyer.

"C-R-I-T—" Anne started.

"No, the machine. The tank. It's a what?"

"A lauter tun," Carrie said. "Ours is a mash/lauter tun." She spelled it out for me, slowly. I appreciated the effort. "We're a small operation, and we want to keep every batch we brew just like the one before. Bigger outfits use bigger lauter tuns, with automated rakes, but we use stirring blades." She laughed. "I'm glad you asked how to spell it, instead of just assuming, Mr. Woodward. I was a philosophy major, for a time. Words and their meanings—their *true* meanings—are important to me. I guess we're both seekers of truth, you and me."

"Please, call me John," I said. "Just because I'm old enough to be your father doesn't mean I want to be reminded of it."

They all laughed at that, and then continued the quick tour and lesson: sparging to remove the sugars from the mash, boiling the mash in a brew kettle and adding hops to make the wort, spinning out the solids and cooling the wort so yeast could be added. That was when the fermentation began. Bacchanal Brewing had two 2,400-gallon fermentation tanks, where yeast converted the glucose in the wort to ethyl alcohol and carbon dioxide, which was continually vented until near the end of the process. At that time, the vent was capped so the CO_2 would be forced into the beer, partially carbonating it.

By the time we had walked through the process, I was desperate for a taste. I swallowed again and again, my mouth as dry as the Sonoran desert in the month before the rains came. My mind was starting to wander once more when Honey grabbed my arm. I'd felt worse sensations.

"Perhaps a drink?"

I'm not exactly sure what my expression was on hearing those words—deer in the headlights of an oncoming Peterbilt, probably. Whatever it was, it made her laugh, a sound that sent a not-unwelcome thrill through me.

"Of *water*, silly. Infused with herbs to offset the taste from the tap."

She waited while I took the proffered glass and downed half of it, then grabbed my arm again, this time linking hers through it.

"Enough of this," Honey said. "The *real* story is outside, in the fields. Let's go, before we lose the light."

§

I had seen the field behind the brewery as I drove up, but paid it scant attention. You didn't have to live long in Arizona (and I hadn't, either time, thankfully) to see enough dried out, sun-yellowed grass to last a lifetime, especially in early summer when the whole world was as parched as a drunk . . . well, anytime his hand was empty. Same was true of Montana, most years. But stepping out Bacchanal's back door, Honey leading the way down two wooden steps and across a small gravel lot at the edge of which the field pressed, as if impatient to march on the building, Carrie and Anne a few steps behind me but present in the sound of their feet crunching across the small stones, the rhythm of their breathing—and it had never before struck me that you could hear a smile in somebody's breath—with the late afternoon sun sending slanting golden beams across the bristled tufts waving at the ends of long, slender stalks, I knew this was no vacant lot gone to seed, no rancher's grazing land.

"Is that . . .?" I began.

Honey let go of me and stepped into it like a beachgoer venturing into the surf. On the far side of the field was a silo, and beyond that a straight line of pines that might have indicated a road. "It's barley!" she exclaimed, running her hands across the spiked heads—awns, I think they were called. I had done a *little* prep for the piece. "Beautiful, beautiful barley!"

"It is," I said. "Beautiful, I mean." I wasn't sure we were talking about the same thing.

Honey whirled, arms outstretched, a human crop circle. "Isn't it? It's two-row barley. Old World barley, which is part of what sets Bacchanal ales apart. Lower protein gives it more fermentable sugars, sweetens the malt. This particular variety is called Summer Isle. Sadly, the crop this year doesn't look to be as robust as in years past." She stopped and looked back the way we'd come, toward the brewery. "Though we think we've found a remedy for that."

"You'll have to forgive Honey," Anne said quickly from somewhere over my left shoulder. "She's a little in love with barley."

I flashed on a tall glass of golden nirvana, foam sliding down the outside. "Who isn't?"

"I apologize, John," Carrie said, coming around to my left side, while Anne stood on my right. "We're not trying to tempt you, here. We're enthused about our process and our product, but we know it isn't for everyone."

"It's okay," I said. "I mean, that's a gorgeous—" I tugged my gaze away from Honey's lush form. "—plant. It's a grass, right?"

"Yes," Anne said. "It's also one of the healthiest foods you can find on the goddess's green earth. The FDA even allows barley-based foods to claim they aid heart health. It lowers blood pressure and can help control blood sugar."

I followed the path Honey had carved into the barley. The spikes were sharp-edged, snagging at my jeans and the discount-store dress shirt I could never quite keep tucked in. "I never knew."

"There's probably a lot you don't know," Honey said. She was walking back toward me now, her gaze fixed on my face. I wondered if there was something between my teeth, or a bug on my cheek.

"I have no doubt," I replied.

She snapped off a piece, just beneath the head, and handed it to me. "See?" she said. "The long ones are spikes, the little ones spikelets."

I glanced at the double row she indicated. "It looks braided," I said.

"Take it, John."

I reached for it, but as soon as my fingers started to close around the awn, she yanked it free. "Ouch!" I said. I opened my hand. A drop of blood beaded on the end of my index finger—my best typing finger.

"Oh, I'm so sorry," she said. She took my hand and lifted it toward her. For a brief, foolish instant, I thought she would press it to her breast, or place it in that delectable mouth to suck the blood away, but instead she brushed my fingertip lightly with the barley.

"There."

I looked at my hand. The blood was gone. "Let me see that." I snatched the barley from her hand before she could react. I expected to see a bloodstained spike; maybe a couple of them, the one that had cut me and the one she had wiped away the blood with.

It was clean. Golden. Not a trace of red.

"It wasn't a lot of blood," Honey said.

"No. Still."

"We told you," Carrie said. "It's a miracle grain."

"And it knows its own, and approves," Honey added with a strange, almost hungry smile. "As do I."

Was it possible to be sexy and a little creepy at the same time? Because she sure seemed to be pulling it off.

"Can you show me the rest now, please? You grow your own hops, right?" I looked at the field as I asked the question, not at any of the women. I suspected my cheeks were flushed, with embarrassment and not a little lust. But I could feel Honey's gaze, boring into me.

God help me, I didn't mind it a bit.

§

"We do," Anne said, answering my question as we walked deeper into the field. "But we're more interested in showing you the harvesting process. If you don't mind?"

"No, of course not," I said, blinking against the light, which was suddenly making my head hurt. My eyes were watering now, too, and my vision seemed to be blurring a little. Allergies? Seemed a little late in the year for them, but then I didn't normally spend a lot of time traipsing through amber waves of grain.

Honey had moved ahead of us, toward something that looked like a tractor with the blade reel from an oversized push mower attached to the front. I watched her climb into the cab and heard the splutter and roar as she started it up.

"Is that a . . .?" I began, but found that I couldn't think of the word. I couldn't think of much of anything but Honey's body and the smooth taste of beer sliding down my throat. I wasn't sure which one I wanted more.

"It's a combine harvester," Anne replied, seemingly oblivious to my mental lapse. "In the old days, all the steps in harvesting barley were done separately, by hand. And while we prefer the old ways for most things, in some cases, the benefits of modern technology are too great to ignore. The harvester reaps, threshes, and winnows, all in a single process, and in much less time than it would take to do each task individually. It's really quite a sight to behold."

It looked like I was going to get to behold it, though, and up close, too, because Anne and Carrie had each taken me by one arm and were guiding me straight toward the thing.

"Shouldn't . . . shouldn't we . . .?" I tried to say, searching foggily for the last words. Move? Out? Of? The? Way?

"Hush, now, John Barleycorn. It will all be over soon."

The sound of the harvester was so loud now I couldn't tell which of the sisters had spoken, so didn't know who to correct. *That's . . . not my name.*

Was it?

I was so confused, and the rhythmic slicing of the harvester blades through the rows of bowing barley were almost like a lullaby, soothing me, making me want to lie down in front of the approaching machine, like an offering.

Wait.

Like a *what?*

The utter foreignness of the thought pulled me out of what I realized must have been some sort of drug-induced stupor. What kind of herbs had Honey put in that water, anyway?

And, more to the point, *why?*

I yanked my arm from Carrie's grasp, but Anne was bigger, stronger. She held on.

"What the hell are you doing?" I demanded, shouting to be heard over the whirring blades.

"Hell has nothing to do with the Craft, John," Anne said grimly, still lecturing, even now. She grabbed onto me with both arms, a grip I fought to break, especially with Carrie clawing at my head and back to regain her own hold.

As I struggled, I heard Carrie start to speak in a strange, almost sing-song meter. After a moment, Anne joined in, matching her word for word. "Seeker of truth," they said. "Lover of barley. Child of the solstice."

I thought my swimming head was playing tricks on me, making me hear them wrong. But they repeated it, in the same tones, the same pattern. "Seeker of truth. Lover of barley. Child of the solstice."

The harvester was coming closer, its engine tearing apart the calm silence that had engulfed the field at first. I didn't know what their nonsensical patter was about, but I was no solstice child. I kept fighting, trying to twist out of their hands.

"Just give in, damn you," Carrie snarled in my ear. "It's an honor to be chosen to bring back the harvest. And you won't even feel anything, thanks to Honey. More mercy than your Puritan kind deserves."

She was right. I could feel her nails tearing at my neck, but whatever herbs had dulled my wits also seemed to be doing the same to my other senses, blocking any associated pain.

Which is probably how I was able to shake her off, plant my foot, and spin around, catching Anne off guard. Pulled off her feet, she slammed into Carrie, releasing me as both women went down in a heap.

Right in front of the harvester.

I didn't bother to see if either of them got up again.

Instead, I turned and ran.

§

They were between me and the parking lot, so I went the other way, cutting through the field toward the silo and the road I hoped was beyond it. My feet felt heavy, as if I'd waded through wet cement, and I was aware that I was stumbling in more of a zigzag pattern than charging straight across. The rasp of the barley was loud, as was my breathing, and I could hear my pulse in my ears. None of it, though, was loud enough to mask the roar of the harvester, that sickening squelching sound, or those horrific screams, which ended as abruptly as the engine noise did.

I didn't look back. I was pretty sure that trying would ensure that I fell on my face. Instead, I kept going, my gaze fixed on the tree line. I hoped the harvester had reaped, threshed, and winnowed both sisters. But whatever luck had allowed me to escape before the harvester reached me had since fled; I heard someone behind me, racing through the field.

Moving faster than me, from the sound of it.

I'd never make the trees. And I still couldn't tell if there was a road on the other side; if not, reaching them would do me no good.

I veered toward the silo. It was closer, and I could hide in there, or perhaps find something to use as a weapon. Make a stand, though I could barely remain upright without the world tilting crazily beneath my feet.

Somehow, I made it, but whoever was coming behind me was catching up in a hurry. I'd been in a grain silo once before, reporting on a story about the dangers faced by children working on family farms. I hadn't spent much time inside; the air was thick and foul, and the owner's warnings of methane gas buildup made me more than a little nervous.

But I remembered some of the basics. I unlatched the lower access door and climbed inside, pulling it shut behind me. It didn't seem very full—this year's harvest had yet to take place—but barley was crusted against the walls, as far up as I could see. Fiberglass panels set at intervals in the upper reaches of the tall structure let in just enough light to deepen the shadows. I stepped carefully over a piece of equipment on the floor, a kind of spiral-bladed, pivoting arm, then remembered its name: sweep auger. It whisked grain from the sides of the silo and toward a conveyor system in the floor. It was powered off, and I didn't think it went that fast to begin with, but I didn't want to take any chances. Leaning against the far wall was a shovel. I had just taken a last staggering step toward it when the door opened.

Anne stepped through. In the dim light I could see her face and neck were spattered with blood, presumably her sister's. She held a steel rod that looked to be at least six feet long. I recognized it as the kind workers used to dislodge stuck grain from silo walls. Suddenly my shovel seemed an inadequate weapon—by the time I could get close enough to hit her with it, she would already have skewered me.

I had the feeling that if I swung the thing, I would only wind up dumping myself on my ass. But I had to try. Her gaze was fixed on me, her hands tight on the rod. Everything about her spoke of menace.

I took a step to my right, her left. She turned with me and came closer. I took another step, and she reached the auger. As she stepped over it, she thrust the rod toward me. I swung the shovel, batting it away, but the motion made the whole place swim and I fell back against the wall. Dust rained down on me.

She charged. I lunged to the right just in time to dodge the rod. It slammed into the silo wall, sending up a reverberation that shook the whole structure with a deep, echoing hum I could feel in my teeth. I tried to catch it with my left hand, hoping to snatch it from her grasp, but I snagged only empty air.

The rod came at me again, and this time I didn't move fast enough. The end scraped my ribs, ripping the shirt that by now was completely untucked and filthy. The absurd thought that the *Standard* didn't pay me enough to replace my clothes flitted through my head in the instant before pain flared through me. The drugs must have been starting to wear off; my side felt like I had walked into the path of a blowtorch.

I took two more lurching steps to the right before she thrust the length of steel at me again. I swatted it with the shovel. I couldn't keep that up forever, though. All she needed was to hit me dead center once, impale me, and I was done.

The next time she tried to spear me, I hurled the shovel. She dodged it easily, but lost her footing as she did. She crashed into one wall, while the shovel clanged off another.

More dust fell, and grain now, too, striking the floor like hailstones. I stumbled toward the door as an ominous vibration shivered through the steel walls.

Anne scrambled to her feet, but her rod had slid beneath the auger and she was trying to wrench it free. My last glimpse, just before I fell outside into the dirt, was of her just as she yanked it loose. But doing so slammed its back end against the wall, and the vibration grew more intense. I heard bigger chunks of crusted barley hitting the floor, and Anne gave a cry as—from the sound of it—another hit her, knocking her once again off her feet.

I made it to my hands and knees and saw the power box right in front of me. Throwing it open, I jammed my finger down onto the switch. The motor engaged instantly. Inside, Anne started screaming. "Shut it off!"

Judging by the racket, she was still trying to regain her footing. Larger quantities of grain were falling with a noise like an entire marching band full of drummers, and her cries were interrupted by grunts of pain. "Come back!" she shrieked. "Come back here, John Barleycorn!"

I stayed where I was, breathing hard, dizzy, seconds away from puking. Anne's shrieks became wails of agony, and I thought maybe I could hear the sound of the sweep augur chewing through her legs, but the falling grain had turned into a rumble. The vibrations as it hit the floor spread through the silo, working more off, and the rumble became thunder. Barley dust puffed out through the open door, followed by a spill of grain. I sat there, a dozen feet away, until the din stopped. Almost reluctantly—sitting felt so good—I found my feet and went back to the door.

All I could see was barley, mounded up high on the floor.

§

The sun was on the last leg of its slow descent, its rays catching the harvester still sitting in the field. I didn't want to go near it. I could have called somebody—911, sheriffs, anybody—but I had just participated in the deaths of two local businesswomen and I was under the influence of some unknown drug. I didn't want to put myself into that kind of meat-grinder until I was free of its effects. I didn't see Honey anywhere, but I couldn't imagine her calling the authorities. Not after what she and her partners had tried to do to me.

I made my way across the field again, toward the brewery and my car parked in front of it. As I walked, the awns poked at me and I batted them wearily away. If I never saw barley again, it would still be too soon. For once, I didn't even crave a beer.

§

I'd intended to circle around the brick building and make straight for my car, but as I neared the closest corner, I thought I saw a flash of movement in the shadows gathering there.

Honey?

I couldn't afford to take the chance. If she was at the corner, going through the building would get me to my car faster than trying to go around the other way.

I changed direction, heading for the brewery's service

entrance, the one we'd all walked out of so cheerfully just a short while ago, a dry drunk improbably surrounded by a trio of beautiful, attentive women, like something out of a dream.

Or, in this case, a nightmare.

Either Carrie or Anne had left the door wedged open with a cinder block, which I shoved inside before pulling the metal door closed behind me. I hoped the click I heard was it locking and that the fact that it had been propped open in the first place meant none of the three women had bothered to take a key. Not that I planned on sticking around long enough to find out.

As I hurried through the darkened brewery, past the two fermentation tanks, I thought I heard footsteps echoing behind me. I tensed and whirled, expecting Honey.

No one.

Christ, John. Get a grip.

I turned back around, picking up my pace. The echoes increased in response, and this time I thought I heard whispers, too.

"Seeker of truth."

I spun so fast I made myself momentarily dizzy.

Nothing but shadows.

I peered into the darkness, trying to see, but it was impossible. If Honey was hiding there, the only way I'd know was if I walked back and bumped into her, and that was *not* happening.

I resolutely turned my back and headed past the long bar for the foyer, just able to make out the flickering light from the candles still burning there. I was running now.

"Lover of barley."

I refused to look, kept my eyes on the arched entrance, ignoring the impossible echoes of many feet, the whispers, the movements at the edges of my vision.

"Child of the solstice."

I fetched up hard at the arch, not because of some unseen wall—though with all the other strangeness tonight, that wouldn't really have surprised me—but because of what I *could* see, just beyond, in the foyer.

Honey knelt there, naked, chanting words I couldn't understand in the center of a circle inlaid in the tiles. Thick black candles stood at five points along its circumference, white lines of

. . . salt? . . . connecting them across the circle's interior, forming a star.

A pentagram.

No. A *pentacle*. I remembered them from my ex's Tarot cards, recalling the distinction only because of her frequent pontification on the topic, something I never thought I'd be grateful for. I guess I owed her an apology.

Assuming I ever made it out of here.

So, a pentacle. And if Honey was kneeling naked in the middle of one, that could only mean she was a . . . I couldn't quite bring myself to think the word, despite what I'd already seen and heard. Been through.

Because I could handle three psychotic women luring me here, drugging me, and trying to kill me for some insane reason that only made sense to them—unfortunately, we lived in that kind of world, and I'd covered worse and more bizarre stories back in New England.

But three . . . *witches*—because that's what they had to be, right?—choosing me to be their . . . *harvest sacrifice*?

I'd had booze-fueled fever dreams that made more sense.

But I couldn't deny the reality—the awns stuck in my pants, the burning pain across my torso, the lovely woman before me.

"You shouldn't have run, John," Honey said softly, her chant finished. She looked up at me with those incredible green eyes, her hair falling about her shoulders in a way that drew my gaze downward . . . I jerked my head back up, met her come-hither look with a glare of my own. "Running only ever makes things worse."

"Only if you get caught."

Honey laughed aloud at that, a sound that still thrilled me, even though I knew she wanted me dead and would do anything in her power to make that happen.

And that was the question, of course.

What exactly *was* in her power?

"Oh, I'd say you've been caught. Quite handily, too." Honey rose as she spoke, and it was all I could do to keep my eyes on her face and not lose myself in the sight of her curves. "The doors are locked, windows barred. And you won't find me as unprepared as you did the others."

She gestured with her hand, taking in the circle and the candles. Behind me, there was a rush of sound, as if a thousand birds had taken flight at once, all of them intent on a single target.

Me.

I winced, bracing myself for an impact that never came.

Honey laughed again, then held both arms out, as if in welcome. A rattling noise sounded on the walls to my left and right, and then suddenly the metal disks flew off the walls and into her waiting hands. In the candlelight, I could see now that the edges of the moons—one half, one a crescent—had been sharpened.

"Are you ready to die now, John Barleycorn?"

In reply, I turned and ran back the way I'd come. As I did, candles I hadn't noticed behind the bar and on the tables flared to life, like lights on a runway, leading me to something I was pretty sure wasn't safety. But what choice did I have? I could hear her bare feet slapping against the wooden floor behind me.

And then I could hear the *whoosh* of something slicing through the air. I couldn't know if she'd aimed left or right, high or low, so I ducked behind the nearest table and heard the *thunk* of metal sinking into wood, right about where the small of my back had been just moments before.

Not quite center mass, but enough to get the job done, if it had connected.

I had little doubt the next one would.

I tried to keep low, working my way through the tables and toward the back of the brewery, where the fermentation tanks were. I thought there were bathrooms there, too, and if any of the windows had escaped the rebar treatment—used in actual urban environments to keep the bad guys out, but here in small-town Montana, as a form of hipster ornamentation—it would be those.

The tables slowed me, but they also kept Honey from getting a clear shot with her Xena Warrior Princess *chakram*, or whatever the hell those things were supposed to be.

Of course, I had no idea if those were the only weapons at her disposal. I had a bad feeling they weren't.

On cue, the echoes started back up, masking her footsteps.

And the whispers, too, though they had a few new refrains this time.

"Are you ready to die, John Barleycorn?"

"Just give in."

And the last, most insidious one, repeating over and over.

"Is your life really so worth living?"

Maybe not, but I'd made it this far, despite myself. I wasn't about to give up now.

And then I was out of tables, and there was nothing between me and the door to the men's room but a long stretch of open floor and the twin silver cylinders of the fermentation tanks.

I'd never make it without something to distract Honey, slow her down.

I looked at the tanks again, considering.

Judging the distance.

Then, with a wordless prayer to my higher power, I took off.

§

I made it to the tanks and had just managed to squeeze myself between them when the higher-pitched *thunk* of metal piercing metal rang in my ears; she'd been going for my head that time, and she'd barely missed.

I had no idea if she was out of throwing moons now or not— she could have pulled the other one out of the table, or even summoned more off the walls as she walked. I had to assume she was still armed and dangerous.

So I did the only thing I could think to do.

I reached around, felt for the valve, and opened it up to full. Then I did the same with the second tank.

The heady scent of beer flooded my nostrils as the cool liquid poured from the tanks in a frothy rush. Hoping that wading through a river of lager would slow her down some, I peeked around the curved edge of the tank to look for Honey. She was standing back near the tables, half moon in hand, ready to throw as soon as I stepped out of my hiding place, unmindful of the beer already sloshing around her ankles.

Damn it. Now what?

As if in answer, the tank that she'd hit with the crescent moon groaned, shook. Weakened by the puncture and with thousands of gallons flowing out from it unchecked, the cylinder was losing its structural stability. Seeing my chance, I wedged myself in between it and the wall, and heaved.

At first, nothing happened, but after a handful of eternities, I felt it give.

Redoubling my efforts, my back and legs braced against the brick wall, clothes ripping and skin tearing, I pushed as hard as I could.

And slowly, like a tree unwilling to admit it had been felled by a logger's axe, the tank toppled.

As it started to fall, I slid out from my hiding place. I watched as it crashed down on the floor and part of the bar, the top splitting open on impact, the remainder of the golden liquid within bursting out across the tables like a flash flood. I saw Honey go down as tables collided with each other. Candles fell from their perches, igniting the alcohol-soaked wood, and flames flared to life across the brewery, turning it into a virtual lake of fire. I watched Honey struggling to rise, her hair brushing up against a burning table, bursting into a fiery corona. She screamed as I turned and ran again, slamming into the men's room door and rushing over to the window above the urinals, chased by fire and ale and a dying witch's curses.

The window was small, and as suspected, unbarred. But I could squeeze through it.

I had to.

Climbing precariously up on two of the urinals, I used my elbow to break the glass, and my forearm to clear the shards from the pane. I was halfway out when the contents of the second tank caught fire and exploded. The blast propelled me from the building onto the packed gravel outside, and the last thing I saw as the world faded from view was the edge of the red solstice sun sinking below the horizon.

§

The inquest raised a lot of questions, but no answers that satisfied anybody. Fortunately for me, there was also no proof beyond the proverbial reasonable doubt that the deaths weren't a series of horrible accidents. I was plenty beat up myself, so it wasn't like I had come out of it unscathed. I got a lot of sideways looks, and for a while heard people whispering until I came within earshot, after which they clammed up and pretended not to stare.

Once it was finished, I tried not to think about it. I buried myself in work, focused on sobriety, met a woman and lost her in the same month. I never went back to the neighborhood where Bacchanal Brewing had been located, and I found that sometimes an entire day could pass without me thinking about Honey, Carrie, and Anne.

Then one day in the latter half of June I was out in that general direction, reporting a story about a survivalist compound being turned into an adventure park, with paintball and zip lines and an obstacle course. On my way back into town, near the day's end, I was approaching the turnoff to the brewery, and almost before I had consciously decided, I was braking and turning the wheel. A few minutes later I was parked on the side of the road, eyeing the remains.

The building was still charred rubble. The winter had been a hard one, and most of what had been left standing had collapsed under the weight of the snow. The silo was gone—dismantled and moved, or razed, I couldn't tell.

But the barley field was lush, the stalks tall, shining like spun gold in the afternoon light. I had found it impressive the first time I'd seen it, but that was nothing like this. I had thought that it would be fallow, abandoned, left to rot. Instead, it looked healthy and rich.

My phone rang once. Glancing at the screen, I realized that I had come on the summer solstice. No number appeared, and it didn't ring again. I stopped, eyeing the crop, knowing what fine beer it would produce, were there anyone around to brew it.

Seeker of truth.

Lover of barley.

Child of the solstice.

Three witches, each fitting one of those descriptions as well as I did—no, better—had died on this ground.

An appropriate sacrifice? Maybe. Or maybe it was nothing but winter snow and late spring sunshine working on soil fertilized by ash.

Sitting there in the car, gazing at the shimmering golden

grass, I felt a pull like nothing I had experienced since those first dry days, when every bar's OPEN sign flashed just for me, every bottle promised salvation, every beer commercial taunted me with what I could no longer have.

I wanted to wade into the barley. I wanted to cup it in my hands, to brew it into ale, to sip, then guzzle, until the field was nothing but bare earth.

Instead, I turned the key, gunned the engine, and left it all behind me, where it belonged. All the way home, I avoided the rear-view, and kept my eyes on the road ahead.

On...John Barleycorn Must Die

"John Barleycorn Must Die" (Roud #164), also called simply "John Barleycorn" or "Sir John Barleycorn," is a song that often worries scholars and folklorists. It's too perfect. As A.L. Lloyd comments: "The song is related to the ancient idea of the Corn King. Perhaps too neatly so, hence the suspicion that it may not be a genuine piece of primitive folklore. It is old (it was already in print c.1635) and has been passed on by generations of country singers. The tune is a variant of Dives and Lazarus."

In the most common beginning three men come from elsewhere (west, east, north) and make a solemn pact that John Barleycorn should die.(1) From there the song describes in detail what happens when a cereal crop is planted. There's plowing and harrowing, planting, the crop absorbs the rain, grows and ripens, is harvested and the grain allowed to cure before [winnowing] removes the grain from the stalk. Then the grain is ground. The song describes this all as if it were inflicted on a writhing man.

In some versions, John Barleycorn now extracts his revenge: "Here's little Sir John in the nut-brown bowl[ale], And here's brandy in the glass, And little Sir John in the nut-brown bowl, Proved the strongest man at last." Without him man cannot hunt or work, proving that no matter what they did to him, he is still the stronger. As Martin Carthy wrote: "Forget the academic stuff about death and rebirth, fertility symbols and corn gods! The reason that this is one of the best known and most popular of all ballads—and one which has crossed a great many musical thresholds—is that it's actually about that other activity which most commonly accompanies the singing of traditional songs—drinking!"

1) Roud Folksong Index. 2014. 22 June, 2014. < http://www.vwml.org/roudnumber/164 >. English Folk Dance and Song Society.

2) Mainly Norfolk: English Folk and Other Good Music. 2014. 22 June, 2014. <http://mainlynorfolk.info/lloyd/songs/johnbarleycorn.html> English Folk Dance and Song Society.

In Arkham Town, Where I was Bound

By
Nancy Holder

It was all on a ghastly, gloomy day that at last I reached the outskirts of Arkham, Massachusetts. After a carriage ride lasting innumerable, endless rainy days and bitterly cold nights, I climbed down at last with time-worn satchel and patched valise, and a chill washed over me with the fog. The moon shone down on a misshapen street crowned with gambrel roofs, and the familiar panic seized my heart as I contemplated why I was there. I walked into the station house on shaking legs in fear for my dear Virginia—Sissy, as I called my little wife. I had failed her again.

The magazine that had employed me had gone bankrupt, and I had no funds. Sissy and I had nothing but molasses and bread to eat, and Sissy—I can admit it now!—was overdue for medical attention. I had not wanted to admit that she had consumption—I had denied it for far too long!—and as a result of my neglect, she was dying, a death made all the harder by our poverty.

As you may well know, my father, David Poe, abandoned my mother, brother, sister, and me before I even knew him, and when I was but two years of age, my mother died. We children were farmed out, and I became the ward (but never son, never that) of John and Frances Allan. My foster mother suffered pitiable heartbreak over the unfaithfulness of my foster father, and I quarreled with him bitterly for her sweet sake. Claiming to find me sulky and ungrateful, he cast me out, and when he died, I was disinherited. He bequeathed his second wife and their children a fortune but for me, not a penny. Owning no property and having been expelled from West Point, I had no employable skills except that I had been raised a gentleman and I was facile with words, and so I determined to make my living with my pen.

I sought through the years to remain gainfully employed as an editor and critic, and to publish my verses. Fame came my way, but not fortune, as had come to others who, I confess, I still consider my literary inferiors (Longfellow comes to mind).

I became shameless in my pursuit of relief. Inquiries on my part revealed that a branch of the Allan family made their home in Arkham. This limb of the Allan family tree had split off two centuries before and spelled their name "Allen." Thus knowledge of them among "my" Allans (though of course they were not mine at all) had been utterly lost.

The patriarch of the Arkham Allens was named Mr. Demeter Allen. I had no claim on him and he and I both knew it, but as I had achieved some repute (others might say notoriety) for my literary work, he agreed that we should meet, and invited me to stay at his home, which was a small distance from the town itself.

Now I waited for him in the milky, thick fog; quatrains sprang into my head as I paced to stay warm. The refrain was ever the same: my love cannot die. She must not, would not; she had endured so much for love of me.

Presently an old woman limped along the cobbles. She was bent over, her face gray and lined, and her clothes tattered. She was wearing no coat. She extended a raggedy glove toward me and said, "A penny, sir? Anything? I'll say a prayer for you and yours."

I gave my head a rueful shake. "I'm sorry for your trouble, missus," I said, "but I barely have a cent to my name."

She wrinkled her brow and when she sighed, it was as if she exhaled a ghost. She shook her head and said, "Woe to you, sir, for my prayers have weight."

"I'm sure of it," I said, and impetuously, I was in a mind to offer her my coat when a fine carriage clopped down the lane, and she vanished into the darkness.

The carriage wheeled to a stop in front of me and a fine, handsome gentleman emerged with hand extended in welcome. Whereas the Allans of Virginia are fair, Demeter Allen's hair, eyebrows, and beard were raven-black, and his eyes were so dark I could discern no color in them as he smiled at me and we shook hands.

"Mr. Poe, so very pleased to meet you," he said warmly. Then he turned to peer into the interior of the carriage and said, "Barbara, say hello to your cousin Edgar from Virginia."

He did me great service, for we were not cousins at all, much less on a familiar, first-name basis, and while it was true that I hailed from Virginia, I did not currently live there. Still, Richmond was the home of the Allans, and I felt that he was attempting to emphasize to me that he felt in some way connected to my life. This gave me hope that at last I might have found sympathetic friends.

After a moment, I heard the rustle of silk, and then a very beautiful young woman appeared in the door of the carriage. Her hair was as black as her father's, and she was fine-boned and quite dainty in appearance. She was brilliant with joy, and I was somewhat taken aback, as I could not imagine her broad smile and flashing eyes were a result of making my acquaintance. Indeed, she barely seemed to notice me.

As she alighted, her father said to the coachman, "Eustace, put Mr. Poe's belongings in the carriage." Then he said to me, "What a cold night this is, cousin. Let us repair to the tavern to warm our blood before we embark on the journey to the house."

I was deeply touched, but all my senses sprang to alert as we walked across the street toward a golden-hued bay window blossoming with shadowed movement. Echoes of laughter and conversation greeted my ears, and I began to worry about how I should manage to pay for refreshments for my two new companions, which was the least hospitality my Southern upbringing required. And in all truth, I was afraid that I should forget my own vow to drink spirits in moderation, and humiliate myself. When upset, I overindulge, even to this day.

My "cousin" Barbara practically bolted ahead of us, as eager to enter the inn as I was hesitant. Soon we were wreathed in a steamy crowd of warm breath and the scent of mulled wine, and Mr. Allen began the introductions. Out of the corner of my eye, I spied Barbara making a quick way toward a tall, handsome youth. She had no eyes for anything but him. But he, on the other hand, was striding past her toward me, his hand extended.

"Mr. Edgar Allan Poe!" he cried. "Oh, sir! I have read everything you have ever written!"

He pumped my hand and tears welled in his eyes. I was at once charmed, for I admit that I have never shrunk from public acclaim, and my poor, distressed heart was grateful for this man's eagerness to meet me.

"Flip!" he called.

This was a beverage of hot rum, I knew, such as they drink in New England. A buxom barmaid arrived with a tray of four steaming pewter mugs. The young man handed one to me, one to Mr. Allan, and took a third off the tray. There was one mug left, and Barbara rustled forward to claim it. But before she could do so, the young man raised his mug and cried, "A toast to the greatest writer who ever lived!"

"Thank you," I said, pausing in hopes that he would give the young lady the fourth mug, but he did not. "Mr...?"

"Jemmy Grove," he answered. "Drink up, I pray you, sir!"

Young Mr. Grove, Mr. Allen, and I drank, and Barbara's face blazed bright red. I wondered if Mr. Grove was ignoring her on purpose—if, perhaps, she entertained false hopes and he was attempting to dash them—and I winced inwardly as she touched an anxious, gloved hand to her hair and adjusted her jet-encrusted shawl around her shoulders. Her uncertainty of her beauty made me think of my own sweet Sissy, who had wondered aloud what I saw in her, as lovelier, grander women had sought my company.

After resolving to take only this one mug of flip, I finally drank, and the pungent rum punch spread throughout my chilled limbs. I found myself surrounded by a ring of faces eagerly calling for me to recite "The Raven," and after quaffing more of my refreshment, I felt eager to oblige.

I was ushered to a small stage at one end of the tavern and as I climbed onto it, I spied Barbara Allen rushing in tears out the tavern door and into the night. Planted firmly in the public center of attention, I could see no way to alert her father without embarrassing the lady, and so I kept my peace and hoped she would come to no harm.

I recited my poem, and then was asked for another. I complied. I was in a fine mood by then, having accepted a second cup of flip, and basking, I do confess, in the adulation. More verses were requested; more, given.

After an interval, Mr. Allen decreed that it was time for us to depart. As if on cue, at that very moment the tavern door opened and Barbara slipped in unnoticed by either her father or Mr. Grove. Her hair was slightly mussed and her exquisite jet shawl was gone.

She and I traded looks; hers said, I beg of you, do not betray me, and I dipped my head ever so slightly in reply. She appeared much relieved.

It was announced that we were to depart, and there was much commotion with fetching "the poet's hat and coat." I made a half-hearted attempt to settle the bill with Mr. Allen, but he would not have it—to my shamed relief.

At long last, Mr. Grove seemed to realize that he had neglected Barbara all evening. He hurried toward her and extended a hand. But she gazed at him with hard, angry eyes, lifted her chin, and showed him her back.

He came up behind her and attempted to place his hand on her shoulder. She shrugged it off. He called her name: "Miss Allen?" and she pretended not to hear.

Then, "Barbara?" And she turned her head in his direction and sneered at him like a queen confronted with a beggar. Mr. Grove was utterly crestfallen, but her features were set as if made of porcelain, and she placed her hand on my arm, clearly preferring my company.

Her father saw none of this, but notice was taken by those in the tavern, and a few knowing grins were exchanged. I smiled faintly as well.

I knew a lovers' quarrel when I saw one.

§

"Arkham's not like other towns. It would suit you, cousin," said Mr. Allen as we headed home. Then he began to recite many of the ghastly legends attending the town—of monsters from other worlds, and curses, and madness, and hideous beings that rise from the sea to mate with the daughters of men. Of witches. I was quite astonished that he spoke so freely of such peculiarities in front of his daughter. Divested of her cloak, she was huddled under the carriage blanket, shivering with cold, and he didn't seem to notice this, either.

As he unfolded tales of horror and more horror, I lifted the carriage curtain and peered outside. Beneath the moonlight, the trees were blasted as if struck by lightning, then twisted into poses resembling grotesque human hunchbacks. Fog congealed into human faces that scowled at me, then dissipated. At a crossroads, I thought I saw a crooked figure in a shroud. It raised a hand in greeting, and I realized it was the beggar woman who had offered to pray for me and mine, wearing Barbara's cloak. I felt a twinge as I ticked my gaze toward Barbara, who clearly had sacrificed her outer garment on this woman's behalf. Miss Allen stared back at the lady, then furtively made the sign of the cross and nervously licked her lips.

§

The Allen home was an imposing country manor house of the same gambreled roof design I saw everywhere in Arkham, its stern gray windows glaring down at us as we alighted. It was not welcoming, but it was large, and I blush to admit that it raised hopes in me of financial help. Even a loan would be welcome.

Lightning flashed as the front door opened and Mr. Allen's man took my coat and hat. I was tired and had imbibed perhaps a bit too much, but Mr. Allen insisted that I accompany him to the parlor, there to meet Mrs. Allen.

Barbara excused herself and went on to bed. We two men entered a poorly lit room lined with oil portraits of dark-haired men and women resembling Demeter Allen. Then, seated before the fire with an embroidery hoop resting in her lap, sat the image of Barbara Allen perhaps some twenty years hence, although somewhat drawn and haggard. Her eyes were focused on the fire; at the sound of our footsteps, she seemed to struggle to blink her eyes and look at us.

"My dear, look. It is dear Mr. Edgar Allan Poe from Richmond," said Mr. Allen, but I noticed that he did not draw near to her.

For an instant, fury glittered in her eyes. I was quite taken aback, but I realized that she was still not looking at me. Mr. Allen was the object of her ire. The exchange was a mirroring of what had transpired between Jemmy Grove and their own daughter, and I wondered at the cause.

"What a pleasure to meet you," she said to me without much enthusiasm.

I inclined my head and made my response as I took the seat across from her. Her husband perched on a settee somewhat more distant from the mantel. Then she called for warm rum and I did not protest. We drank to her health and then to mine.

"Tell me, Mr. Poe, how do you like this wicked place?" she asked me.

"Begging no disrespect, ma'am, but as a gracious lady such as yourself lives in this place, surely it cannot be too wicked."

She smiled at my pretty gallantry and said, "Let us not forget that Eve turned the Garden into Hell."

"Adam found paradise with her," I rejoined, even though that wasn't entirely accurate. But I am a writer, after all, and writers often varnish the truth. And, I confess, the imp of the perverse within me goaded me to see what her response might be.

But she only smiled neutrally and called a servant to refill my goblet. I was weary, and I knew I was drinking too much. When at last I was released from the obligations of a visitor and shown to my room, I could hear the rain pounding on the roof. The wind wailed against the glass of my window, in a room of dark wood and burgundy velvet. Lightning crashed.

I wandered to the window, drew open the curtains, and started at the sight of a figure down below in the carriage yard. It wore a greatcoat and a top hat, and stood utterly still with its head tilted back. When lightning illuminated its features, I saw that it was Jemmy Grove, Miss Allen's sweetheart.

His mouth was moving; I unlatched the window and tilted my head in an effort to catch his words through the whistling tempest.

"Barbara," he pleaded. "Barbara Allen." He wailed as if suffering the greatest of torments.

I wasn't sure where her room was situated, and I considered whether I should alert her to the fact that her beau—if beau he still was—was serenading her like an Irish banshee. For some moments I debated and had just made up my mind to seek her out when Mr. Grove dejectedly strode to a horse tied up at a gate.

Thunder rolled and the miserable, sodden horse reared. The young man was obviously an accomplished horseman, for he gentled the steed with some ease, then mounted. He cast one last longing look at the house, and then he cantered away.

§

I slept heavily, for I was exhausted and half-drunk. The sun had barely risen when there was a knock on my door. I expected a servant, but after putting on my dressing gown, I opened the door to Barbara Allen. High color gave her a rosy glow, and I saw that she was fully dressed in a coat and bonnet.

She said, "Papa has gone. There's a fire at the mill. And I beseech you, Cousin Edgar, will you escort me to Mr. Grove's? I've had a message that he is quite ill."

I was much astonished by her request, but not at all surprised that the young man had suffered from standing in the storm. I was about to say as much when she reached out and squeezed one of my hands with both of hers.

"I beg of you, please take me to him. Mama, well, you see, sir, she has a condition and in order to sleep she must take…It will be hard to rouse her and I need to go now!"

It was utterly imprudent of me to assent. In the first instance, it was most improper to go at all, but for me to whisk away the daughter of the house without consulting her parents? Unpardonable. I had come with hat in hand to look for money from her father. My wife was starving, dying.

No, my love cannot die.

But in my life, I have often done the one thing I should not. I have sought out the dramatic in situations that other, wiser folk shun. So I told her I would escort her, dressed, and had a quick breakfast and very strong coffee.

The day was chill but we took two horses rather than a carriage. She pushed her mare and I had trouble keeping up as we charged through a blasted, black-and-white landscape so dank and dreary that I wished with all my heart to be back in New York. Then we came upon a cheery country home surrounded by pines, such a contrast to its surroundings, that my heart lightened upon seeing it.

True love shall win the day, I thought as a boy came forward to gather our horses and assist Miss Allen. She scarcely waited for me as she hurried to a large red wooden door set between two white columns. A fine black carriage with matching horses sat in the drive. I surmised that a physician had come.

Her gloved hand was on the knocker when the door opened and a young lady stopped on the transom. She was as fair as Barbara Allen was dark.

Miss Allen's eyes widened and I saw the rage of the mother reflected in the daughter; the other woman raised her chin, and said, "He is asleep. It would be better if you did not disturb him."

The fair young lady looked at me haughtily, then walked past us both to the carriage. Barbara Allen's fury did not abate and she stomped into the house without invitation. I followed hesitantly behind.

A maid appeared and curtseyed. I prepared to give her my coat and hat but Miss Allen walked right past her and started up a staircase. I raised a brow and the maid curtseyed again. Tears were streaming down her face.

"You may as well go up, sir, if you wish to say good-bye to our boy," she said, and then she fell to weeping.

I wondered where the rest of the household was. A well-mannered gentleman would have waited in the foyer. But I followed Barbara Allen up, then trailed behind her as she ran down a hall and pushed open the door at the end of it.

I knew it was a sickroom before I was one step inside. The odor made my heart clench. I thought of my love, my beautiful Sissy.

"Barbara," said a voice from the bed. It was young Jemmy Grove, blankets up to his chin. I was shocked at his appearance. His sunken cheeks and eyes gave him the aspect of an elderly man, older even than the beggar woman of the night before. His rheumy eyes ticked toward me, and he smiled with thin, bluish lips. "Mr. Poe. You do me such an honor."

"Why was Jennet Swanson here?" Barbara Allen demanded, and I caught my breath, astonished at the depth of her jealousy in the face of Mr. Grove's grievous condition. "You told me she meant nothing to you."

Evidently he means something to her, I thought, but did

not say. Instead, I drew a bit away and thought to quietly walk back out the door in order to give the man his dignity. He fell to coughing so violently that I saw in my mind's eye droplets of blood upon a handkerchief, and the world whirled around me. What was I doing here? Oh, why had I come to Arkham? For all I knew, my love lay in similar agony, forsaken by me because of this foolish quest!

"I went to your window. I called for you," he said. "Forgive me, love, I was so thrilled that Mr. Poe had come to Arkham—"

"Why was she here?" Barbara demanded. "You are all alike! You men, you faithless devils!" This last she cried in a scream like that of a spoiled child who had been refused a plaything. "I have laid a curse on you, Jemmy! Death to a faithless lover!"

She hissed at him like a cat and whirled on her heel. I was so shocked I stood rooted to the spot. She did not wait for me. I heard her dash down the stairs, and still I did not go. I went to the young man, who was doubled over in coughing. Tears and sweat were pouring down his face.

"I was never…I am not faithless," he managed to grind out, through it took him some time. I heard Barbara Allen galloping away. "She fears it most because her father…Forgive me, Mr. Poe, I am a gentleman." And then he fell back against the pillows, gasping.

"Help! Mr. Grove needs his physician!" I cried, and started for the door, but Jemmy Grove grabbed my forearm, and his grip was uncommonly strong.

"Tell her I loved her. I always loved her," he pleaded, and then I was firmly moved out of the way by a gray-haired gentleman, who was indeed his physician.

I went downstairs and the little maid saw me. She threw her arms around me and sobbed as if her heart would break.

"Please, send any news, any change, to the Allen home," I asked her. "I—we would like to know."

She shook her head against my chest. "It will be the bell, sir. In our little chapel. When you hear it toll, you will know he's gone." She burst into fresh tears.

I stayed until she composed herself, and then I quitted the house, grateful to be gone, but sorry for the lad inside it. I was angry with Barbara, so very angry, until I remembered what had been said about her father, and I thought of my own faithless foster father. My foster mother had had no recourse but to endure John Allan's mistresses and bastards. She had died a broken woman. Perhaps it was the same with Demeter Allen and his wife. I knew the kind of special hell that brought to battered hearts.

The melancholy sight of the Allen house presented itself to me just as the sound of a bell tolled in my ear. I drew my horse up short and cocked my head to make sure I heard it true, and not simply in my poetic imagination. It rang. Dolefully, mournfully, endlessly. Jemmy Grove was dead then. I murmured, *"Requiescat in pace."* Rest in peace.

A scream echoed like thunder across the yard where Jemmy Grove had caught his death. Barbara Allen came flying out of the house, and limping after her was the old woman, Barbara's jet-encrusted shawl wrapped around her.

I could not hear their conversation, but their voices were raised. Then Mrs. Allen appeared in the doorway, and as I dismounted and ran to the trio of women, she saw me and swayed, tumbling to her knees.

"Demeter is dead!" Mrs. Allen cried. "In the mill fire!"

I approached. The old woman looked my way, and across her face spread the most evil, malevolent smile I have ever seen and hope never to see again. It was inhuman. Her eyes glistened like the jet of the shawl.

"He was unfaithful," the hag decreed. "A curse was laid."

Mrs. Allen seemed not to hear or else to not comprehend. She was lost in her misery.

Barbara Allen clutched her bosom as if her heart would burst from her chest. "Jemmy, Jemmy," she moaned. "Could you not be true?" And then she fell to hard, heavy sobbing in cadence with her mother.

"He was true," the woman said. Her hideous smile bore down on Barbara Allen. "A true love stands in the rain to beg forgiveness. A true love uses the last of his strength to tell his beloved that he loves her. But tell me, girl, what kind of lover asks for a death curse on a young man like that? What kind of faith does she show? No faith."

The woman pointed a gnarled finger at the distraught girl and said, "And a curse has been laid that the faithless would die.

This curse must run its course."

Barbara Allen's sobs turned to gasps. Her eyes went wide. Then I heard the rattle in her throat as she fought to draw breath. She clamped her hand around her neck and reached out to her mother, who roused from her frenzy to rush to her daughter.

"Barbara! Barbara!" Mrs. Allen screamed. Then, as her daughter collapsed in her arms, she shouted at the woman, "What are you doing to her, you old witch? Stop it, for the love of God!"

"She did it to herself," the woman replied. "And not for any sort of love at all." And she burst into merry peals of laughter.

§

You know, of course, that I did not return to New York with money. The mill was not properly insured, and Mrs. Allen was ruined. It is not true that Jemmy Grove and Barbara Allen were buried near each other, but it is true that flowers blossomed on their graves mere days after their coffins were lowered into the earth.

On his bloomed a calla lily, for innocence, and rich, green grass, and a weeping willow tree.

And on hers, deadly nightshade, and nothing else, ever—no grass, nor nettle, nor weed.

Jennet Swanson married her fiancé a fortnight after Jemmy Grove's death. Mr. Grove was to have been her fiancé's best man. The old woman was never seen again in Arkham town.

And I wish down to my immortal soul that I had asked her to pray for Sissy.

On...Barbara Allen

One of the best known of all ballads is Child #84 (Roud 54), Barbara Allen. It is also known as "Bonny Barbara Allan," "Sir John Grehme and Barbara Allan," and "Barbara Allens' Cruelty." This ballad can be traced back at least three and a half centuries— Samuel Pepys writes in his diary on January second, 1666, that at a gathering Mrs. Knipp, an actress, sang the "little Scotch song of Barbary Allen."

In the ballad a man, sometimes named Sir John Graeme, (and sometimes, Jemmy Grove,) is dying. In some versions he's dying for the love of Barbara Allen, in others, it's of an undisclosed ailment. He sends for Barbara Allen who eventually arrives. In one version she's angry at him for slighting her, in others she is simply unmoved by his condition. He turns his face to the wall, she leaves and he dies. Upon hearing of his death, Barbara Allen feels remorse for her treatment of him and in all but one version death takes her as well. (1)

Recently Barbara Allen has been sung by Bob Dylan, on the 2nd Gaslight Tape in late 1962, as well as Jean Ritchie, Shirley Collins, Joan Baez, and Pete Seeger.

1) Child, Francis James. The English and Scottish Popular Ballads Vol. 2. Mineola: Dover, 2003.

DRIVING JENNY HOME

BY
SEANAN MCGUIRE

NOVEMBER

Jenny can you hear me, I am driving in the rain,
I am looking for you darling, I am calling out your name,
For I'll do as much for my true love as any lover known—
Let the rain fall on the highway. I'll be taking Jenny home.

§

I t only took three days for them to let me out of the hospital,
but that was long enough. Jenny was already in the ground.
So I stayed in my room, "recuperating," until my parents
told me that I was going back to school whether I liked it or not.
"Homecoming was a month ago, honey," they said, and "Leigh,
this isn't healthy," they said, and I didn't have a choice.

I told them there was something I had to do before I could go
back, and while they didn't like it much, at least they understood.
I missed the funeral, after all.

It's raining when I walk into the cemetery where they buried
my girl. That's right. That's exactly right. It should be raining
because Jenny is dead, and it's all my fault. It should keep on
raining forever.

Walking between the rows of graves is like something out of a nightmare or a dream—a bad dream, the kind that escapes nightmare territory by dancing on the razor's edge between surrealism and insanity. The kind where the walls bleed lobsters and the sky burns to ash when it touches the horizon. But the flowers I've brought to place on Jenny's grave are just flowers. They don't sing or whisper prophecy or turn into butterflies and fly away. When I finally find her tombstone—a simple granite rectangle that can't possibly summarize everything she was and should have been—and lay them down beneath the line that lists her date of birth and death; they don't bring Jenny back to me.

"God, Jenny," I say, sinking to my knees in the grass. "This is like some sick joke, only no one's telling me the punch line, and nobody's laughing. I'd take it back if I could. I'd take it all back if it would bring you home."

Jenny doesn't answer me. Jenny's never going to answer me again.

I stay where I am for what feels like an hour or more, the rain running down the back of my jacket and soaking my hair as I bow my head and cry. This can't be true. This can't be my life. It feels like just yesterday that I was picking her up for homecoming. She wore that dress the color of moonlight on the snow, and she fit in my arms like the missing piece of a puzzle. She's not fitting into anyone's arms now. She's dead and gone and she's not coming back to me.

They lock the cemetery gates at sunset. I don't want to spend the night here among the graves, and so when the light starts to fade, I force myself to move, wiping my tears away and leaning forward to press a kiss against the cold granite of Jenny's headstone.

"I love you," I say. "I'll see you soon."

Then I stand, wet clothes sloshing with every step, and start toward the distant gates. The rain is slacking off a bit, which is good since the setting sun is making it hard to see, and I'm starting to feel like a teenage emo cliché: sad lesbian in the graveyard in the rain. Jenny wouldn't like seeing me like this.

Maybe that's not the best train of thought because Jenny's never going to see me again, not like this, and not like anything else.

I'm crying again by the time I reach my car, a 1978 Volvo Bertone I inherited from my father when I turned sixteen and Mom made him dig it out of the garage. It handles like a tank and guzzles gas like nobody's business, but the collision that killed Jenny and put me in the hospital didn't even bend its frame. Jenny would have been fine if she'd been wearing her seatbelt, instead of twisted around and rummaging through the back seat. I guess I should hate the car for taking her away from me, but I like being able to get to school, and Jenny always loved the Bertone. She said it was just the right combination of old-fashioned and ugly as hell, and that she appreciated the contrast.

"That's my girl," I said, putting a hand gently on the door. That's when I see the ticket fluttering against the windshield like a trapped bird in the process of beating itself to death. It hasn't been there long; it's not even soaked through. I grimace. "Fucking cops," I mutter, and reach for it, only to freeze when another hand snatches it up before I can get there. A hand with long, slender fingers, the nails painted a shade of perfect moonlight gold that didn't come out of any bottle. Jenny always mixed her own nail polish. She said wearing anything off-the-rack, from clothes to cosmetics, showed a lack of commitment.

I lift my head. Jenny is standing next to the car in her moonlight dress, her homecoming corsage still tied around her wrist. She smiles, and she looks so sad that it makes me want to die, even though the sight of her is making me want to live like nothing has in weeks.

"Hi, Leigh," she says, and oh, God, her voice is the same as it always was. Nothing has changed. Everything has changed. "Can I get a ride home?"

What is there for me to say?

"Yes," I say, and unlock the car.

But she doesn't get in. Jenny doesn't get in. She just looks at me, her smile fading away a little bit at a time, until she finally says, "There are rules."

"Rules," I echo dumbly. My dead girlfriend is standing in front of me, and she's telling me there are rules. I don't understand why there should be since I'm clearly losing my mind.

"You have to drive me straight home," she says. "No stops— we're not going to the movies or going to Taco Bell or anything like that. You can't ask me why I'm here. And you can't give me a kiss good night."

It's an odd set of restrictions to get from a hallucination. I frown at her for a moment, trying to figure out what my subconscious is telling me—and then I decide that I honestly don't care. Jenny's here. Whether she's a hallucination or a ghost (and the fact that she's still holding the parking ticket is a vote for "ghost," unless I'm hallucinating that, too) doesn't matter. All that really matters now is driving Jenny home.

"Okay," I say, and we both get in the car, and I drive us away from the cemetery, and everything's okay again, if only for a little while.

DECEMBER

Jenny was gone when I turned onto her street, disappearing in the moments between checking my mirror and looking back at her. She left the parking ticket in the seat where she had been. She was always thoughtful that way.

That was a month ago. The ticket's been paid, and the shock waves have mostly finished washing through our school. I'm off the cheerleading squad, of course—even if the rest of the girls had sort of known about Jenny and me back when I was a base and she was a flyer, even though they'd been cool about the fact that we were lesbians, I was responsible for the death of one of our own. They couldn't look at me without seeing her, and I couldn't look at them without seeing her, and we were all tired of being haunted. So I quit the squad, and now no one's trying to use Jenny to define me. They're too busy using her to define everything else.

Jenny's dress at homecoming was moonlight satin? Fine, then, the theme for prom is going to be "Love Under the Moon," and everyone already knows Jenny will be awarded the coveted crown—the other girls who should be talking about campaigning by this point lower their eyes and murmur her name whenever the position of Prom Queen is mentioned, like wanting it would mean wanting what Jenny got: a brutal death and an early grave. They're canonizing her with memory, wearing away her hard edges bit by bit until all that's left is something perfect that they can tell their own children about someday when they're telling them not to drink and drive.

Jenny hadn't been drinking. Neither had I. Tyler did all the drinking for both of us, big muscle-headed football asshole who thought he was so great—thought Jenny was his for the taking—but learned he was so beneath her notice when he saw her dancing with me on the far side of the gymnasium, the fat girl in the tuxedo pressed up against the high school fantasy. We were both cheerleaders, but she was the one everyone remembered. I was just the one who made sure she didn't fall. I had one job. I couldn't even accomplish that.

But God, she was so beautiful that night. She was like the goddess of the moon, come down to hold hands with a mortal girl until the sun came up and the fantasy burned to ash. She was a fairy tale, she was a fiction, and I still felt like I had mud under my fingernails, despite the hours I'd spent scrubbing them clean. I guess that was why I let Tyler and his asshole friends get to me when they cornered me by the punchbowl. "Be the bigger person" and "just ignore them" is all well and good for people whose own high school days are fading in the rearview mirror of adulthood, but in the moment, when you're wearing teenage skin...

I didn't throw the first punch. I didn't throw the last one, either. I would probably have been beaten to a pulp if Jenny hadn't thrown herself into the middle of things, shouting at Tyler for being a Neanderthal idiot and shouting at me for letting myself be baited. I said I was sorry. I said I was stupid. I said I wouldn't let it happen again.

She said, "Take me home."

I drove home angry. That's the worst part. That's the part I'm never going to forgive myself for. Jenny wasn't speaking to me, just flipping through the radio and sulking, right up until she decided she was cold and undid her belt so that she could rummage through the backseat for my discarded tuxedo jacket. That was when Tyler came around the corner behind us, drunk and angry and driving a Prius that didn't stand a chance against my ancient bruiser of a Volvo. He slammed into my bumper, crumpling his car like a tin can and putting Jenny through the windshield.

The impact was enough to knock me out, even though I was wearing my seatbelt. By the time I woke up, it was too late. Jenny was gone.

How could I have been so stupid?

It's been two months since Jenny died and a month since I saw her. I've parked next to the cemetery gates every goddamn day since then, listening to a playlist of her favorite songs—too much country, too many teenage death ballads from the 1950s, and not nearly enough good old-fashioned rock and roll—and waiting to see her again. Even if it's just a glimpse, I need to know I'm not losing my mind. I need to know I wasn't hallucinating when I saw her before.

But the sun is going down, and there's no sign of Jenny. The grassy lawn is empty; the cemetery gates are closed and locked, as impassable as the wall to some forbidden city. I sigh. She's not coming. I'm losing my mind. I've had a month to think about what happened here, what I heard and saw and smelled. There's no way it was real; things like that don't happen. I close my eyes and lean back in my seat, breathing in through my nose and out from my mouth, and wait for the urge to wait for her to pass away.

It doesn't pass.

But someone's knocking on the window.

The sound is enough to make me yelp, twisting in my seat… and there's Jenny in her dress like moonlight with her hair pinned up just so, long gold curls anchored in an elaborate updo by little pins with glittering silver stars on them. My fingers itch to plunge into that hair and unwind it strand by strand, until the smell of her shampoo fills the world. I don't move. I can't move. Jenny frowns and knocks on the glass again.

I don't answer. Instead, I open the car door and get out, my eyes fixed on her face the whole time. I can see her—fine, the mind plays tricks. I can hear her, I can smell her, and that doesn't prove anything, that doesn't prove anything except that I miss her so badly I can taste it, and every day that I wake up and Jenny's not there is like another needle in my heart. I keep thinking it'll run out of room, and then the morning comes and proves me wrong. She's not real, she can't be real, and I'm going to prove it to myself here and now. I'm going to—

My hand catches her wrist. Her skin is cool, like she's been standing outside without a coat for too long, but it's still her skin, soft and familiar and real. My breath catches in my throat. I try to speak. Nothing happens, and Jenny daintily pulls herself free.

"You haven't answered," she says.

"Jenny, God, what is going on here?" I grab for her again, but she's too quick for me—she steps back and out of the range of my questing fingers, leaving them to close on empty air. "Why are you doing this? Do your parents know that you're not dead? Why are you hiding?"

"Because all I'm doing is asking for a ride home, and I'm only doing it because you keep coming here and wanting me to," she replies. She looks at me, eyes wide and sad and pleading, and I know the truth. There's no other explanation. "I died, Leigh. I died, and you didn't get me home. Even though you promised. You didn't get me home."

"I'll get you home, I promise." I'm making promises I can't keep—I'm making promises to a dead girl, and I've seen enough horror movies to know that this is a terrible idea, but fuck, what do I care? A week ago I was thinking about killing myself. At least this way I'll do something useful with what's left of my life. Any promise in the world is worth making, if I'm making it to Jenny.

"You can try," she says, and disappears, leaving the scent of vanilla in her wake. Vanilla, and something darker, something wet and green and old, like the moss that grows on gravestones.

Somehow, I'm not surprised when I turn around and find her sitting in the car, belt already buckled, hands folded primly in her lap. This is a dream, I think, and I'm opening the car door, I'm sliding back into my seat, and Jenny is there, Jenny with her corsage on her wrist and a sad, distant look on her face. This is a dream, and I never want to wake up again.

"Drive, Leigh," she says, and there's a sudden tension in her voice, like she wants to say so much more, but she doesn't know how. "You have to drive, or I can't stay."

"What?"

"Drive."

There's no denying the urgency in the word, and so I start the engine and hit the gas, and we're rolling, moving away from the cemetery and starting on the long road back to Jenny's house. She

SEANAN McGUIRE

lives—she lived, she's dead, and I can't let myself forget that, not even with her sitting next to me, the smell of her vanilla perfume rolling through the cab like a storm front—on the other side of town. We have twenty miles to go, and that's if I take the short way.

She never said I had to do that. I turn left when I should have turned right, going for the route we always used to take when we were thinking that maybe a brief stop by the side of a wooded road would be a good way to spend a little of the afternoon.

Jenny is silent for the first part of the drive. I glance her way, but her attention is on the window, watching as the housing developments that ring the town like mushrooms melt away into forest, the semi-untouched wood that still owns this part of the state. If it weren't for her perfume, I'd think I was hallucinating. Maybe I could still be hallucinating. Do hallucinations have a scent?

I'm mulling that over when Jenny says, in a small, wounded voice, "You were supposed to drive me home. That was the deal, when my parents said that I could go to the dance with you. You told my father you would get me home by midnight. Remember? You promised."

I glance at her, startled, and startle myself all over again when she fills my field of vision, Jenny in her moonlight dress, Jenny with her golden hair, Jenny not under the ground and filling the bellies of a million worms. "I didn't mean to have an accident. You should have been wearing your belt," I say. The words are mulish, sullen; they fall into the space between us like clots of earth onto her grave.

"It scared me when I saw Tyler hitting you," she says and turns away from me, looking out the window. "He was so much bigger than you were, and he'd been drinking, and I just wanted to get away before somebody got hurt. I knew it would piss him off, seeing us there, and I didn't care, because I loved you. I should have cared. All-American boys get the All-American girls, right? That's what the Founding Fathers died for." Scorn drips from her voice. I flinch from it. I can't help myself. "I knew it was stupid. I knew I should have yelled for one of the chaperones and told them that we wanted to stay, and that he needed to go. But I was so mad. You made me so mad, Leigh. Why couldn't you keep your temper for just one night? It was supposed to be our night."

"I'm sorry," I say, and it's small, and it's stupid, and it's not enough.

"So am I," says Jenny.

She doesn't say another word during the drive. I have to look away from her when I turn onto her street—it's an unprotected left, if I watched my dead girlfriend, I'd be joining her in the ground—and when I look back, Jenny's gone, leaving only the faint scent of vanilla and the feeling that I've lost her all over again.

I drive by her house without slowing down. There's nothing for me there.

Nothing at all.

JANUARY

It's apparently been long enough since the funeral for public opinion to have shifted. I come back from Christmas break and the shrines to Jenny are gone, and the plans for the prom theme to match her homecoming dress have all been forgotten, replaced by something cliché about Greek gods and the beauty of Olympus. I should be happy. I'm not being reminded of Jenny every time I turn a corner or go into the school office. Instead, rage paces and snarls under my sternum like a captive animal. How dare they forget about her? How dare they go on with their lives like nothing has changed? Jenny is dead. She's not coming back to school tomorrow, or the next day, or ever, and it's not right for them to let go of her like this.

The school counselor says this is healthy. Says they're "moving on" and "coming to terms," and that maybe it's time my parents start paying for some independent counseling services for me since it's pretty clear she's not going to be able to help me properly through my grief—not with me refusing to let go of Jenny's memory. I call her a bitch and get thrown out of her office with a week's detention and a letter to take home to my mother. I should probably feel bad about that. I can't find the energy. I'm walking through a school that was haunted by Jenny only a few weeks ago, and now seems content to go on as if she'd never existed.

Three months: that's apparently the lifespan of teenage grief. That's how long our fickle hearts are meant to hold on to someone who's not there anymore. Anything more than that is cause for concern.

Poor, absent Tyler is the new darling of the student body. Tyler, the football hero who may never play again; Tyler, who was just trying to have a good time when he got drunk and crashed into my car, killing my girlfriend almost instantly; Tyler, who was the sort of guy every one of us should aspire to be.

I'm starting to think about murder.

I'm thinking about murder when I park at the curb in front of the cemetery, my hands resting lightly on the wheel and my eyes fixed on the middle distance, visions of Tyler's tortured face dancing like sugarplums through my daydreams. There's no rap on the window, but there's the smell of vanilla, and the sudden, definite feeling that I am not alone in the car. I start the engine before I turn to flash a smile at Jenny, and say, "I'm happy to give you a ride home."

"This isn't healthy," says Jenny, a frown on her face and a curl of golden hair hanging across her forehead like a banner. "You shouldn't still be showing up here."

"Why wouldn't I?" I pull away from the curb, turning my attention back to the road at the last possible moment. I don't want to take my eyes away from her, but I'm coming to learn the rules of our monthly encounters: I have to drive. That's what matters more than anything else. "You need a ride home. I promised."

"Leigh…"

"How could I live with myself if I knew you weren't at peace because I broke my word to you?"

"But I'm not at peace, Leigh." She sounds like she's in pain. I start to take my foot off the gas, automatically turning to reach for her and try to hug that pain away. I see her face when she recoils, when she cries, "Drive! You have to drive!"

My foot presses down almost of its own accord. The car lurches forward, my heart pounding against my ribs, and for a moment, I think this is it: this is how I die.

But the moment passes, and the car is back under my control, and we're rolling easy down the road as Jenny says, "I can't rest in peace. You won't let me. Everyone else is starting to let go, they're starting to ease up on my memory—even my parents. And then there's you."

"I miss you." The words are small and stupid and big enough to encompass the entire world. I miss her. That's all that I'm capable of doing anymore.

"You have to let me go."

"Or what?"

"Or this keeps happening over and over again," she says. "I keep showing up. You keep driving me home. I keep disappearing. Over and over."

"For how long?"

"I don't know. Forever, I guess."

I think about that as I drive, the streets melting away around us. The air in the cab smells like vanilla. At some point Jenny realizes I'm not going to say anything else, and she turns on the radio, spinning through the stations until she finds a channel that's playing the kind of music she likes, all soft country ballads and too much auto-tune. One of her favorite bands is on, performing a song that hadn't been released yet when she died. She makes a small, wordless sound of delight, and that's it: that seals the deal. I love her and I want her to rest easy, but that doesn't mean I can let her go. Not yet. Maybe not ever.

"I'll have their new album when I pick you up next month," I say, as we turn onto her street. "You can listen to it during the drive."

"Leigh—"

"I'm sorry you're not resting in peace. But I'm not resting in peace either, so at least we can not rest in peace together for a little while longer. If that's selfish, I don't really care. I miss you too much. I can't just stop."

Her hand touches my cheek, fingers cool. I don't turn. I don't want to see her disappear.

"I love you," she says.

"I love you too," I answer, and she's gone, and I drive past her house without slowing down or stopping. Forever is a long time. I'm not sure it would be long enough.

FEBRUARY

Now they say that love is ended by betrayal or the grave,

SEANAN McGUIRE

And they tell me to give up on her, the one I couldn't save,
But I'll do as much for my true love as any lover known—
I will know no rest or solace 'til I'm taking Jenny home.

§

Valentine's Day without Jenny is another word for Hell. I stay home sick, choosing another black mark on my attendance record over the school halls festooned with paper hearts and filled with girls giggling over their discount chocolates and wilting roses. Two weeks later, when Jenny appears in front of the cemetery, there's a bouquet of daisies—her favorite flower—waiting for her on the dashboard, along with the CD I promised her.

She's still my Valentine. Death doesn't change that.

Death doesn't really change anything.

MARCH

It's been four months since Jenny died, and I'm starting to think about the mechanics of suicide. It can't be that hard to kill somebody, can it? Tyler managed it, and Tyler's a dumb jock with more muscles than brains. Or he was, anyway; they still don't know whether he's ever going to wake up, and even if he does, there's no way of knowing whether he'll ever walk again. His football career is over, buried alongside Jenny's body, and that might be a comfort to me if I didn't miss her so goddamn much, if his teammates didn't glare at me when they pass me in the halls, like I was the one who suggested he try to put the make on my girlfriend at the homecoming dance. None of this was my idea, I want to scream. None of this is the way that I wanted my junior year of high school to go. But try telling them that. Too many words, too many syllables, too many concepts for their atrophied little brains. Tyler, Jenny, and I wound up in a weird sort of triangle on the night of the dance, two of us competing for one girl, and now Jenny's dead and Tyler's in a coma and I'm still here, which makes me the perfect target.

I guess if I were as suicidal as I feel I'd bait them and let them beat me to death behind the school. At least that way they'd get punished for it, and I'd finally get to stop living in a world that doesn't have Jenny in it anymore.

…but I don't really live in that world, do I? I just exist there. It's four months since Jenny's funeral, and here I am again, parked in front of the cemetery, waiting.

The sun reaches the horizon and again, Jenny—Jenny in her moonlight gown, Jenny with her golden hair, and her corsage still fresh on her wrist. Mine is just so many fallen petals now, sitting in a dish next to my bed where the smell can chase me down into my dreams. Jenny, looking at me with fond exasperation, one satin-toed foot tapping on the grassy knoll.

"Again, Leigh?" she asks, and before I can answer her, she chases the question with a question, asking, "Can I get a ride home?"

"Always," I say, and then she's in the car, appearing like a miracle, and my foot is on the gas, and everything is right with the world. As long as I'm with Jenny, everything is fine.

Again, I take the long way back to her house, choosing more time with her over the expediency of city streets. It's better this way, I tell myself, and I realize I actually mean it: if this is a dream, I know it'll end when I make the final turn onto her block, and if it's not a dream—if my dead girlfriend is really riding in my front seat like this sort of thing happens every day—then the last thing I want is for someone to see us. They might react the same way I did, with confusion and disbelief and denial. Or they might decide I didn't deserve this, and give someone else the task of driving Jenny home.

"Tyler's still in a coma, you know," I say, because I have to say something; I have to fill the silence between us with words, or it's going to drown me. "They're not sure whether he's ever going to wake up again."

"Good," she spits, with such venom that it startles me. "He deserves to be caught that way. Not living, not dead. Just lost, for as long as their machines can keep him there."

I worry my lip between my teeth before asking, "You really mean that?"

"Yes," she says, and "no," she says, and "I would be here with you if it weren't for him. I would be here with my family. Really here, I mean, with skin and bones and a heartbeat, not drifting through every time I need someone to drive me home. I'd

SEANAN McGUIRE

be getting older. You know, I read this book once, about a unicorn who'd been turned into a human? And she hated it. She said that she could feel her body dying all around her. I know what she meant now, Leigh, and I miss it. I miss the feeling of my body dying, because it meant that I had a body that could die. It meant that I was real. More than just a memory. It meant I belonged to the world. I'm never going to have that again, and it's all Tyler's fault."

There are so many words that it's almost overwhelming. It takes me a moment to process them all, and we're moving the whole time, getting closer and closer to the point where she leaves me again. I want to ask the best question in the world, I want to stun her with how well I understand, but when I open my mouth, what comes out is, "So stay."

"I can't," she says. "I'm dead, remember?"

There's laughter in her voice, and pain too, like she likes remembering what she is as little as I like being reminded of it. I don't say anything, but I hit the gas just a little harder, and neither one of us says anything for the rest of the drive.

It's just like before. I turn onto her street, and the smell of vanilla fills the car, and when I turn to look at her, she's gone like she was never there. I may as well have been driving a hallucination across the city. I pull up to a stop sign and lean over to touch the seat. It's warm. She was there enough to warm up the seat with the body that she doesn't have.

Maybe that means something.

I hold that thought firmly as I drive myself back home. Jenny could still warm a seat, and maybe that means something...but what, I just don't know.

APRIL

Jenny's already standing on the curb when I pull up, her arms clasped tight around herself like she's cold. I find myself wishing she'd died wearing something warmer, which turns quickly to wishing she'd never died at all, and that's dangerous; that's the kind of thinking I can chase down the rabbit holes of my mind all night long. So I just stop the car and roll down the window and wait for her to ask the question.

"Can I get a ride?"

"Always," I say, and she disappears, leaving me alone. This time, my heart doesn't stop. I've learned enough to know what comes next. I turn, and there she is in the passenger seat, her seatbelt already fastened, a smile on her perfect lips. Trying to be casual, I say, "You look good today."

"One good thing about death: no more bad hair days," she says with a laugh that isn't a laugh at all, more a close cousin to a sob. Kissing cousin, even, the two so tangled together that I couldn't pry them apart if I tried. "I'm really glad I like this dress."

"I wonder if that's what you'd be wearing if they'd buried you in something else." The words are thoughtless. I cringe.

Jenny doesn't seem to mind. If anything, she looks relieved. She's been dead for six months, and this is the first time I've talked to her like that mattered at all, like it changed anything about our relationship, apart from how often we get to see each other. "I think so," she says. "It's different for everybody, but most of the ghosts I've met have been wearing something that really mattered to them when they were alive. Lots of wedding gowns, tuxedos, graduation robes…this was the prettiest dress I ever owned. It only makes sense that I'd be wearing it now."

"I'd say that wearing it made you the prettiest girl in the world, but you didn't need a dress for that."

Jenny laughs without the sob this time, and leans forward to turn on the radio. "Just drive," she says.

So I do, and everything is perfect, and I could go on like this forever, just me and Jenny and our monthly date, her in her homecoming dress, me in whatever I threw on that day, driving into eternity.

MAY

Now they say that love is something you'd be lucky to forget,
But I say that I was lucky on the day that we first met,
And I'll do as much for my true love as any lover known —
I will roam the lonesome highways 'til I'm bringing Jenny home.

§

The halls are buzzing with the news that Tyler—elevated in his absence to young god, deified like Jenny was, but without the absence of flesh to allow his memory to erode—has started responding to treatment. Why, he opened his eyes yesterday, which is nothing short of a miracle as far as his legion of adoring fans is concerned. If this continues, he could actually wake up soon! Imagine! Tyler, All-American high school god, walking among us mere mortals like we have the right to glory in his physical presence and breathe his rarified air!

It makes me want to vomit, or punch someone, or scream. But all these things are anti-social, and the school counselors are still watching me more closely than I like, since apparently my inability to "move on" from the death of the first girl I ever loved means that I'm a potential suicide risk or school shooter or something. I'm not really clear on what the problem is, and no one else seems to be either. They just know I'm not fitting easy into their pre-fab high school mold anymore, and so they watch me, and they wait for me to make a mistake.

Tyler's name is on everyone's lips today, even the teachers, who urge us to focus on our studies because "that's what Tyler would want us to do." By seventh period, I've had enough, and when my history teacher invokes Tyler's name in an effort to quiet us down, I stick my hand in the air and ask, "Do you think Tyler was quiet when he was committing vehicular manslaughter? Or do you think he had time to scream at the sight of Jenny's corpse before his brain damage kicked in?"

I'm sent to the principal's office for my trouble, a red detention slip clutched in my hand, and it's not until I see the sun setting through the study hall window that I realize what this means—that I won't reach the cemetery until hours after I usually arrive. I bolt to my feet.

"Sit down, Miss Winslow!" barks the Vice-Principal, and my knees buckle, years of trained obedience ordering me back into my seat before my conscious mind is invited to the party. I shoot another panicked glance at the window, but it's too late, it's too late; the sun is dipping down below the horizon. I don't know much about the strange dance that I've been locked in since homecoming, and still something tells me that this is a line that should never have been crossed. She appears at sunset. Well, the sun has set, and when I reach the cemetery, Jenny won't be waiting.

Even knowing that, I run for my car as soon as we're released, breaking speed laws all the way down to the cemetery gates. But Jenny isn't there. I stay until midnight, listening to her favorite CD over and over again and praying to a god I don't entirely believe in, and Jenny never comes. I broke the rules. I broke the chain.

What if Jenny never comes again? What am I going to do then?

JUNE

I skip school on the day Jenny's due to appear, even knowing she won't be there until sunset. I missed her once. I can't run the risk of missing her again. Not when we only get one night a month, and that night is limited to however long it takes to drive from the cemetery to her house—not exactly the kind of dates I used to lay awake dreaming about. I haven't kissed her since the night she died. I ache to hold her in my arms, kiss her cheek, and tell her how much I've missed her, how much I miss her every single day. But if I can't do that, I can at least do this; I can be here, I can wait for her until she comes.

I have to move the car three times when the security guard comes by and gives me the hairy eyeball, suspicion written plainly on his face. What's a chubby teenage girl in a beat-up Volvo doing parked in front of their cemetery? What mischief am I planning?

No mischief, sir, I want to say, but I can't imagine he'd take well to being told that I was just here to pick up my girlfriend, who's been dead for seven months—don't worry, she looks just fine, on account of how she doesn't have a body anymore. I'd be lucky if he called the cops. It's more likely he'd call the local loony bin, and I'd be hauled away by men in white coats, screaming for my ghost girlfriend all the while. No. Nuh-uh. I don't have time to be committed, and so I move the car again and again, wasting gas and wasting time as I wait for the magic moment when Jenny will appear.

Then I'm coming around the corner and there she is, blazing

up in the headlights like a fairy tale princess, all moonlight gold and helpless longing. I stop the car, roll down the window, look out at her, and smile.

"Hey," I say. "You need a ride?"

I'm trying to sound cool and smooth and like the sort of person who belongs in a place like this. All I really manage is sounding like my dorky self. Jenny still smiles as she walks toward the car. That's all the validation I need.

"Where were you last month, Leigh?" she asks. "I thought maybe you were getting over me."

"That's never going to happen," I say. "I had detention." She disappears, and then she's in the car with me, and my heart hurts from the reality of her. I know that what I have to say will hurt her, but I have to say it anyway. "Tyler's waking up."

Jenny goes still, and it's not until that moment that I realize she isn't breathing, she's never been breathing, not any of the times I've seen her or any of the nights when I've driven her home. The realization changes something. It's like for the first time I can't pretend that she's not dead, not on any level. There is only one living body in this car, only one person who's getting older, only one unicorn trapped in a human form. The other person, the Jenny-shaped person…she's dead and gone, she's dwindling into dust underground, and she's never coming back to me. This is the closest we're ever going to get, these strange moments of stolen time in my car.

"He shouldn't get to wake up," she says finally. There's a bitterness in her voice that runs all the way down to the bone, the kind of dark, resentful hatred that used to be reserved for people who abused animals or argued against gay marriage. I bite my lip and keep driving, not wanting to see the look on her face as she continues, "I didn't get to wake up. Why should he?"

"He may never walk again."

"Well isn't that a shame—oh, wait. I'm definitely never going to walk again because I'm dead, and it's his fault, and I can't even rest easy in my grave and forget about all this, because you won't let me go. So what do you want me to do, Leigh? Be happy for him? Oh, hooray, the man who killed me is waking up, and maybe his life's been changed forever, but it's still a life. He still gets to have a life. He gets to grow up and get old and I get to keep asking you to drive me home. How is that fair?"

"It's not," I say quietly.

"Then what are you going to do about it?" There's a challenge in her voice that I don't know quite how to answer, and so I don't. I just drive her home.

What else am I supposed to do?

JULY

Well, I'm supposed to commit murder, for one thing.

It's a little surprising that I didn't think of it sooner, but as the days stretch out and the school year winds to an end, the thought preys on me more and more often. How hard could it be, really, to kill someone who's bedridden, slipping in and out of consciousness, and incapable of fighting back? Not that hard. Getting to him is going to be the difficult part...and wouldn't it make Jenny happy to know that I loved her enough to kill for her? I want to see her smile, really smile, just one more time. And not just from her memorial page in the yearbook, where they've used a picture of her in her homecoming dress—the only dress she has anymore—and her corsage. None of the pictures in her memorial collage have me in them. Without Jenny and the cheerleading squad to drag me into the school's social limelight, I'm fading from everyone's memory, another high school weirdo worthy only of dismissal.

Maybe that's a good thing, given what I'm planning to do.

It wasn't a plan at first, just an idle thought, a continuation of that half-conversation that I hadn't been able to finish with Jenny. But it's grown, bit by bit, into something bigger and more powerful than it was when it began. Tyler killed Jenny. Tyler doesn't deserve to have any kind of a life, not when Jenny doesn't get to. Tyler needs to die, and if I want to show her that I'm still a good girlfriend, I need to be the one who kills him. It's as simple as that.

I don't say anything when I go to pick her up; I just smile, and hand her a copy of the yearbook so she can see all the nice things people said about her after she was gone and in the ground, and then I drive her home. It's the least that I can do, all things considered.

AUGUST

Jenny, I was foolish, I was selfish, I'm ashamed,
And I'm praying you'll forgive me, though I know I should be blamed,
For I'll do as much for my true love as any lover known—
I will never know salvation 'til I'm taking Jenny home.

§

Tyler has his own room—naturally he does, his parents have money and they've never been shy about spending it on their only beloved son. That makes things a little easier. Finding it is easy; our classmates have sent offerings of flowers and stuffed toys in such great numbers that when I walk up to the admission desk with a bouquet of roses in my hands, the nurse barely even looks up from her romance novel before spitting out his room number, three little digits that don't seem like nearly enough information to lead me to murder. But there they are, and there I go, walking down the hall unquestioned, the roses in my hands somehow serving as an all-access pass.

I've heard they don't allow flowers in the ICU, but apparently, Tyler's far enough along the road to recovery that they've moved him into a lower security grade. That, too, works in my favor.

His door isn't locked. Three strikes, Tyler, you're out.

The room is dim and quiet, save for the soft, steady rasp of the machines that keep him alive. He's a wasted skeleton of a man, all that football muscle melted away to reveal the scarecrow that was sleeping for so long inside his skin. I stop at the foot of the bed, looking at him. Maybe this isn't about unicorns at all; maybe this is some kind of strange *Wizard of Oz* parable with Jenny just trying to get home and Tyler trapped in the echoing cavern of his own mind. I can't decide whether that makes me the Lion or the Tin Man. Am I looking for courage or am I wishing for a heart?

Now that I'm here, I don't know what to do. I don't have a syringe; I can't inject air bubbles into his arm like they do on Dad's crime shows, and I wouldn't know how to do it even if I could. I'd put a pillow over his face, but he has machines to do his breathing for him, and I'm pretty sure they'd start beeping like crazy if I pulled them loose.

The door opens and closes behind me. "More flowers?" asks an unseen woman. "Well, put them with the rest. Poor boy's lucky he doesn't have allergies. That would just be one more problem on top of a mountain of them."

"Is...is he going to be okay?" I'm not really concerned about Tyler's welfare—I'm not—but I'd expected him to look more like, well, himself. A great big bear of a teenage boy, briefly bedridden, gathering the strength to jump right back into his life. Not this wasted bundle of bones and sickness.

"That depends on how you measure 'okay,' I suppose." The owner of the voice is a middle aged woman in pale pink scrubs. She takes the flowers from my hands, apparently able to sense that I can't bring myself to move. "Is he going to live? At this point, the prognosis is good. His folks have paid for the very best care, and he's got a strong will. He's stubborn. Stubbornness counts for a lot in cases like these. But is he ever going to walk again? Throw a pass or kick a ball or anything like that? No, I don't think that's likely."

"Oh." I pause then, frowning. "Should you be telling me this?"

"A pretty little thing like you only sneaks into a hospital with a bunch of flowers for two reasons: love or hate. I read the papers. I know which one it is." The nurse looks over her shoulder at me as she sets my roses down amongst the rest. "She won't rest any easier if you kill him, and neither will you. Are you sticking to the rules? Do you drive her home when she asks you to?"

My throat is a thin straw through which only air can pass. I squeak a few times, trying to speak, and finally settle for a nod.

"That's good. Have you tried to kiss her?"

I've dreamt about it. That isn't the same thing. I shake my head.

The nurse nods approvingly. "That's good. That's real good. It's not safe for a girl like you to be kissing a girl like her. There are consequences, when the living love the dead. Now I'm going to ask you one more question, and I'll thank you to find your voice, since your answer is going to determine whether or not I call for security. I'm assuming you came here to kill this boy. You can go ahead and correct me if I'm wrong, but that's not my question. Are you still planning to try?"

"N-no, ma'am," I manage. "He shouldn't be alive when Jenny's not, but it's not my place to change that. I guess the worst thing I can do to him is leave him alive."

"Good girl." She smiles at me, and then glances meaningfully to the clock above the door. "You'd better hurry if you want to pick her up on time."

I want to stay and ask her what she knows about ghosts, how she understands my arrangement with Jenny...who she's been driving home. But she's right; the sun will be down soon, and if I want to make it to the cemetery, I need to go, and I don't really want to be here, in this room where time is rotting on the vine. So I turn and run, leaving the hospital, leaving Tyler to his own living hell, and it's not until Jenny is sliding into her place beside me that I really wonder what that nurse knew, or why she asked if I'd been trying to kiss my girl.

I go back to the hospital the next day. The nurse I met in Tyler's room isn't there.

Somehow, that's not really a surprise.

SEPTEMBER

School starts up again in an explosion of cheerleaders and football players wearing orange and green uniforms and smiles like they just won the universal lottery. It's freshmen slinking in the halls and sophomores seeming suddenly easy in their skins, it's juniors with their chests puffed up with upperclassman pride and seniors smiling beatifically, rulers of their small, time-delineated kingdom. It's all so stupid, and there was a time when I would have loved it. I would have been walking in formation with the rest of the cheerleaders, Jenny by my side, and we would have been queens of the world. Homecoming last year was supposed to be our grand declaration of love, and by now, everyone would have been used to the idea that we were together. We could have had one perfect year of high school, me and Jenny, Jenny and me.

Instead, I'm just another nobody at the edge of the crowd, wondering why this ever seemed to matter. All the memorials to Jenny are gone, and there's a whole new class of freshmen who never knew her, and will never know that they're supposed to miss her. Summer has restored the campus, sweeping its ghosts away, and now I'm the only one who's haunted.

I don't know how long I can live like this.

I'm still dwelling on that when it comes time to pick Jenny up again; she slides into the car, all vanilla and moonlight, and asks, "Well? How's senior year?"

She still loves the idea of the future we crafted for ourselves, back when we were lying on our backs behind the tumbling mats, hands entangled, and both of us were breathing. I shake my head and start the car. "Same shit, different semester," I say. And then, because the question is burning me, I ask, "Why am I not allowed to kiss you?"

Jenny is silent.

"I mean, I get to drive you home. I know you're solid. I've touched your hands and seen you hold things. So why can't I kiss you? What makes it so wrong to want to kiss my girlfriend?"

"I'm dead, Leigh." Her voice is the whispering of wind among the gravestones, barely audible, impossible to ignore.

"So what? You're still my girl. I'm not giving up on you."

"I'm dead, and you're not."

I've thought about changing that so many times. "And?"

"And if I kissed you, it would…" Jenny sighs. "Everything dies, Leigh. Everything. But some things make you die faster."

"Like kissing dead girls?"

"Like kissing dead girls." Jenny reaches over and touches my hand, gentle as a promise, cruel as a prayer. "Homecoming is next month. I've been buried for almost a year. Don't you think it's time you let me go?"

I don't answer her because that question is every answer I've been seeking for the last eleven months. "I think it's time that something changed, yeah," I say, and we drive on.

OCTOBER

My tuxedo still fits. Grief either bulks you up or slims you down, and I guess I've gone for the latter—too many days when I couldn't bring myself to eat, too many nights spent crying until I threw up. It was a little snug when I wore it the first time and now it's a little loose, but I look okay. I think Jenny will appreciate it.

SEANAN McGUIRE

"Are you going to homecoming?" asks Mom when she sees me coming down the stairs. She sounds surprised and maybe a little hopeful, like this is a sign that things are changing for the better.

"Yeah." Homecoming isn't tonight—it's always on a Saturday, and it's only Monday now—but this is the anniversary of Jenny's death, and I don't feel like correcting my mother. I finish descending the stairs and press a kiss against her cheek, sweeter than a note left on my dresser, crueler than an explanation. I don't think there's any way to explain what I've decided to do. "Don't wait up, okay?"

"I won't," she says, relief plain on her face. "Who's the lucky girl?"

"It's a surprise." My new boutonniere is already pinned to the front of my tuxedo. I figure Jenny doesn't need a corsage—she still has hers from last year—but I bought her daisies, just to make the symbolism clear.

"Have fun tonight."

"I will." I should feel bad, I know I should, but I can't. There's nothing for me here, and I still have to keep my promise. I have to finish driving Jenny home.

I pull up to the cemetery just as the sun is starting to go down, and Jenny's there, my Jenny, in her dress like moonlight. She gasps a little when I get out of the car and she sees me in my tuxedo. That's what I was hoping for, that moment of shock, when she's too busy staring to react as I stride toward her, the daisies held out in my hand.

"These are for you," I say, pressing them into her hands. She takes them—she's solid, she's solid, because she's holding the flowers—and is still looking at them when I lean forward and press my lips to hers.

She still tastes like vanilla lip gloss, but there's something else there, something dark and sad and dry as dust. She pulls back, eyes wide and filled with dismay. "Do you know what you've done?" she demands, and I do know, I do know what I've done.

So I smile and say, "Too late now," and this time when I kiss her, she doesn't pull away. We'll get into the car soon; I'll drive her home, and this time, when whatever happens, happens, I won't survive. That's all right. That's what I wanted.

I made her a promise, after all. I promised that I'd get her all the way home.

§

Jenny, darling Jenny, there is no need to explain,
I have seen your lonely graveside, I have waited in the rain,
And I'll do as much for my true love as any lover known—
Though my family will grieve me, I'll be driving Jenny home.

On...The Unquiet Grave

The Unquiet Grave is Child Ballad 78, Roud #51. Child wrote that, like Sweet William's Ghost, it sprang from the belief that excessive grieving for the dead would disturb their repose.

Child quotes many traditions that believed too many tears or too much mourning by the living would hurt the dead. In Scotland there is a story where a sister cried night after night for her brother. He finally appeared and reprimanded her for the "extravagance" of her sorrow and its "rebellion" against the decrees of Providence. He told her that every tear made him cold and weighed him down. Child also cites a story in the Grimm records of a child coming to its mother and asking her to stop her tears because they make him wet and he cannot sleep. She stops and he later returns to inform her he's now dry and at peace.

In what is the strictest ban against grief, Child wrote that the ancient Persians forbid weeping for the dead. It was against the express command of the Almighty and as such was a heinous sin and caused the dead to be trapped in a river, where they constantly experienced the "agony" of drowning.

The plot of the ballad has someone (male or female) mourn on the grave of their love for a year and a day. At the end of that time, the dead love appears and asks why they are not being allowed to rest. The mourner requests a kiss good-bye to which the corpse replies that their breath smells foul and if you kiss me you will soon join me. (1)

The Unquiet Grave has been sung by the British folk band Lau, by Ween, as well as by Joan Baez, Kate Rusby, Bobby McMillon, and The Dubliners. Composer Ralph Vaughan Williams wrote several arrangements for the song.

1) Child, Francis James. The English and Scottish Popular Ballads Vol. 2. Mineola: Dover, 2003.

HOLLOW IS THE HEART

BY
SIMON R. GREEN

B radford-on-Avon is an old town, in an old country. Sick and feverish with centuries of history. And some things older than history. Older, and more foul.

My name is Jason Grant, and if there were any justice in this world, you'd already know my name. My books would be everywhere, my name on everyone's lips, and my face on all the chat shows. Instead, I make a precarious living researching dubious articles for partwork magazines, and generally hacking it out for pitiful returns. I grub about for work wherever I can find it, cranking it out by the yard to pay the bills. It's been a long time since I've written anything just to satisfy my soul.

I did write a whole bunch of novels and screenplays, but nobody wanted them. I was a journalist, once, doing my bit for a small but respected local paper, the *Wiltshire Record and News*. But that was then, and this is now. I finally have a story worth the telling. A story to prise open the eyes of the world, and make them see things in a whole new way if only I dared submit it. It has been made very clear to me that silence and obscurity are the price of my survival. But I'm not sure I care anymore.

It all started when I made one last attempt to get my old job back.

I sat in the outer office of the *Wiltshire Record and News*, waiting to see the editor. Being calm and quiet and not making any trouble, playing the part of the prodigal son and the penitent return. Returned to the scene of my crime, like a dog to its vomit, to beg a few crumbs from the editor's table because my cupboard was bare, and I was getting hungry. My old boss, Samantha Walsh: editor, publisher and Conscience in Chief of the local weekly rag. There was no way in hell she was ever going to give me my old job back, I knew that. But if I could just get my foot in the door, hold her attention with some fast talking... I might yet walk out of here with a story assignment. Do a good enough job, and it could lead to regular work. And I wanted that.

Not a staff position, obviously, but a local stringer with local connections is always going to be a useful asset. The odds were stacked against me. I couldn't have blotted my copybook more thoroughly the last time I was here if I'd pissed in the printer's ink.

I sat politely on my fiendishly uncomfortable visitor's chair and glowered at the clock on the wall. The editor was deliberately keeping me waiting, to make sure I understood my place in the scheme of things. That I was not needed, or even welcome. Everywhere I looked in the outer office, something old and familiar looked back at me. It was as though I'd never been away. The same dreary old fittings and furnishings, cheap but durable. The carpet worn thin from people pacing up and down as they waited to be summoned into the inner sanctum to learn their fate. Dusty plastic venetian blinds at the windows, cutting the sunshine into strips. The same framed front pages proudly displayed on the walls; names and faces and news from a time when people actually read the paper to learn what they needed to know. Significant stories and excited headlines, forgotten moments from the county's past, going all the way back to the First World War

I sat forward in my chair and stared at the floor. So I wouldn't have to look at anything else. There had been a time... when this had felt like home.

There's nothing like visiting an old haunt to make you feel old and unwanted. The surroundings might not have changed, but I had. I look back at the person I was then, and I barely recognise him. I looked at my reflection in the long mirror on the other side of the room. A man in his late thirties who looked older. Thinning hair and a hard-used face, more than a little scruffy. I should have shaved before I came out or at least found the time to force a comb through my hair. But it had been a long time since anyone cared what I looked like, including me.

The door to the inner office opened suddenly, and the editor glared at me. As though I was the one who'd kept her waiting. She nodded briefly as though she didn't trust herself to speak, then turned around and stomped back to sit behind her editor's desk. Her place of power. Leaving me to trail into the inner office after her and shut the door very quietly and politely behind me. Being careful not to slouch. She always used to yell at me when she caught me slouching. There was a time I could have got away with it, but not now. I sat down on the bare wooden chair set out before her desk piled high, as always, with papers overflowing her In and Out trays. She just sat there and waited for me to speak. Because, after all, I was the one who wanted something from her.

Samantha Walsh was middle-aged with prematurely grey hair and deep lines etched around her eyes and mouth. She dressed neatly and conservatively, in a way that didn't so much ignore fashion as bypass it completely. The ultimate authority figure, the iron hand in the iron glove. Who'd spent so much time occupying the moral high ground, it was a wonder she didn't get nose bleeds from the altitude. I was amazed she could even see us poor mortals down below. The editor fixed me with her usual steely gaze, and I gave her my best respectful smile.

"Hello, Sam. Been a while, hasn't it...?"

"It's Ms. Walsh to you, Grant, and don't you forget it. You have no friends here. And sit up straight. You make the place look untidy."

So that was how it was going to be. I sat up straighter, squared my shoulders, and did my best to look like a professional. The editor sniffed as though reluctantly giving me credit for trying.

"All right, Grant. I read your e-mail. You haven't forgotten how to grab a reader's attention, I'll give you that. So against all my better judgment, I'll admit I'm intrigued. Hit me with your proposal, but make it quick and succinct. I've got a paper to run and a deadline to meet. Just because we're a weekly, it doesn't mean I've got time to waste on the likes of you."

"You'll like this one," I said, doing my best to sound confident. "I've got a new local take on a very old legend. A story that used to be on everyone's lips, in this town and around, that no one has talked about in centuries. I stumbled across this particular piece of

SIMON R. GREEN

local history while looking for something else, which is always the way. I was doing research on a story for *Hidden Worldz* magazine. A story that will not be appearing because the magazine had the bad manners to fold before I could hand it in. Or get paid. Do you remember the old story of the Hollow Women?"

"Refresh my memory," said the editor. Which was her way of saying that she didn't, but was prepared to listen.

"Women who can only be seen, and only appear to have substance, from the front. If you look at them from the back, they're just an empty, hollow husk. A shell of a woman, no depth to her at all. The old legend tells how they prey on young, unattached men. They win the men's hearts and then break them, seduce them and make a child with them to continue their own kind... and then disappear. Always girl children... never been a Hollow Man. These women were predators, giving every appearance of being human. But inside they were empty, emotionless, inhuman.

"Obviously, this was designed as a moral warning for young men back then. Don't go off with strange young women or there might be unfortunate consequences. Avoid shallow types, stick with a real woman and make a commitment to home and family."

"Funny how, in these old stories, it's always the men who have to be warned, and the women who are presented as the villains of the piece," said the editor.

"Well, quite," I said. "The point is, I have uncovered evidence that strongly suggests this old legend had its roots and beginnings right here, in the town. A basis in truth and real history. I started with an old folk song from 1815. 'The Foggy Foggy Dew.' I went jumping from link to link across the Net and ended up with a series of stories coming out of that old disreputable part of Bradford-on-Avon, back when we had real slums. The Hollows. I think... this all goes back to women from the Hollows."

The editor sniffed loudly, but I knew I had her. Sam does love the old folk stories, thinks they're part of what shapes local character. Add a local connection, and she was hooked.

"You might have something there," she conceded. "Not enough for me to offer any advance money, or even a guarantee of publication when the story's completed, but... I am interested. If you do good work on this, turn in something good enough to demand publication... I might be able to do something for you."

"Can't say fairer than that," I said.

"What do you want from me?" said the editor. "Access to the paper's archives?"

"I've already been through the old editions," I said tactfully. "It's all online these days. No, what I need from you is to be able to say I represent the *Wiltshire Record and News*. People will talk to the paper, where they wouldn't talk to me."

"Agreed," said the editor. "On one condition. You work on this story with an assistant I will provide."

I looked at her. I hadn't seen that one coming. "What?"

"Emma Tee. Girl reporter, new to the paper, young and enthusiastic and on her way up. Like you used to be. Work with her. If she can survive you, she'll make a great reporter. And just maybe some of her youthful integrity will rub off on you. But, James, listen to me. The story might be based on a legend, but I expect you to keep your prose tight and factual. No flights of fancy."

"Understood," I said.

"You'd better," said the editor. "Go on. Get out of here. Emma's waiting in the outer office. And be nice to her! Don't frighten her off. Bright, young reporters are getting hard to come by."

She really was waiting for me, sitting in the chair I'd just vacated, reading last week's edition of the paper. I could barely see any of her, behind the *Wiltshire Record and News*. Because she was such a small thing, and the paper remained an old-fashioned broadsheet, despite financial pressures. The editor still believed that readers still believe you can't trust anything you read in a tabloid. *And we*, she was fond of saying, *are the local paper of record. If we say it happened, it happened.*

The paper lowered abruptly, revealing a fresh, young face with a big, beaming smile. The kind that would probably have been irresistible to anyone else. Emma Tee was barely out of her teens with fluffed-out blond hair, a cheerful, young face without even a trace of makeup, shining blue eyes and a sweet demeanour. She was so full of youth and energy I felt old and tired just looking at her.

"Hi!" she said brightly, folding up the paper and tossing it casually to one side. "I'm Emma Tee, and you must be Jason Grant.

Don't worry. I've already been warned about you by practically everybody, so let's just take that as read and move on."

She bounced up out of her chair and extended a small hand for me to shake. I did so solemnly. She still hadn't stopped smiling.

"So!" she said. "What are we, as journalists of record and reporters of fact, doing investigating an old fairy tale?"

"The things we choose to believe," I said carefully, "the stories we cherish and preserve, tell us who and what we really are. That's what makes old folk tales so important. We are going to investigate which local people and conditions gave birth to this particular legend, of the Hollow Women."

"Marvellous!" said Emma. "Where do we start? General search engine or something more specific?"

"I've already tried that," I said. "And beyond the basics... there's nothing there."

"But that's not possible!" said Emma.

"Not on its own," I said. "Which is what started me thinking. Someone seems to have gone to a lot of trouble to erase all but the original story of the Hollow Women. And I want to know why. Some old scandal perhaps? Featuring, or maybe even implicating, some old established families in the town?"

Emma grinned happily. "We can but hope. Nothing like a good local scandal to sell the local paper! How far back do we need to look to get to the beginning of this legend?"

"If I'm right, the eighteenth century," I said. "And for that we need access to the old records, the original sources. The books and papers that make up the church and parish records. The kind of thing you can't erase or delete. I already approached the local church, but the vicar wouldn't talk to me, let alone allow me access to his precious historical archives. Not as long as I was just a local hack. But since we are now official representatives of a respected local paper..."

"Does it have to be the church?" said Emma, her sunny face suddenly clouded. She'd finally stopped smiling. "Don't like churches. They give me the creeps."

"If you want to report the news," I said solemnly, "you have to go where the news is. Or in this case, where the news was."

On the way to the church, I filled Emma in on what I'd

already turned up. A series of stories in the local press, about that most disreputable area, the Hollows. Stories from the eighteenth century, of drunkenness, debauchery and bad behaviour in the streets. Nothing in the least supernatural or fantastical. Just... warnings for men of good character to stay away from the bad women of the Hollows.

The Saint Laurence Church was mostly blocky Norman architecture with later Gothic flourishes, and a handful of stone gargoyles up by the guttering, showing their bare stone arses to the world. The church was surrounded by an old graveyard so packed full of the eternally resting there was no room left for new arrivals. Stones and crosses and monuments were jammed so close together there was hardly any room to pass between them. Wild flowers blossomed in profusion, where they weren't being choked by weeds. I led the way down the narrow gravel path with Emma hanging back and scowling mutinously in the rear.

I couldn't see what the problem was. The sun was shining brightly, and as graveyards went, this one seemed open and cheerful. A pleasant enough setting in which to contemplate eternity. I've always liked graveyards. Always a good place to go teenage drinking, late at night, with a few convivial friends. Secure in the knowledge no one would come barging in to bother you.

The vicar emerged abruptly from among the headstones, and came bustling forward to meet us. Oliver Markham had to be in his late seventies, but he still had a great mane of grey hair, and a bristling grey beard. It gave him something of the air of an Old Testament prophet, somewhat undermined by his cheerful smile and vague eyes. A pleasant enough sort in a dotty and distracted kind of way. He kicked his way through the last few weeds and stepped out onto the gravel path. He remembered meeting me before, but had to be reminded of my name. And he made enough of a fuss over meeting Emma that she quite forgot she didn't want to be there. He went to shake my hand, and only then realised he was still holding the trowel he'd been using for a bit of weeding. He tossed the trowel casually away and made a point of giving me a good hearty handshake. And a more careful one for Emma.

"Well, well, Mister Jason Grant," he said finally. "Back again! Yes, yes... The local archives, isn't it? I'm glad someone's taking an interest in them. They're all stored away in the church basement. Because no one else wants them. I keep hoping the local historical society will take the damned things off my hands and spend the money it will take to preserve them properly. I don't have the budget, you see! No, no... Sorry I had to drive you away, earlier, Mister... Grant! Yes! But I needed to be sure you represented the right sort of people. The archive records are very old, very valuable... and very fragile. So I have to be careful about who gets to see them. Oh yes! As long as they're in the Church they're in my care, you see...."

And yet, all the while he was saying this, he seemed to have trouble concentrating on me. His gaze kept sliding away, to Emma. Which was only natural in that she was a great deal prettier than me, but still...

The vicar finally stopped talking not long after he ran out of things to say and produced a large ring of old-fashioned keys, great solid metal things. He sorted carefully through them, muttering cheerfully to himself until finally he separated out one particular key and presented it to me. Slapping the heavy thing into my palm with enough emphasis to make me wince.

"There you go!" he said happily. "All yours! I'll leave you to it, if you don't mind. All that dust in the basement does terrible things to my sinuses. And I have work to do... work that needs doing... Where did I put my trowel?"

The basement under the church turned out to be a dank and gloomy place with no windows and just the one bare light bulb to push back the heavy shadows. All four walls were covered with shelves, packed full to bursting with old books and folders of even older documents. Some of the folders were labelled or dated, most weren't. More books tottered in piles across the stone floor. Dust and cobwebs to all sides suggested it had been some time since anyone had been down there. Emma didn't like the look or feel of the place, and I didn't blame her. So much history in one place has an oppressive weight.

It took us hours to locate the necessary volumes of town history, written out in longhand in a series of over-sized leather-bound books. Emma and I piled them up on the single reading desk, and then I sat down on the only chair (as the senior partner in this team) and worked my way through the volumes. With Emma standing right behind me, peering over my shoulder, and getting just a bit agitated when I didn't finish reading a page fast enough to suit her. I worked steadily through the old records, making notes where necessary. After a while, Emma started to fidget.

"If someone did go to all the trouble of removing knowledge of the Hollow Women from the Net, why didn't they destroy these old archives as well?"

"Because that might have drawn attention to them?" I said, scowling at the handwritten pages. My eyes ached. "Any attack on local records might make people think there was something important in them... Okay, this is it. A whole series of incidents in the town from the late seventeen hundreds onwards. Reports of certain unruly women from the Hollows preying on unfortunate young men. Taking their innocence and their valuables and sometimes sending them home in just the clothes they stood up in. This is the source of the legend! These terrible predatory women from the Hollows. The Hollow Women!"

"Well, yes," said Emma. "But isn't there anything more recent? You know how Ms. Walsh always wants to tie stories to modern settings and people. Makes it more accessible for today's reader."

To keep her happy (and because she was right, the Editor would want that), I skimmed through the more recent volumes. There were any number of incidents in the Hollows, everything from public drunkenness to open riot... but the stories of the Hollow Women just seemed to fade out. And no matter where I looked, I couldn't turn up any actual names, addresses, or anything that would serve as hard evidence.

Nothing to tie a scandal to any local family name. Unfortunately...

I slammed the final volume shut, sat back in my chair, and stretched my aching back.

"I think we've done all that can be reasonably asked of us," I said. "We've connected the dots and made a reasonable connection. Enough to put together a solid story for our beloved editor."

"It's a good, strong story as far as it goes," Emma said

SIMON R. GREEN

carefully. "But we still need to show a link to the town today. I think we need to pay a visit to what's left of the Hollows. The last mention of the Hollow Women was in the nineteen twenties. There might still be some people living there who heard the stories firsthand from their grandparents. I think we should check this out if only because..."

"Because if we don't, Ms. bloody Walsh will ask why we didn't," I said. "All right, then. To the Hollows it is. I wonder if there's time to buy a Kevlar jacket and update my immunisation shots?"

Of course, the Hollows as such didn't exist anymore. The slums of old were pulled down long ago, replaced by a series of run-down Council houses. Entering the Hollow Estates was like crossing a line into new and dangerous territory. Overgrown lawns with old refrigerators and other large objects just dumped in the gardens. Ugly graffiti on every wall and lots of peeling paint. No attempt to smarten the place up because nobody cared. Small groups of youths lurking around in hoodies, waiting for something to happen. And ready to start something if it didn't. Emma and I were careful to stick to the main roads, and took it in turns to brave the awful gardens, knock on doors, and talk as charmingly as we could to whoever answered. No one wanted to talk to us. They were all suspicious of strangers, particularly snooping strangers. We might be the law or social services or looking for money. We got a lot of doors slammed in our faces, and I would have given up if Emma hadn't been there. But finally, we struck gold in the form of an old woman called Alicia Tiley.

A very old woman who lived alone in a crumbling wreck of a house with far too many cats. She scowled all through Emma's cheery and engaging questions until she realised we were only interested in stories about the Hollows women, and then her head came up and she fixed me with a sharp look before stepping suddenly back, and inviting us in.

The narrow entrance hall smelled of damp. And cats. And damp cats. Dozens of them hurried back and forth, excited by the arrival of strangers, darting between our legs and jumping from one high spot to another. Alicia Tiley led us through into her pokey little parlour, stepping over and around the cats without looking while they did their best to trip us up. The parlour was crowded with all kinds of colourful junk and tatt. It looked like Alicia hadn't thrown away anything in years. She bustled around, making us a cup of tea, while advising us to just turf the cats out of any chair we fancied. The first cat I approached bared its teeth and hissed at me, but Emma chased the animals out of two chairs with effortless efficiency.

I sat down gingerly. The chair smelt very strongly of cats and not in a good way. To take my mind off that, I studied Alicia surreptitiously. She had clearly been a tall woman once, but age and presumably infirmity had bent her right over. She was large-boned, but still slender to the point of scrawny, her hard-edged face more full of character than anything else. She wore her thin grey hair scraped back in a tight bun. Her hands were bent almost into claws by arthritis, but she still managed the tea things easily enough. She moved slowly and steadily, pacing herself, so her strength would still be there when it was needed.

She put an old-fashioned china tea service down on the table before us. I took one look at the state of the cups and decided immediately there was no way I was drinking anything that went in them. Even if it did involve boiling water. Alicia finally finished pouring out the tea, thrust a cup into my hand and Emma's and then lowered herself carefully into a chair facing us.

"The Hollow Women," she said, harshly. "The ruiners of men. Seducers and betrayers. And murderers too, sometimes. If there was a thing that needed keeping quiet. Or men who should have known enough not to go back after them. The Hollow Women could make any man love them and give up their hearts just so they could have the fun of breaking them. Was a time, everyone around here knew, to beware of the Hollow Women. But people forget...

"I lost my dear Jack to them, long and long ago. He was never the same, afterwards. Oh yes... I was young once, and a young man loved me. Until one of them got him... If you want to know the truth, you need to talk to the nuns. They know."

"I'm sorry," I said. "Nuns? Which nuns are these?"

"The Holy Sisters of Saint Baphomet," Alicia said sharply. "You know the ones. They all live together at Barrow Farm, down by the river."

"Oh... yes," I said. "An order of reclusive nuns. They bought Barrow Farm and moved in... how long ago? Must be years..."

"More than twenty years," said Emma. "I'm not surprised you forgot about them. Most people have. They don't get out much."

"I sort of got that, from reclusive," I said.

"They keep themselves to themselves," said Alicia, sipping loudly at her tea. "But there's no denying they know things."

"Why would nuns know anything about the Hollow Women?" said Emma. "One of the few things we know for sure from the old legend was that these women had a violent antipathy for all things religious. And apparently, vice versa. It was always the church who spoke out most strongly against the sinful practices of the Hollows women."

"They know things," Alicia said darkly. "Know thy enemy and all that."

"I still don't think we should go barging in on an order of reclusive nuns," said Emma.

"We're reporters," I said sternly. "And that means we go where the story is."

"Then you can go on your own," said Emma. "Churches are spooky enough. I'm not doing anything that might get a whole bunch of nuns mad at me."

At first, I thought she was joking, but she just sat there stubbornly and refused even to discuss the matter. Alicia looked on, quietly enjoying the argument. So in the end, I got up and left Emma there to see if she could get any useful information out of Alicia. I hated to do it, not least because the editor had made it very clear I was supposed to work this story with Emma, but it wasn't my fault if the little girl reporter couldn't keep up. You have to go where the story leads you.

Barrow Farm was a sprawling old stone building, right on the bank of the River Avon, where it cuts through the centre of the town. No telling how old the place was, but the local creamy grey stone was deeply discoloured from the ravages of time and weather, and the tiled roof looked like it could use some serious repairs. There was no bell at the front door, just a large, black iron knocker in the shape of a wolf's head, the ring hanging from its snarling mouth. Not exactly the most welcoming first impression from a company of nuns. I looked around for signs of life, but there didn't seem to be any. All the windows were covered by heavy wooden shutters as though the nuns felt they were under siege from the modern world and were determined to keep it out.

I banged the iron knocker heartily. It raised a hell of a din, but there was still a really long pause before the door finally opened just enough for a single nun to stare out at me with a cold and entirely unwelcoming gaze. The black robes and starched white wimple gave her a nun's usual anonymity. Her face could have been any age, and the only expression I could read was open disapproval. I nodded and smiled politely, introduced myself, and explained why I was there. The nun showed no interest at all, until I mentioned the Hollow Women. She fixed me with a firm stare and then opened the door wider.

"I am Sister Joan. I know the story of the Hollow Women. We all do. We are the Holy Sisters of Saint Baphomet and sin is our business." She smiled briefly, and I realised that was meant to be a joke. "You'd better come in, Mister Grant. And we will discuss the matter further. I should make it clear, none of us are at all interested in publicity."

I assured her it was the Hollow Women who were the story, not the sisters, and she stood back to allow me to enter. She locked and bolted the door very carefully and then led me through a series of narrow rooms that finally opened out onto a large hall. Sunlight fell in through a number of tall narrow windows, but still it seemed to me that the room had too many shadows for my liking. For all its size, the hall felt... isolated, cut off, not part of the world. A very private and very secure place. A long wooden table took up the middle of the room, and around it sat a great many nuns in full regalia. All of them looking at me with cold eyes and tightly pursed mouths. None of them got up to greet me.

Sister Joan explained who I was and why I was there and not one of the sisters even nodded to me. Sister Joan pulled out a chair for me at the head of the table and I sat down. The presence of so many staring eyes would probably have been intimidating to anyone else. I just smiled politely back at them while Sister Joan sat down beside me.

She then proceeded to interrogate me on the subject of the

SIMON R. GREEN

Hollow Women, hitting me with question after question, drawing out everything I knew. She didn't challenge or correct anything I said. I got the impression she was checking what I had discovered against what she already knew. The other nuns remained silent throughout, never taking their eyes off me.

More and more, the great open hall made me feel uneasy. It was all very clean, nothing out of place, but it was just so... characterless. The nuns had been here for twenty years and more, but they'd made no impression on their surroundings. No religious paintings or texts on the walls, not even a single crucifix. This had to be a really austere order.

In the name of self-defense, I interrupted Sister Joan's questions to ask a few of my own, including the lack of religious items on show. Sister Joan smiled tightly.

"Our order does not believe in idolatry or the need for religious paraphernalia. Our belief is pure without distractions. Let the world go its own way and we shall go ours."

"I've told you everything I know," I said. "Now it's your turn. What can you tell me about the Hollow Women? And why are you so interested? I thought the Hollow Women couldn't abide religious people and vice versa."

"It's all about faith," said Sister Joan. "So lacking in modern times. The legend of the Hollow Women is old... They have existed alongside civilisation under many names. Before this town was a town, there were Hollow Women preying on the men. Before there were people, there were Hollow Women. They learned to look like people, the better to prey on them. Perhaps these days they have learned to look like something else. It's hard to be sure of anything where the Hollow Women are concerned. They are very secretive. They've had to be to survive so long. The church has tried to stamp them out many times."

"Which church?" I said.

"All of them, Mister Grant! Perhaps because only those of true faith can see through the illusions that hide the Hollow Women from the eyes of the world. It is a war, Mister Grant. Make no mistake. There can be no forgiveness for things that prey on men."

"You've clearly amassed a great deal of information during your researches," I said carefully. "Would it be possible for me to take a look at what you've discovered?"

Sister Joan was already shaking her head, even before I finished speaking. "No, Mister Grant, it will not be possible."

"May I ask why not? My story wouldn't have to quote you or mention the Sisters in any way if that's what's worrying you."

"Information is ammunition, Mister Grant. And as I said, there is a war on. We guard what we know most jealously for when it might be needed."

"You seem convinced these Hollow Women of legend still exist," I said. "Do you see them as supernatural creatures? Like vampires or ghosts?"

"Those are dead things, Mister Grant. The Hollow Women are as real, as natural, as you. Every species has its predator."

"But you do believe they still exist, here in the town?"

"Oh yes, Mister Grant, we know they do. Hiding in plain sight. Only emerging to prey on the weak and then disappearing again. Any woman could be a Hollow Woman. That's the point. And be warned, Mister Grant. If you go looking for them, you can be sure they will come looking for you."

I looked up and down the table to see if the other nuns were taking this as seriously, and everywhere I looked, cold eyes and cold faces stared implacably back at me. There's nothing scarier than a faith backed up with utter certainty. They believed. Sister Joan stood up and indicated it was time for me to leave. And I couldn't get out of there fast enough.

The door closed firmly behind me. I heard the lock turn and bolts slamming into place as Sister Joan sealed Barrow Farm off from the intruding world again. I breathed in deeply and shook my head to clear it. Sometimes intense beliefs can be... catching. I had to remind myself I only got into this story to prove the mythical Hollow Women had a real world source in the Hollows women. The Holy Sisters of Saint Baphomet had been locked up together for too long. Stewing in their own conspiracy theories and the need for someone who needed punishing. I suppose, if you believe in devils and possessions and miracles, it's not too big a leap of faith to believe in women who can only be seen from the front.

I shuddered suddenly despite myself. When faith turns inwards, it becomes unhealthy. I did not believe in anything supernatural. I'd spent enough years writing and researching the

SIMON R. GREEN

weird shit to know it was all just bullshit and wish fulfilment. Whatever the Holy Sisters knew, or thought they knew, I didn't need to know it. They were just a dead end. I needed to put them behind me and press on with my research into historical records. The church archives had been a good start, but where next? The vicar had mentioned a local historical society...

I turned my back on Barrow Farm and strode determinedly away, not looking back once.

I reached for my phone to call Emma and bring her up to date only to realise she hadn't given me her number. So the editor couldn't blame me if her precious new reporter wasn't a big contributor to what was, after all, my story.

I walked back into the middle of town and headed straight for my favourite watering hole, the Dandy Lion, for a quick drink and a think. It's always been my experience that the two go well together as long as you don't overdo either of them. The Dandy is a cosy and comfortable drinking establishment with traditional fixtures and fittings and absolutely no piped music. I can usually find someone worth talking and drinking with. But I really wasn't expecting that when I walked through the doors, the first person I found waiting for me was Emma Tee.

She was sat by a table right by the door with a drink in front of her that she'd barely touched. She smiled winningly at me. I looked briefly past her to where a group of old friends were sitting round a table farther in, but I had promised the editor I would work with Emma. And Sam Walsh was perfectly capable of spiking my story out of hand if I didn't. So I got myself a pint of good cheer from the bar and sat down opposite Emma. She gave me her best happy smile, backed up by bright shining eyes... and it was hard to stay mad at her.

"How did you get on with the Holy Sisters?" said Emma, smiling perhaps just a little mischievously.

"Don't ask," I said. "I'm sorry about just going off and leaving you to cope with the mad old cat lady."

"Oh no, I should apologise to you!" Emma said immediately. "For not following the story. You were completely right. The story must come first. I just didn't want to meet the nuns. Nuns are creepy. Even more than old churches. So you didn't get anything useful from them?"

"Not a thing," I said. "Except that they seem convinced the Hollow Women of legend are still a real and present danger."

"Let them think what they like," Emma said firmly. "Our story will prove the Hollow Women are just an urban legend, mistranslated and misunderstood down the years. That's what reporting is supposed to be about, isn't it? Shining a light into dark places and uncovering the truth."

"Yes," I said. "That is what it's supposed to be about."

We sat and talked, and drank our drinks, and talked some more. She was very easy to talk to. And somewhat to my surprise, I found we were getting on really well. She had an endless interest in all things journalistic and was fascinated by my tales of researching weird stuff for strange magazines. And it helped a lot that she thought my jokes were funny. All my cynicism and world-weariness seemed to just evaporate in the face of her youthful enthusiasm. I'd forgotten how it felt to get properly excited about a story. But then it had been a long time since I had a story worth getting excited about.

Emma was quite open about why she wanted to become a journalist. She'd left her home, and her family, to make her own way in the world. I got the impression this had been very much against her family's wishes. That they were very strict, very traditional, and apparently believed they had a right and a duty to map out her life for her. And Emma wasn't having any of it. She wanted to be a journalist so she could tell the truth about things, things that mattered. Because her family had tried so hard to hide the truth about the world from her because it conflicted with what they believed. Emma wanted to know everything there was to know about the world. So she could tell everyone else. My heart went out to her. Looking at Emma was a lot like looking at my younger self.

"My parents never wanted me to be a writer," I said. "No money in it, that was what they said. Get a proper job with prospects. So I sort of drifted sideways into journalism. I did quite well for a while."

"What happened?" said Emma. "I know something happened. Ms Walsh said... some things when she told me I'd be working with you. What went wrong, Jason?"

"I did," I said. "I had my chance, and I blew it because I

couldn't stand the hard discipline of real journalism. I decided it was more important to tell a good story than sticking to the facts. So if facts got in the way, I just changed or suppressed them to make the story more sensational. I wrote some really great stories—they just weren't entirely true. On a modern daily tabloid, that wouldn't have been a problem. That would have been business as usual. But here, in the local paper of record..."

"Ms. Walsh fired you."

"Hell yes. More in sorrow than anger, I like to think. But it was definitely 'Go and never darken my doors again.' It's taken me years to get this opportunity. And years to understand that she was right. People need to be able to believe what they're told is the truth."

"Even when a little white lie can be so much more comforting?"

"Perhaps especially then. You can't base decisions that matter on someone telling you what you want to hear. No other local paper would touch me after word got out as to why I was fired, and without a good local history, the dailies didn't want to know. And that's how I ended up hacking it out and phoning it in for any rag that would have me." I smiled, briefly. "It does feel good to be working on a real story at last."

"I did get some more information out of Alicia Tiley after you left," said Emma. "After a little encouragement and open pleading..."

"You didn't actually drink that tea, did you?"

She winced. "Please. Don't remind me. And one of her cats pissed on my shoes. Anyway, Alicia remembered a part of the legend of the Hollow Women that was new to me. Apparently they only emerge, only reveal themselves as their true selves, at night. And only when the fog rises to blur reality... and hide them from prying eyes. That's when they go forth to prey on unattached young men. And strike down their enemies, anyone who might be getting too close to the truth about them."

"You mean they kill people?"

"Oh yes," said Emma. "They kill people."

"You're right," I said. "That is a new twist. Makes sense, I suppose. The women from the Hollows were probably professional women, plying their trade away from the light of day. And because what they were doing was illegal, they or their protectors would kill anyone who threatened their livelihood, or their territory. The Holy Sisters said the Hollow Women would come after me if I went after them."

"They actually said that to you?"

"Yes. Very sternly."

Emma looked at me for a long moment. "Do you really think you might be in danger, Jason?"

"From a supernatural myth?" I said, grinning despite myself. "Hardly. You mustn't take any of this too seriously, Emma. It's just an old moral fable that's outlived its significance. Don't let the material spook you."

She forced a smile. "As long as you don't go hanging around the Hollow Estates at dawn."

"Don't worry," I said. "I never get up that early. Another drink?"

"Don't mind if I do," said Emma.

Time passed in a pleasant fashion. When Emma and I finally left the Dandy Lion, leaning on each other in a companionable sort of way and giggling a bit, it was well into the evening. A fog was slowly forming on the air, a pearly grey haze, swallowing up the distance and spreading milky halos around the street lights. It seemed to thicken slowly even as I looked at it. There was no one else about, not even any traffic passing. It was like staring off the edge of the world. Everything seemed vague and uncertain. As though if I went walking off into the fog, the places I expected wouldn't be there anymore.

It was all very quiet, the fog soaking up sound. I put an arm around Emma, protectively, and looked about me. Suddenly feeling a hell of a lot more sober. The foggy evening seemed the perfect setting for some old legend to come walking back into the world. I glared into the curling mists. I was damned if I'd let my own story get to me. I looked at Emma, and she was staring into the fog with wide, worried eyes. She turned suddenly to look at me, and she seemed genuinely scared.

"Don't worry," I said. "We're a long way from dawn."

She didn't smile. Not even a little bit. "You don't understand," she said.

"Come on," I said. "I think you've had a few too many. I'll

walk you home. You've nothing to worry about as long as I'm with you. And tomorrow, when the fog's all gone, you'll see how silly you were. It's just a story!"

"It's a long way to where I live," said Emma. She looked at me. "Where's your place, James? Is it near?"

"Yes," I said. "Just a few streets away."

"Can I stay with you tonight?" said Emma, her wide eyes fixed on mine. "That's what I want, James. I want to stay with you, tonight. Can I?"

And I said yes.

I took her back to my place. Nothing special, just a reasonably comfortable flat above a newsagent's. It wasn't until I unlocked my door and ushered her in that I realised how much of a mess I'd let the place get into. I was a man who lived alone and let things lie where they fell. I made a token effort to clear some of it up, while Emma looked around her, not commenting.

She was nervous. I could tell. I stopped what I was doing and went to her.

"You haven't done this before, have you?" I said.

"No," she said.

"It's been a while for me. Emma... you don't have to do anything you don't want to."

"I want to do this, Jason."

"There's a spare bed. I just need to sort out some sheets for it..."

"I want you, Jason."

I put my arms around her. And she put her arms around me. Our faces were so close now; I could feel her breath on my mouth.

"You're so much younger than me," I said. "And so beautiful. You deserve better than me..."

"Hush, Jason. You deserve me. I'm here for you."

She hugged me tightly, pressing the side of her face against my shoulder. The smell from her hair filled my head. She held me as tightly as she could, as though afraid someone might drag her away.

"Hey," I said. "It's all right. Really. Everything's going to be all right, Emma."

"Yes," she said. "It is." She looked up at me, and smiled.

"Take me to bed, Jason. Take me to bed and love me so we can forget everything except us. That's what I want."

And that's what I did.

Sometime later, I lay on my back in bed, the sweat drying on my bare skin, stretched out and relaxed, feeling more at peace with myself than I had in a long time. Emma was sat up beside me, her back against the headboard, staring out across the room. I couldn't read the expression on her face. She suddenly swung her legs over the side of the bed, and padded silently across the bedroom, entirely naked, to stand before the window. She opened the curtains just a little, and looked out.

Nice arse, I thought.

"What is it?" I said.

"I thought I heard something." She didn't look back at me.

"Come back to bed," I said. "It's nothing. Just the night. There are always noises, at night."

"Yes," she said. "There's always something happening in the night."

I glanced at my alarm clock, on the bedside table. "Getting on for ten o'clock. The night's barely started. Come back to bed, Emma."

"In a minute."

She was still staring out through the crack in the curtains at the street below. I rolled over onto my side, thinking vaguely about getting out of bed to join her and that was when I saw her back reflected in the wardrobe mirror. She had no back. Seen from behind, in the mirror's reflection, there was just a hollowed out shell. A concave depth, all ridges and whorls. As though something had reached in and scooped out everything that made her human. It was like looking into the husk of a dead insect or the hollow trunk of a diseased tree with all the insides eaten away.

I cried out. I couldn't help myself. And she spun round to look at me. She saw the truth in my face and I saw the truth in hers.

She looked at my wardrobe mirror and then back at me. For a moment she seemed to shrink in on herself, and then she drew herself up again and faced me squarely. She seemed entirely human. As long as I looked at her from the front. But I couldn't forget what I had seen. And what I had just done with something that only pretended to be human. She started towards me. I sat up sharply and put my back against the headboard. She stopped at the foot of the bed.

"I'm sorry, Jason," she said. "I'm so sorry. I was so happy I let my concentration slip, just for a moment. I never meant for you to know."

"You're real," I said. "They're real. The Hollow Women. The ones who prey on men."

"Yes, Jason."

She reached out a hand to me, and I flinched back. She looked at me sadly and let her hand drop again.

"I could have loved you, Jason. Don't you know that?"

"How long...?"

"All my life. Hollow Women are born, not made. Just like you. I had no choice in the matter. That's why I left home. Left my family and my own kind because I didn't want to be like them. I wanted to be what I wanted to be." She smiled, briefly. "The name they gave me, that I never thought to change, should have been a clue. Emma Tee. Empty. I tried so hard, Jason! Trying to live as a human, among humans. I do care for you in my way."

"You can't stay here," I said.

She looked at the curtained window behind her, and then back at me. She seemed scared.

"Please, Jason. Don't make me go. Don't throw me out. It's night, and there's a fog, and I'm so scared about what might happen..."

"Scared of what?" I said. "Why were you so determined to spend the night here with me?"

"Because they're out there. Looking for me. I know it. You've been asking too many questions, Jason. Getting too close to the truth. Despite everything I could do to distract you."

"What is the truth, Emma? Really?"

"If I tell you everything, will you let me stay?"

"Tell me everything," I said. "Tell me all about the Hollow Women."

She turned her back on me and got dressed. It looked like a perfectly ordinary human back now. I got dressed too. And then we sat down on chairs a respectful distance apart, facing each other. And she told me what I needed to know in a calm, emotionless voice.

"I saw something moving, down in the street," she said. "Something in the fog. A human shape that didn't move like anything human. In the fog, in the night, the only time when Hollow Women appear as themselves."

"How do they... pass, normally?" I said. "How can they, how can you walk among us, and not be seen for what you are?"

"A glamour. A broadcast telepathic illusion. It can be undermined, seen through, if someone has more faith in their religion than they do in the illusions of the world. That's why I was so nervous at the church, earlier. The vicar kept getting glimpses of me out of the corners of his eyes. That's why he was so jumpy. Only his refusal to believe what he was seeing with his own eyes protected me."

"Where are you from?" I said. "I mean, you said you left your home and your family. A family of Hollow Women. Where are they?"

"You don't need to know, Jason. It's safer for you if you don't know."

"I need to know! This isn't my story anymore. It's my life!"

"They'll kill you to keep their secret safe."

"It was the old woman, wasn't it?" I said. "Alicia Tiley. She was a Hollow Woman!"

"No, you fool," said Emma. "She was just an old woman. She didn't know anything. I already knew everything. All the Hollow Women, all that are left, live together in one place now because they're not human and when they're alone, they don't have to act human. You've already met them, Jason. At Barrow Farm. The Holy Sisters. Hole-y. Get it? What better disguise..."

"Where do you come from originally?" I said. My throat was tight. It was getting hard to breathe. "I mean, if you're not human, what are you? Mutations? Aliens? Supernatural? What?"

"I don't know," said Emma. "If the sisters ever knew, they forgot long ago. We're just predators. That's all you need to know."

"How is it that you're so... human?"

"Television," Emma said simply. "I'm the first generation of Hollow Women to be exposed to television. It really is a window on the world. A better world, a better way of living. And I wanted it." She glanced back at the window. "They'll know I've talked. They'll come for me. And for you. I was only allowed to stay away as long as I kept my head down. Didn't get noticed. I was doing so well. And then you came to Ms. Walsh with your idea for a story. I was the one who convinced her to go for it with me attached. So I could watch over you, steer you away from the truth. Towards a nice, safe historical interpretation that would help hide us. You can't defend yourself from something you don't believe in. But you wanted this so much and I..."

"You need to leave town," I said. I got to my feet. "Come on. You need to get away. Start over, somewhere else. I'll see you safely away, and then later, I can come and join you. With both of us gone maybe the sisters won't feel so threatened."

"You'd come with me?" said Emma, getting to her feet. She looked at me wonderingly. "You'd do that, for me? After... everything?"

"Of course," I said. "I care for you in my way."

I put out my hands to her, and she grasped them tightly, like a drowning woman.

"It's the human thing to do, Emma. I'm sorry I freaked out at first. It's just... I never had one of my stories turn on me before."

"I'm sorry too," said Emma. She didn't say for what, though I didn't realise that till later.

"We can't go by car," I said. "They'll be expecting that. Looking for that. No—I'll take you to the railway station. It's not far. There's still time to catch the last train out of here and you'll be safe among the other passengers. Just... keep going, keep changing trains until you're far away. You can hide yourself properly in a big city. They'll never find you."

"Will you come and find me if I call for you?" said Emma.

"Do you want me to?"

"Yes. More than everything."

"Good. Because that's what I want too."

We held each other for a long moment. In the end, she pushed me away.

"I have to go, Jason. It's not safe here. For either of us."

Outside in the street, the fog had come down hard. Thick,

grey walls surrounded us on every side, cutting us off from the rest of the world. There was no one about. Not even a single passing car. As though everyone somehow knew it wasn't safe to be out and about this night. Emma held tightly to my arm, staring frantically about her.

"I've never seen a fog this thick," I said.

"I have," said Emma. "It's them. They're here."

"It's all right!" I said roughly. "I'll get you to the station."

I set out confidently enough, but in the fog, all the streets looked the same, and without landmarks to guide me, I soon lost my way and all sense of direction. I kept going anyway, striding out, Emma clattering along beside me, still hanging tight to my arm. And then, one by one, they appeared. Just dark shadows at first, appearing and disappearing in the mists around me like sharks circling silently in murky waters. Bursting out of the mists in front of me just long enough to turn me aside, guiding me, herding me, closing in from all sides. I kept going, even broke into a run, but it did no good. They were everywhere. Moving faster than I could because they didn't have human limitations. They never made a sound, just appearing and disappearing, until finally they all came out of the fog at once, forming a great circle around me and Emma. The Holy Sisters. The Hollow Women.

The black and white of their disguising robes stood out starkly against the grey mists. They stood very still, inhumanly still, watching me with their cold, empty faces. Sister Joan loomed up suddenly before me. I struck out at her, but she was gone before the blow arrived, vanished back into the mists. She reappeared while I was still off balance, and her fist came flying at me impossibly fast. She hit me once, clubbing me down with sudden, vicious strength. I hit the ground hard, driven to my knees by the force of the blow, all the strength knocked out of me. I cried out in shock and pain. When I looked up, she was standing over me, studying me with cold predator's eyes.

Dark shapes rushed in from every side, and just like that they were all over me. Lashing out with large, hard fists driven by more than human strength. Blood flew from my battered face. I tried to defend myself, but I couldn't even touch them. I ended up curled in a ball on the ground, hurting all over. And suddenly, they stopped. I slowly uncurled and looked up. Sister Joan was standing over me, her face entirely unmoved, unconcerned. She wasn't even breathing hard.

"Forget your story," she said. "Forget her. Forget any of this ever happened. And we will let you live as a cautionary example."

"All right," I said shakily, blood spilling from my mouth. "All right..."

"He lies," said another voice, from one of the Hollow Women looking on. Others took it up. *He lies, he lies...*

"You can't forget us because you won't forget her," said Sister Joan. "Such a pity... Say your prayers, Jason Grant. Your story has come to an end."

"No!"

I turned my head, slowly, painfully, and there was Emma. Standing beside me, her hands clenched into fists, glaring defiantly at Sister Joan.

"If you kill him, I'll never forgive you! Never!"

"You forget yourself, child," said Sister Joan. "You forget what you are. When he is gone..."

"No. I won't let you kill him."

Sister Joan considered her thoughtfully. "How will you stop us?"

"By giving you what you want. If you'll let him live, I'll come home again. I promise. I'll come back to you, and I'll never try to leave again. That's what you want, isn't it?"

"Come home?" said Sister Joan. "No more arguments, no more running away?"

"Yes," said Emma. She didn't look at me. "That's what I want."

It was the bravest thing I ever saw. A Hollow Woman, demonstrating her humanity. Giving up her life for mine.

Sister Joan looked at me, and then at Emma. "Did you...?"

"Yes," Emma said steadily. "I slept with him. And made a child with him."

I looked at her speechlessly. I had no doubt she was telling the truth. That she knew. It was, after all, what Hollow Women did.

"Then come home, child," said Sister Joan. "Your place is waiting for you."

Emma walked away from me, into the ranks of the waiting

Hollow Women. And together, they turned sideways and disappeared, back into the fog. Only Sister Joan remained.

"I could still tell the world all about you," I said.

"But you won't," said Sister Joan. "Not if you want Emma to stay safe. Silence and obscurity are the price of your survival, and hers." She smiled, very briefly. "And anyway, who would believe you? A hack writer of so many wild stories? No one believes in the things you write. The world only likes its legends in stories these days. We have what we came for. Nothing else matters."

She walked away and left me. I caught a last brief glimpse of Emma standing alone in the mists. She looked at me and didn't smile or wave good-bye. She took one last look at me and then walked away forever. As she turned away, I saw her back was empty. Just a hollow shell.

And I was left alone, in the fog, and the night. Alone, with my hollowed out heart.

On...The Foggy, Foggy Dew

Roud #558 denotes the British ballad The Foggy, Foggy Dew (not to be confused with the Irish ballad The Foggy Dew). Reading through the nearly fifty late nineteenth/early twentieth century versions in the Vaughan Williams Memorial Library as posted by The English Folk Dance and Song Society one finds that the plot of this ballad tends to go one of four ways.

1) At night a girl is frightened by "the foggy dew," or a "bugaboo" and comes into a young man's bed for comfort.

2) A young man, a weaver, courted a girl who, frightened of the "foggy dew" came into his bed. Part of the night they "sport and play." In the morning she worries about being undone but he says she is not to worry since the foggy dew is gone. From then on whenever she gives him a wink or a smile he thinks of the foggy dew.

3) This version is similar to #2 except later in life the now older man is with his son, with the inference being that the son was the result.

4) Again this is similar to #2, except that afterwards the girl asks, what if they should have a child? They marry and are happy and forever more when he looks at her he thinks of the foggy, foggy dew. (1)

Alan Lomax mentions on the sleeve notes for Shirley Collins' 1958/1959 recording that this is one of the few "frankly erotic songs" that made its passage from Southern England to America more or less uncensored. (2)

"The Foggy, Foggy Dew" has been sung by Burl Ives, Shirley Collins, Martin Carthy, A.L. Lloyd, and in countless pubs.

1) Roud Folksong Index. 2013. 6 November, 2013. <http://www.efdss.org/efdss-the-full-english>. English Folk Dance and Song Society.

2) Mainly Norfolk: English Folk and Other Good Music. 2013. 6 November, 2013.

<http:// mainlynorfolk.info/lloyd/songs/thefoggydew.html> English Folk Dance and Song Society.

THE CONTRIBUTORS

CHRISTOPHER GOLDEN is the award-winning, bestselling author of such novels as *The Myth Hunters, Wildwood Road, The Boys Are Back in Town, The Ferryman, Strangewood, Of Saints and Shadows,* and (with Tim Lebbon) *The Map of Moments.* He has also written books for teens and young adults, including *Poison Ink, Soulless,* and the thriller series Body of Evidence, honored by the New York Public Library and chosen as one of YALSA's Best Books for Young Readers. Upcoming teen novels include a new series of hardcover YA fantasy novels co-authored with Tim Lebbon and entitled The Secret Journeys of Jack London. A lifelong fan of the "team-up," Golden frequently collaborates with other writers on books, comics, and scripts. In addition to his recent work with Tim Lebbon, he co-wrote the lavishly illustrated novel *Baltimore, or, The Steadfast Tin Soldier and the Vampire* with Mike Mignola. With Thomas E. Sniegoski, he is the co-author of multiple novels, as well as comic book miniseries such as *Talent* and *The Sisterhood,* both currently in development as feature films. With Amber Benson, Golden co-created the online animated series Ghosts of Albion and co-wrote the book series of the same name. As an editor, he has worked on the short story anthologies *The New Dead* and *British Invasion,* among others, and has also written and co-written comic books, video games, screenplays, the online animated series Ghosts of Albion (with Amber Benson) and a network television pilot. The author is also known for his many media tie-in works, including novels, comics, and video games, in the worlds of *Buffy the Vampire Slayer, Hellboy, Angel,* and *X-Men,* among others.

DAVID LISS is the author of eight novels, most recently *The Day of Atonement*. His previous bestselling books include *The Coffee Trader* and *The Ethical Assassin*, both of which are being developed as films, and *A Conspiracy of Paper*, which is now being developed for television. Liss is the author of numerous comics, including *Mystery Men, Sherlock Holmes: Moriarty Lives* and *Angelica Tomorrow*.

DEL HOWISON Along with his wife Sue, Del owns Dark Delicacies, "America's Home of Horror." He is a Bram Stoker Award winning editor and multi-nominee as well as having been nominated for a Shirley Jackson and the Black Quill awards. His short story "The Lost Herd" was retitled to Sacrifice and released as the premiere episode of the horror television series Fear Itself on NBC.

GARY BRAUNBECK is the prolific author of 25 books, as well as nearly 250 short stories. He is a multiple Bram Stoker Award winner and as won the International Horror Guild Award. He is a past-president of the Horror Writers Association. His fiction has been translated into Japanese, French, Italian, Russian and German.

GREGORY FROST is a writer of dark fantasy, SF, Young Adult, and historical thriller fiction. He has been a finalist for every major fantasy genre award. His latest novel-length work is the YA-crossover "Shadowbridge" duology; voted "one of the four best fantasy novels of the year" by the ALA. His historical thriller, *Fitcher's Brides*, was a Best Novel finalist for both World Fantasy and International Horror Guild Awards. Other Frost short stories appear in Ellen Datlow's *Supernatural Noir* anthology, and in *V-Wars*, edited by Jonathan Maberry. He directs the fiction writing program at Swarthmore College. He is the co-founder of the Liars Club.

JACK KETCHUM is an American author. He is the recipient of four Bram Stoker Awards and three further nominations. Many of his novels have been adapted to film, including *The Girl Next Door* and *Red*.

JONATHAN MABERRY is a *NY Times* bestselling author, multiple Bram Stoker Award winner, and comic book writer for Marvel, Dark Horse and IDW. His novels include *Code Zero, Rot & Ruin, Fall Of Night, Ghost Road Blues, Patient Zero, The Wolfman,* and many others. Nonfiction books include *Ultimate Jujutsu, The Cryptopedia, Zombie Csu,* and others. Several of Jonathan's novels are in development for movies or TV including *V-Wars, Extinction Machine, Rot & Ruin* and *Dead of Night* He's the editor/co-author of *V-Wars,* a vampire-themed anthology, and is editing a series of all original *X-Files* anthologies. He was a featured expert on The History Channel special *Zombies: A Living History.* Since 1978, he's sold more than 1200 magazine feature articles, 3000 columns, two plays, greeting cards, song lyrics, and poetry. His comics include *V-Wars, Rot & Ruin, Captain America: Hail Hydra, Bad Blood, Marvel Zombies Return* and *Marvel Universe Vs The Avengers.* He lives in Del Mar, California with his wife, Sara Jo and their dog, Rosie. www.jonathanmaberry.com

JEFFREY J. MARIOTTE is the award-winning author of more than fifty novels, including supernatural thrillers *Season of the Wolf, Missing White Girl, River Runs Red,* and *Cold Black Hearts*, horror epic *The Slab,* the *Dark Vengeance* teen horror quartet, and others. He also writes comic books, including the long-running horror/ Western comic book series *Desperadoes* and original graphic novel *Zombie Cop.* With writing partner Marsheila Rockwell, he has published short fiction and is working on more. He has worked in virtually every aspect of the book business, as a writer, editor, marketing executive, and bookseller. He lives in southeastern Arizona. Visit him at www.jeffmariotte.com.

JEFF STRAND is the four-time Bram Stoker Award nominated author of such books as *Pressure, Dweller, A Bad Day For Voodoo,* and *Wolf Hunt.* He lives in Tampa, Florida, and because he cares about your ears, he lets others do the singing where folk ballads are concerned.

KEITH R.A. DeCANDIDO is the international, best-selling, award-winning author of more than 50 novels as well as dozens of short stories, novellas, comic books, and blog entries. His many works of fiction in media universes such as *Star Trek, Supernatural, World of Warcraft, Doctor Who, Spider-Man, Buffy the Vampire Slayer, Farscape, Leverage,* and more won him a Lifetime Achievement Award from the International Association of Media Tie-In Writers in 2009. Recent and upcoming work ranges from the *Sleepy Hollow* novel *Children of the Revolution* to the acclaimed "Precinct" series of fantasy police procedurals (*Dragon Precinct, Unicorn Precinct, Goblin Precinct, Gryphon Precinct* and *Tales from Dragon Precinct*) to the *Star Trek* coffee table book *The Klingon Art of War* to the short story collection *Ragnarok & Roll: Tales of Cassie Zukav, Weirdness Magnet* (which features the protagonist of "Fish Out of Water"). He has also contributed to the anthologies *Bad-Ass Faeries: It's Elemental, More Tales of Zorro, Stargate: Far Horizons, V-Wars* Volumes 1 & 3, and *The X-Files: The Truth is Out There,* and he's also a regular blogger for Tor.com, doing a twice-weekly rewatch of *Star Trek: Deep Space Nine.* Find out more at his web site at DeCandido.net.

KELLEY ARMSTRONG is a #1 New York Times bestseller. She has published eighteen fantasy novels to date, set in the world of the Women of the Otherworld and the Darkest Powers series, also two crime novels in 2007 and 2009.

LISA MORTON is a screenwriter, author of non-fiction books, award-winning prose writer, and Halloween expert whose work was described by the American Library Association's *Readers' Advisory Guide to Horror* as "consistently dark, unsettling, and frightening." Her most recent releases include the novella *By Insanity of Reason* (co-authored with John R. Little) and the novel *Zombie Apocalypse: Washington Deceased.* She lives in North Hollywood, and can be found online at *www. lisamorton.com.*

MARSHEILA (MARCY) ROCKWELL is the author of *The Shard Axe* series, the only official novels that tie into the popular MMORPG, Dungeons & Dragons Online. She has two collections out now (*Tales of Sand and Sorcery and Bridges of Longing and Other Strange Passageways)*, and is currently hard at work on the second book in a trilogy based on Neil Gaiman's *Lady Justice* comic books. "John Barleycorn Must Die" is her second published collaboration with writing partner Jeffrey J. Mariotte. The first, "A Soul in the Hand," can be found in the *Neverland's Library* anthology from Ragnarok Publications. Learn more here: *http://www.marsheilarockwell.com/*.

NANCY HOLDER is a *New York Times* bestselling author (the dark fantasy series Wicked) who has written over seventy novels, and two hundred short stories, essays, and articles, many of which have appeared in "Best of" anthologies. She has received five Bram Stoker awards and a Scribe award for her supernatural fiction, as well as a Pioneer award from Romantic Times for her young adult fiction. She also received a Special Sales Award from *amazon.com*. She is well known for her work on such fantasy properties as *Buffy the Vampire Slayer, MTV Teen Wolf, Saving Grace, Hellboy, Hulk, Highlander,* and many others. She has written two retold fairy tales for Simon and Schuster's Once Upon a Time series, and a nursery rhyme retelling ("The Lion and the Unicorn") for Month 9 Books. Many of her MFA students have explored dark fantasy retellings in their third semester projects. She will be the Author Guest of Honor at the 2014 World Horror Convention.

SEANAN McGUIRE is the *New York Times* Bestselling fantasy author of the October Daye series, and the InCryptid series, both published by DAW Books. She won the John W. Campbell Award in 2010, and was the first person to be nominated for the Hugo Awards five times in a single year. Seanan majored in folklore and mythology at the University of California Berkeley (go Bears!), and periodically vanishes into haunted corn mazes for days at a time. She lives in Northern California, where she writes stuff. She also writes as Mira Grant, author of the Newsflesh series, and talks about horrible things at the dinner table.

SIMON GREEN was born in Bradford-on-Avon, Wiltshire, England (where he still resides), in 1955. He has obtained an M.A. in Modern English and American Literature from Leicester

University and he also studied history and has a combined Humanities degree. His writing career started in 1973, when he was a student in London. His first actual sale was a story titled "Manslayer," back in 1976, but it didn't appear till much later; *Awake, Awake....* was his first sale to a professional editor in 1979. Furthermore, he sold some six or seven stories to semi-pro magazines before that market disappeared practically overnight. After years of publishers' rejection letters, he sold an incredible seven novels in 1988, just two days after he started working at Bilbo's bookshop in Bath (this after three and a half years of being unemployed!). This was followed in 1989 by two more, and a commission to write the bestselling novelization of the Kevin Costner film *Robin Hood: Prince of Thieves*, which has sold more than 370,000 copies.

NANCY KEIM COMLEY has a degree in English and a Master's in Folklore from Western Kentucky University. She has written about and been published on diverse topics such as the death, burial and funerary rites of an African American community and a storyteller in Tennessee.

JONATHAN MABERRY,
JOE R. LANSDALE, GARY BRAUNBECK,
HARRY SHANNON and JOE McKINNEY

LIMBUS
INC.

—— BOOK II ——

EDITED BY BRETT J. TALLEY

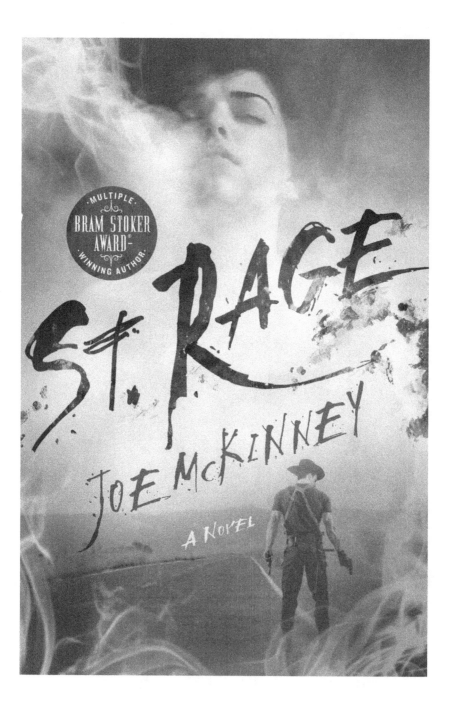

St. Rage

JOE McKINNEY

A NOVEL

CPSIA information can be obtained
at www.ICGtesting.com
Printed in the USA
LVHW040339140623
749669LV00002B/175